Death of a Ba

Revenge is Crimi

CW00502971

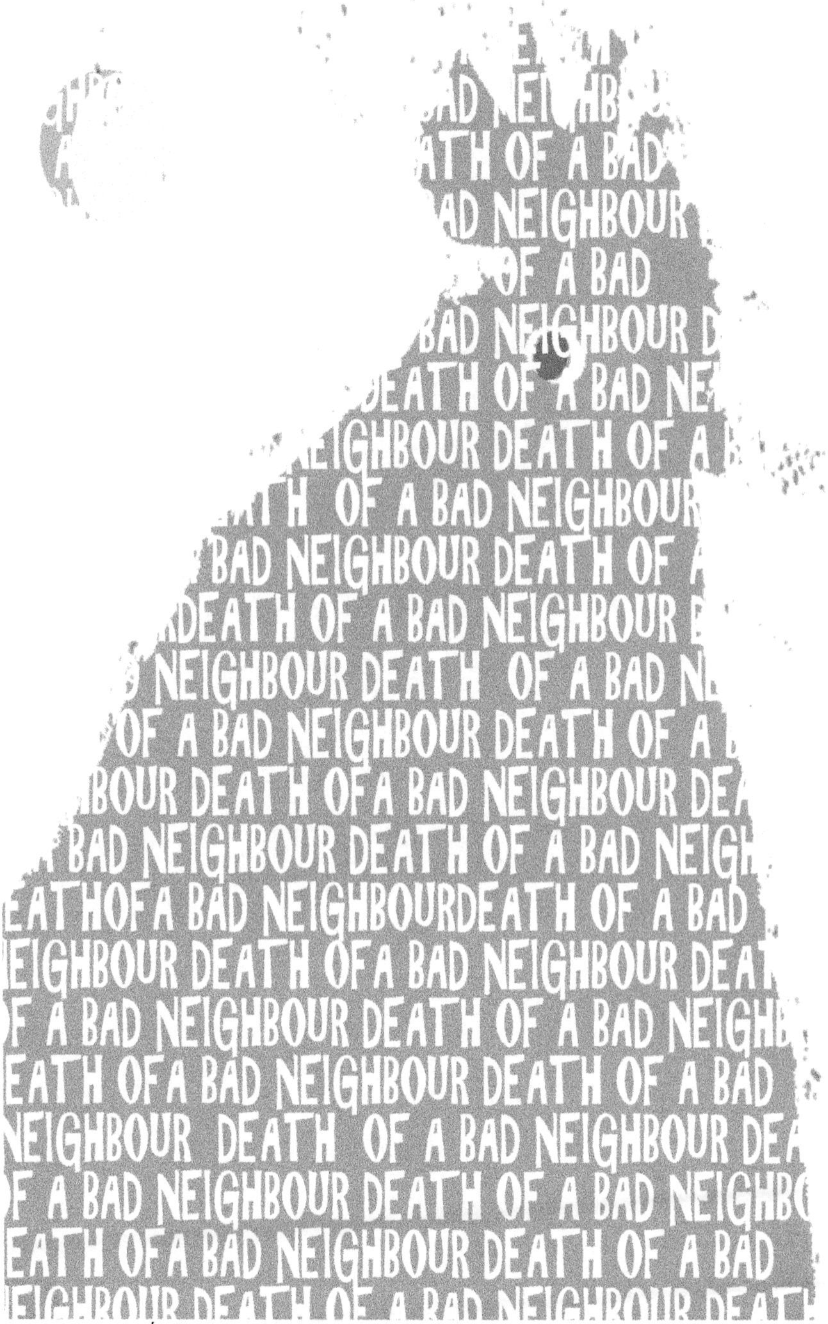

ATH OF A BAD
AD NEIGHBOUR
OF A BAD
BAD NEIGHBOUR
DEATH OF A BAD
NEIGHBOUR DEATH OF A
OF A BAD NEIGHBOUR
BAD NEIGHBOUR DEATH OF
DEATH OF A BAD NEIGHBOUR
NEIGHBOUR DEATH OF A BAD
OF A BAD NEIGHBOUR DEATH OF A
BOUR DEATH OF A BAD NEIGHBOUR
BAD NEIGHBOUR DEATH OF A BAD
EATH OF A BAD NEIGHBOURDEATH OF A BAD
EIGHBOUR DEATH OF A BAD NEIGHBOUR
F A BAD NEIGHBOUR DEATH OF A BAD
EATH OF A BAD NEIGHBOUR DEATH OF A BAD
NEIGHBOUR DEATH OF A BAD NEIGHBOUR
F A BAD NEIGHBOUR DEATH OF A BAD
EATH OF A BAD NEIGHBOUR DEATH OF A BAD

Death of a Bad Neighbour:
Revenge is Criminal

An Anthology
of CRIME AND MYSTERY STORIES

Edited by Jack Calverley

Death of a Bad Neighbour: Revenge Is Criminal
First print edition. April 2022.
Amazon paperback ISBN: 9798790964015
Logic of Dreams paperback ISBN: 9781739688707

Published by The Logic of Dreams.
Requests to publish work from this book should be sent to:
anthology@jackcalverley.com

While every precaution has been taken in the preparation of this book, the
publisher assumes no responsibility for errors or omissions, or for damages
resulting from the use of information contained herein.

Book and cover design by Jack Calverley.
Real life cockerel photograph copyright © 2019 by David Cain on Unsplash.
Fonts copyright © 2021 Arphic Technology co., Ltd, Taiwan.

This is a work of fiction. Names, characters, places and incidents either are
the product of the authors' imaginations or are used fictitiously, and any
resemblance to actual presons, living or dead, business establishments,
events, or locales is entirely coincidental.

Copyrights

Contents

The Authors

Hilary Davidson

HILARY DAVIDSON is the bestselling author of seven crime novels. Her work includes the standalones *Her Last Breath* and *Blood Always Tells*, the Shadows of New York series (*One Small Sacrifice* and *Don't Look Down*), and the Lily Moore series (*The Damage Done, The Next One to Fall*, and *Evil in All Its Disguises*). Her fiction has won two Anthony Awards and a Derringer Award. Her short stories have appeared in *Thuglit, Ellery Queen's Mystery Magazine, Beat to a Pulp, Mystery Tribune*, and other dark places. Before turning to a life of crime-writing, Hilary was a journalist and the author of 18 nonfiction books. Originally from Toronto, she has lived in New York City since October 2001. Visit her online at: **www.hilarydavidson.com** Instagram: **@hilarydavidsonbooks** Twitter: **@hilarydavidson**.

Eve Elliot

EVE ELLIOT is a voice actress, fiction writer and essayist who has recently discovered the thrill of writing crime fiction. Her short stories and creative non-fiction have been published in ten anthologies and journals in Europe and North America, and she recently wrote and produced her first radio play, *The Death of Dr. Davidson*, as a full cast, twelve-part audio series. She is also currently completing her second romance novel, releasing it one chapter at a time to her Patreon supporters. *One Spye After Another* is her first attempt at mixing humour and crime. She lives in Dublin, Ireland. Find out more at **www.eveelliot.com**.

Kay Hanifen

KAY HANIFEN was born on a Friday the 13ᵗʰ and lived in a haunted castle for three months, so naturally, she has a taste for the strange and macabre. She is a graduate of Emerson College with a BFA in Creative Writing. Her articles have appeared in *Ghouls Magazine*, *Screen Rant*, *The Borgen Project*, and *Leatherneck* magazine; and her short stories have appeared in *Strangely Funny VIII*, *Crunchy With Ketchup*, *Midnight From Beyond the Stars*, *Dark Shadows: The Gay Nineties*, *Wicked Newsletters*, *Fearful Fun*, *Death of a Bad Neighbor*, *Enchanted Entrapments*, and *Slice of Paradise*. When she's not consuming pop culture with the voraciousness of a vampire at a 24-hour blood bank, you can usually find her with her two black cats or on Twitter **@TheUnicornComi1**.

Wendy Harrison

WENDY HARRISON's fascination with mystery began with Nancy Drew and continued with real-life experiences as a prosecutor in Florida. Now retired, she spends her time solving crimes of her own creation as a published mystery short story writer. Her publications include stories in the anthologies *Peace, Love & Crime: Crime Fiction Inspired by Songs of the '60s*, *Autumn Noir*, *Holiday Hijinks*, *Crimeucopia: Tales from the Back Porch* and *The Big Fang*, as well as the upcoming *More Groovy Gumshoes*. She shares her home with Brooks, her first-reader husband, and with a rescued Shepherd mix dog and a calico cat who bark and purr respectively as she writes.

Steve Hockensmith

STEVE HOCKENSMITH's first novel, *Holmes on the Range*, was a finalist for the Edgar, Shamus, Anthony and Dilys awards. He's gone on to write five sequels (so far) as well as the New York Times bestseller *Pride and Prejudice and Zombies: Dawn of the Dreadfuls* and the tarot-themed mystery *The White Magic Five and Dime*. He's also authored a number of books and graphic novels for children, including the Edgar finalist *Nick and Tesla's Super-Cyborg Gadget Glove*. A widely published writer of short stories, he's appeared in *Ellery Queen* and *Alfred Hitchcock's Mystery Magazine* more than 30 times. You can learn more about him and his writing at **stevehockensmith.com**.

Robert Lopresti

ROBERT LOPRESTI is the author of more than eighty short stories, some of which have won the Black Orchid Novella Award, and the Derringer Award (three times), as well as being reprinted in *Best American Mystery Stories* and *Year's Best Dark Fantasy and Horror*. His latest novel, *Greenfellas*, is a comic caper about the Mafia trying to save the environment. He is a retired librarian, lives in the Pacific Northwest, and is the current president of the Short Mystery Fiction Society. He can be found online at: **roblopresti.com**.

Nick Manzolillo

NICK MANZOLILLO is the author of the Lovecraftian horror novel *Moon, Regardless*. His short fiction has appeared in over sixty publications, including: *Switchblade*, *TQR*, *Red Room Magazine*, *Grievous Angel*, and the *Tales To Terrify* podcast. He has an MFA in Creative and Professional Writing from Western Connecticut State University and currently lives in Rhode Island. You can find out more about him at **nickmanzolillo.com**.

Warren Moore

WARREN MOORE is Professor of English at Newberry College, in Newberry, South Carolina. His novel *Broken Glass Waltzes* was published in 2017 by Down&Out Books, and his short fiction has appeared in numerous anthologies and small publications. Moore blogs at **profmondo.wordpress.com**, and can be found on Twitter as **@profmondo**.

Eve Morton

EVE MORTON is an author, poet, academic, and educator living in Ontario, Canada. Her latest mystery/suspense story is *The Serenity Nearby* (Sapphire Publishing, 2022). She teaches university and college classes on media studies, academic writing, and genre literature, among other topics. Find more information, including more short stories and poetry on **authormorton.wordpress.com**.

Shiny Nyquist

SHINY NYQUIST lives on a narrowboat on the canal system in England 'cruising the cut' while working as a website designer, thus sharing vicariously in enterprises as diverse as a private academy, a portrait artist, and a sex shop, and then writing fiction as time allows, with a web presence here: shinynyquist.wordpress.com/

Kevin Quigley

KEVIN QUIGLEY grew up in suburbia and knows a thing or two about the protective nature of cat owners... and of bad neighbors. He is the author of the novels *I'm On Fire* and *Roller Disco Saturday Night*, as well as the short story collections *Damage & Dread* and *This Terrestrial Hell*. His stories have appeared in the Cemetery Dance anthologies *Halloween Carnival* and *Shivers*, and Lawrence Block's upcoming *Playing Games*.

Quigley is also known for his monographic work on Stephen King (*The Stephen King Illustrated Movie Trivia Book*, *Chart of Darkness*, *Stephen King Limited*), which has earned him expert status on the subject. His latest nonfiction book is a deep exploration into the Oregon folk-rock band Blitzen Trapper, and their seminal album, *Furr*. He lives in Boston, Massachusetts with his husband, Shawn, in a building that does not allow pets.

Marilyn Todd

MARILYN TODD is the award-winning author of twenty historical thrillers, three anthologies, and over a hundred short stories. A regular contributor to *Ellery Queen's Mystery Magazine*, she was also nominated for a *Private Eye* Writers of America Shamus Award. Her latest series features Britain's first crime-scene photographer—"which brilliantly evokes the darker side of Victorian London." Born in London, Marilyn now lives with her husband in France, and when she isn't killing people, she enjoys cooking—which is pretty much the same thing. Catch her online here: **www.marilyntodd.com**.

F. D. Trenton

F. D. TRENTON has worked as a silicon chip tester and a fintech programmer, and has had articles published in *Computing* and *Computer Weekly*. F.D. lives in the northernmost outskirts of London, England, within earshot of numerous motorways, none of which are much use to even the most devoted cyclist.

L. C. Tyler

L. C. TYLER is a former chair of the Crime Writers Association and the author of two detective series: the Herring Mysteries (recently optioned for television) and a historical crime series featuring seventeenth century lawyer and spy, John Grey. He has twice won the Goldsboro Last Laugh Award for the best humorous crime novel of the year and has been shortlisted for the Edgar Allan Poe Awards and for the CWA Historical Dagger. He also writes short stories, for British and American anthologies, and was awarded the 2017 CWA Short Story Dagger. He has lived and worked all over the world, including postings to Hong Kong, Malaysia, Sudan and Denmark, but has more recently been based in London and West Sussex. He can be found online at **lctyler99.wixsite.com/mysite** on Twitter as **@lenctyler**.

Dave Zeltserman

DAVE ZELTSERMAN is an award-winning writer whose crime and horror novels have been chosen by NPR, Washington Post, Booklist, WBUR, and American Library Association for best books of the year. His crime novel, *Small Crimes*, has been made into a Netflix film, and his novel *The Caretaker of Lorne Field* is currently in film development.

Introduction

Jack Calverley

I AM TOLD that a criminal gang built the house I live in.

I'm talking wide-shouldered men wearing orange and white stripes who, as prisoners under supervision, poured the concrete into upright moulds—the house is neither brick built nor timber framed—and they hung rust-red tiles across the building at the front, and across the pitched roof, painting the rest of the house white, aside from the window frames and outside doors which, front and rear, they painted black. They equipped kitchen and bathroom, although their initial shrines to gushing water have long since been swapped out for whatever has, over the years, captured the fashion-conscious home-owner's eye (I inherited a peppermint green bathroom suite upstairs and a kitchen of black marble downstairs).

The man who told me this lives next door in a similar house. When he told me, it was in hushed tones, with his head bent.

His name is Bob.

Bob is all tortoise head and tortoise neck with a few wisps of lemon grass hair. And while he habitually wears a light shirt and blue jeans you can't help feeling it is a lightweight disguise for loose-fitting heavy-duty tweed.

It was Bob who told me that the previous occupants of my home were a couple who quarreled, split up, and divided the house between them. The wife moved upstairs; the husband took up residence on the ground floor. She used the front door; he the rear. She took up graphic design. He took to drinking, and to playing heavy metal music twenty-four hours a day. But, soon after they split up, he died in a motorcycle accident. He had been hammering down the Edgware Road at thirty-something miles an hour when a London black cab driver opened the cab door into the path of the bike...

Thus died a chronological neighbour of mine, he occupying the same house as me, but for a neighouring period of time.

The house on the other side of mine, so Bob tells me, used to belong to a couple and their teenage daughter. The couple split up after the husband fell into bed with a German teacher (she was German and a teacher; whether she taught German or geography or something entirely other, no one seems to know). The husband, having cleaved himself from his erstwhile loved ones with an emotional axe, was subsequently diagnosed with a rare incurable illness, told he had not long to live, and the NHS could do nothing for him (this was some years ago, you understand, and treatments move ever onward. As to what would happen today, who can say?). Anyhow, upon hearing the bad news, the German mistress whisked the husband off to Germany where some treatment was at least forthcoming.

Bob had me hooked up to this point, but he was unable to report a final outcome and I felt that, rather than tell me about the neighbours, he was trying to make a political point, a sour triumphalism—for or against the NHS or its funding, I couldn't say—but it dulled my interest.

The current occupant of that house on the mother-and-daughter side has recently extended the roof, turning the attic into an oversized brutalist bedroom without seeking planning permission and, according to Bob, you wouldn't believe how many locals have written to the council to complain about what amounts to a concrete block the size and shape of a shipping container being impaled upon a traditional red-tiled pitched roof.

The council, whose job it is to do something, has done nothing.

Then there is the house across the road, built by regular folk from bricks the colour of burned toast, and there are the people that people it: a middle-aged upholsterer [grey-clad, string-vested, shambling, and bald]; a midnight DJ who announces every last return home in booming bass [dreadlocked and besmocked, in green and yellow and red, who chatters a million words a second like your best-of-breed racetrack pundit]; and there's some mother's cast-out son, who is never seen to work, but wherever he goes he trails the garden brazier smell of home-grown marijuana, and is probably growing it, converting it to cash, and calling that a good living [pale as death, mind you, flimsy as rice-paper, and with panda eyes].

But if the council can't be moved to visit a noisy, muddy building site to view an architectural abomination in the making, for certain: an over-stretched Met Police is even less likely to visit a minor cultivator of a drug that many would claim merely stupefies and pacifies its users and, thereby, the primary offender—the perp I hear you correcting me—remains untroubled by Justice.

Nonetheless I have to say (because there are other stories too), mostly, Bob has me hooked by these glimpses into local life; he has me convinced by these little yarns. Every time we meet at the gate, or in the street, or when swapping each other's wrongly delivered mail—yes, I admit, he has me mesmerized as he keeps me up to date with all the comings and goings, all the histories that give rise to the human landscape, and what happens when I am away, at work, or travelling, and cannot see for myself.

You see when I'm around, nothing much ever happens; I must absent myself from the neighbourhood for the least mischief to occur.

As if I were some kind of hi-viz officer of the law.

Of course, I don't know how much of anything dear old Bob says is true. But it seems that all that is needed for his stories to gain some traction is for them to persist in the minds of his audience.

Had he not had me hooked, I could hardly report these histories to you now, could I? And yet how much of what he says is fiction? How much is deliberately shaped—designed, even, using a skill he has honed over many years—to make it plausible, and memorable? To make it true.

Well, allow me to go one or two steps further:

Would it surprise you to learn that Bob's late son was a Motörhead fan and motorcycle enthusiast? Or that the unfaithful and once gravely-ill husband was an upholsterer? How intertwined might this local world turn out to be?

However:

Have I succeeded in persuading you that tortoise-headed Bob actually exists?

You see, for sure, I must denounce all of this as fiction. I have to. Heaven forfend that anyone I have ever known thinks I am writing about them, and takes offence—feels demeaned, or diminished in any way, especially in the eyes of the public, to suffer reputational damage, or an intrusion of privacy.

Anyone so demeaned might sue.

So, no. No! No! No! *None of the above is true!*

Necessarily, everything I have written here is make-believe. And the people who people this make-believe are make-believe too, for the sole purpose of my fictitious examples.

So also, this must be true for all that follows in this anthology.

More so since the theme is bad neighbours. Those people whom we could all happily do without. For whom money trumps decency. Arrogance and personal convenience trump consideration or good manners—never mind generosity of spirit—and as for morality, who he? Not these neighbours, not the rental landlord who ignores all complaints when the noise and mess his tenants make, at all hours of the day and night, is the bane of someone else's life; not the entitled daughters of the rich and famous who press their good fortune into service to manipulate due process; not the twisted freeholder who turns every marginally legal trick in the book to extort fees from leaseholders who cannot then sell because they would have to reveal just how bad their freeholder is (the leaseholder-freeholder thing being a feature of the UK).

And if you think for one moment these bad neighbours care, you are as unhinged as they are. Making them care is the problem. Decent people cannot conceive how bad people can be bad, while bad people cannot conceive why decent people bother being decent. And beware, because if ever you vent your frustration, these neighbours are the experts in the complaints procedures and they are *the* great manipulators and you will find yourself unwittingly painted as the irredeemably guilty party. Bleak indeed.

So...The stories in this anthology are mostly about some kind of comeuppance, and of course in real life the scum-sucking pond-life never get their comeuppance (if they did they would not be scum-sucking pond-life, rather, they would be the criminals, duly convicted and behind bars, set to learn housebuilding, or some other socially useful skill).

So is there the least modicum of truth in anything I have set out in these pages?

No! No! No! None of this is true!

What's more: the contributing authors all assure me that the stories they have submitted and which follow this introduction are pure fiction and to the best of their knowledge and belief their characters bear no resemblance to any real life characters, nor their story events to any real life events.

Read on dear reader, read on, for good fiction carries with it the emotional impact of truth while brushing with fact in nothing more than imaginary caresses, soft touches of mind's-eye colour, and evocative almost-scents.

I kid you not.

Jack Calverley
March 2022

Lambs and Wolves

Robert Lopresti

THE FIRST TIME he saw the bald guy in the woods, Garmo figured: *This is it. They found me.*

Of course, he wouldn't have been surprised to spot hunters with shotguns out there, hoping to blast coyotes or rabbits or whatever the hicks in these parts liked to kill. But this guy was nothing like that.

Baldy was ex-military, or wanted to look like it. Six-foot-plus, muscles rippling under black clothes. No visible weapons, but plenty of room for a gun under his turtleneck.

Garmo had been doing the dishes—washing his coffee cup, really—when he looked out the kitchen window and spied the man prowling through the woods just beyond his backyard.

He stepped away from the window, too far back for Baldy to see him. The whole emergency plan vanished from his head in a heartbeat.

Calm down, dammit.

Should he call Meisengill? Wasn't that the first step?

His right hand flexed involuntarily, grasping for a gun that wasn't there. A gun would bust the deal, get him sent to a prison where he would be whacked as surely as if Baldy—

Where was the bastard now?

There. He had slipped past Garmo's little house and was peeking over the fence at the colonial home next door.

Garmo's shoulders sagged in relief.

I'll be damned. He's just stalking Kathy.

MEISENGILL DIDN'T BUY it. When Garmo told him about the bald guy at their next scheduled meeting—in the back room of a sub shop half an hour outside of town—the deputy marshal was furious.

"I don't believe this. You saw a possible shooter doing reconnaissance of your house and you didn't think that was worth giving me a little ring-a-ding? What sort of death wish do you have, anyway?"

"Relax," said Garmo. He bit into his lunch, the so-called Sicilian sub, which was a sad thing. What he wouldn't give for a meatball hoagie, but nobody within a hundred miles of this place knew Italian food from Spanish fly.

"It turns out the guy was just your average perv, spying on the chick who lives next door."

"And that's another thing," said Meisengill, red in the face. "You're supposed to report changes in your environment. This woman moved in almost a month ago and you just mention her today?"

Garmo shrugged. "If she was gonna kill me she'd have done it by now."

"Oh, brilliant." The marshal's eyes narrowed. "You didn't want us looking too close because you had plans for her, right? Are you keeping it in your pants?"

Garmo snorted. "I'm just trying to stay alive out here in freaking no-man's land."

THE FACT WAS that when he first saw the blond woman carrying bags of groceries in from her car his first thought had not been about security rules.

He reached her driveway just as she stepped out of her house, ready for another load.

"You must be the new neighbor," he said. "I'm Jeff Clancy."

That name bugged him. He didn't look like an Irishman but the experts at the Marshal Service said anything Italian was too obvious.

The blonde smiled back and held out her hand. "Kathy Whitehill. Pleased to meet you."

"Can I help with your bags?"

"That would be great. I just moved in so I have to get, you know, all the stuff you'd expect a kitchen to have, spices and herbs, and..."

All Garmo expected from a kitchen was a fridge to store leftover take-out and a microwave to reheat it, but he nodded and started hoisting sacks.

"I rented the place furnished," Kathy had said. "Which is my way of saying that ugly lamp isn't my fault. And, oh lord, the wallpaper."

"Mine is furnished too," said Garmo. "There's a picture in the living room that looks like someone tried to paint a horse through a beer bottle."

She laughed. "Have a seat and watch me unpack. What brought you to your furnished home, Jeff?"

It was no pain watching her. She was maybe thirty, a few years older than Garmo. Clearly she worked out, but was not a body-builder. Garmo approved; he hated muscle-bound women. She wore tight jeans and a t-shirt that said HOOSIERS. An Indiana thing, he supposed.

"Got laid off from my job in Rhode Island," he said, "and wanted a change. My cousin runs an auto parts store here in town and needed some help."

Actually Tom Parnell was no relative, and what he had really needed was a deal with the IRS to pave over some creative accounting he had done, so he had agreed to hire Jeff Clancy, no questions asked.

"What brings you to our thriving metropolis?"

Kathy laughed again. She had finished putting beef and vegetables in the fridge and was now storing things in the pantry.

"I'm an advance scout. Ed, that's my husband, is a construction manager. Do you know what that is? When a skyscraper's going up somebody has to run the office. Make sure the portapotties and girders show up on time, not to mention the workers. That's my Ed."

"Sounds interesting," Garmo lied.

"He loves it. The problem is that every few years he builds himself right out of a job. He's finishing one right now in Bloomington, and he'll be starting another one here next month."

"I can't believe they're raising a skyscraper here in hicksville."

"That would stand out like the proverbial sore thumb, wouldn't it? No, they're building a new hospital over in the county seat."

She turned around and smiled at him. "Okay, the rest of the stuff can wait. Want a beer?"

"That would be nice."

"Coming up. So I got here, rented this place for a couple of months and now I'm looking for a home we can live in long-term. By the time he gets here I'll have a house all fixed up and our stuff in it."

"Doesn't he want to see the place first?"

"Ed likes surprises. Besides, I know what he likes."

"You must get lonely when he's in the next state."

"Oh, we make up for it when he's here." The way she smiled told Garmo there was no point in putting the moves on her. Meisengill would approve.

"And what do you do when you aren't scouting the jungles of Indiana?" he asked.

"Technical writer," she said with a shrug. "I write those boring manuals nobody wants to read. And here I thought I would be the next Margaret Atwood."

MEISENGILL WAS IGNORING his own sandwich, jotting notes. "If you spot the bald guy again, try to get a picture of him. We'll see if he's got a record."

"Should I warn the girl about him?"

The deputy looked startled. "I told you, damn it. Stay away from her! You're trouble on the hoof and you won't make things any better by getting involved. Get it?"

Garmo shook his head. "I don't understand you, Deputy."

"Why? What isn't clear?"

"Oh, I understand what you're saying. It's you I don't get." Garmo waved a hand. "Me, I don't much care for my job at the auto parts store, but I don't resent it like you do yours. You're always mad. You've got a good job with benefits and a pension. So what's your problem?"

Meisengill went cherry red.

"You want to know the truth, *Jeff*?" He gave the new name a mocking tone. "I love part of my job and I hate the other part. It depends on whether I'm dealing with lambs or wolves."

Garmo frowned. "What does that mean?"

The deputy sighed. "Let's take a hypothetical, okay? Say there's this woman, a schoolteacher with a husband and two kids. Never had so much as a parking ticket. One night she's walking her dog and she hears a fight going on across the street."

Garmo put down his sandwich.

"She sees this guy take a gun and shoot some other clown in the head three times. Bang bang bang."

Garmo's throat had gone dry. He sipped soda.

For once Meisengill seemed to be enjoying himself. "The teacher managed to keep her dog quiet and get back to her apartment house without being seen by Johnny Gunslinger. And being a good citizen who believes in the American system of justice, this little lamb called the cops and reported what she saw."

Garmo had heard a dog *yip* that night but he had been too busy concentrating on Fabrizzi, bleeding on the pavement, to worry about it. One in a long line of mistakes.

"So," said Meisengill, with mock cheerfulness. "This poor woman and her whole family wound up in the witness protection program, having to uproot themselves, change their names, their jobs, abandon friends and family, all because of that trigger-happy fool."

All because she was a snitch.

"But it gets better!" said the deputy. "Because our idiot friend put three bullets in the vic's skull and didn't even kill him. Quite a marksman, huh?"

Fabrizzi had found Garmo in bed with his wife and chased him with Anna's peashooter of a gun. Garmo wrestled it away from him, but how could he know those little bullets wouldn't finish the job?

"Now," said Meisengill, "you'd think the victim would have been happy to testify against the man who banged his wife and almost killed him, and that might have left the schoolteacher off the hook. But no, the near-sighted shooter's daddy was a mob boss, and the vic was so terrified he wouldn't say a word."

Garmo nodded. His father had paid Fabrizzi's medical bills and given the man and his wife a pile of dough to leave town. A much better deal than they would have gotten if he had stuck around to testify.

"So, wrapping things up," said Meisengill, "the idiot with the gun was facing a long prison sentence, and, since there is no honor whatsoever among thieves, he decided to cooperate with the feds."

It was the hardest decision Garmo had ever made, even though his father had insisted on it. "I don't want to die knowing you're in prison," he had said. "Talk. You don't owe those jackals in our family anything. Hell, they won't let you run my business anyway."

"What I can't understand," Meisengill went on, "and what I can never forgive, is that the geniuses at the Justice Department agreed that you didn't have to testify against your father. You sent a bunch of small fry to prison but that bastard Don Garmo is still strolling around free as a goddamned bird."

"My father isn't strolling anywhere. He's in a bed dying."

The deputy snorted. "I'll believe that when I piss on his tombstone. I know plenty of Mafia kingpins who had certificates from a dozen M.D.s that they were on death's doorstep, and most of them were still kicking when their prosecutors died of old age."

Garmo realized he was squashing his sandwich between tightening fingers. He put it down again and wiped his hands. "I'm sorry my father isn't dying fast enough to suit you."

Meisengill snorted. "Oh, have I hurt your tender little feelings? Gimme a break. If I'm going to get sentimental it's about all the people who died young because of your old man."

He drank his orange juice. "But I digress, don't I? You were asking about my job satisfaction. I like my work fine when I'm protecting the lambs, like the teacher and her family. And I have no idea where they are, so don't you dare ask.

"What gives me acid indigestion is when I'm taking care of wolves like you. Believe me, I would be happy to leave you to the hit men your so-called friends have set on your tail. But that would discourage future turncoats from seeing the light. So here I am babysitting a tattletale jerk who couldn't even kill the man he was cuckolding. Lucky me."

Garmo released a breath. "Lucky you."

Meisengill shrugged. "It's a living. You have anything else to report except your new lust object and the bald guy chasing her?"

"No. Listen, could I write a letter to my father?"

"Jesus." The marshal straightened up. "You really do have a death wish. Anything you send will be read by half of a dozen of your dearest enemies before it reaches the old man's sick bed. If it ever does reach him."

"I'm not that important."

"Damn right. You're a bug on the windshield. But all the paisans you put in jail, and their loving relatives outside, they all want revenge."

Garmo shrugged. This was not news. "There's some stuff I want to get off my chest before he passes. Is that so wrong?"

Meisengill sighed. "Tell you what. Go ahead and write your letter. Not a word about where you are or how you spend your days. Give it to me next time we meet and if the people upstairs approve it I'll have it typed up and sent along to the old bastard."

"A typed copy?"

"The original might give somebody a hint as to where you are." He shrugged. "Ink. Paper. Pollen. That ain't gonna happen."

Garmo smiled. "Thanks. I appreciate it."

Meisengill raised a bony finger. "But only if you keep your nose clean, Jeff Clancy. No speeding tickets. And don't miss a day's work."

"Got it."

"And stay away from your sexy neighbor. Chasing a married woman got you into this mess."

"WHAT'S YOUR PROBLEM today?" asked Parnell. The owner of the auto parts store was a beefy man, although Garmo never saw him eating a thing. He usually had a stick of nicotine gum in his mouth, chewing automatically when he wasn't complaining. Today he was desperate to close the store early to get to a basketball game. A high school game. Apparently that passed for entertainment out here.

"I had to ask you three times to get those plugs. Are you on vacation?" Then he grinned nervously.

Parnell's attitude to Garmo was a study in mixed feelings. Obviously he resented having "Jeff Clancy" forced on him by the feds. And he was the kind of a man certain to pick on any sucker unlucky enough to work for him.

But after giving Garmo a dressing-down he would invariably remember that this was a guy with a past, probably a bloody one. Suddenly he would be all smiles, as if the insults had just been a joke.

"Sorry," said Garmo. "Got a lot on my mind today. Sick relative."

Parnell frowned.

Garmo figured he was thinking: *This man's not supposed to be in touch with any relatives. Is he lying or breaking the rules?*

No doubt the boss would soon be calling Meisengill in a panic, worrying that Jeff Clancy's mysterious past was about to show up in the store with an AK-47.

Well, let 'em whine. For once Garmo was telling the truth. He was worried about his father. And besides, he had been following the rules like a freaking boy scout.

As he manhandled cartons into place in the back room of the store he thought about what he wanted to say to his old man.

There was no way he could apologize for being such a screw-up. But at least he could say thanks for all his father had done for him. Maybe reminisce about the good times when he was growing up, when his mom was still alive.

Before he really understood what his father did for a living. Before he was eager to join up.

"Clancy! Get your ass up here now!"

He sighed.

GARMO SAW HIS neighbor twice in the next few weeks. The first time it happened while he was mowing the lawn. That was another chore he had never had to do in the city, but at least he understood it. This was not true about some of the other yard work.

When he had arrived in town there was a twenty pound sack of top soil near the front door. What were you supposed to do with that? Next to it were half a dozen black steel stakes, each seven feet long. It was clear you were supposed to put the pointed end in the ground and hang something from the hook on the other end. He had no idea what. So they still leaned against the wall, mocking the city boy.

He was dragging the lawn mower over to trim the sidewalk edges when Kathy popped out of her house, pretty as a picture in halter top and shorts. She waved as she headed to her car.

"House hunting!" she said.

"Good luck." But he didn't mean it. When she disappeared this dreary edge of suburbia was going to be even more depressing.

THE NEXT TIME he saw her was downtown. It was his lunch break and he was strolling to a burger joint—what passed for pizza out here was too tragic to consider—when he saw Kathy on the other side of the street, coming out of the post office with a big envelope in her hand.

Garmo was about to call her name when, damned if he didn't see the bald guy again. He was dressed in jeans and a gray sweater this time, and he was at the far end of the block. He was absolutely staring at Kathy.

"Hey!" yelled Garmo, and stepped into the street.

A horn blasted and he heard the screech of brakes. A white SUV slammed to a stop a foot in front of him.

The driver shouted as Garmo ran past.

Kathy was wide-eyed. "Jeff, be careful! You could have gotten killed!"

The bald guy was gone. "Damn it."

"Jeff? What's wrong?"

"You have any stalkers? Ex-boyfriends following you?"

"What? No!"

"I just saw a guy watching you, down by the drug store. A bald-headed man."

"What makes you think he was watching me?"

"He was looking right at you."

"So? He was looking down the street. That's nothing to get run over about."

"Yeah, but I saw him once before."

Kathy frowned. "When was that?"

"A couple of days after you moved in. He was skulking around in the woods behind your yard."

She stared at him for a moment. Then she smiled. "Skulking."

Garmo felt his face reddening. *She thinks I'm coming on to her.* "I mean it, Kathy. This is real."

"Then why didn't you tell me about it then?"

Good question. He couldn't explain that a U.S. deputy marshal had told him to stay away from her.

"I forgot about it until I saw him again."

She patted his arm. "That's very sweet of you, Jeff, but I can take care of myself."

"Look." Garmo felt helpless. "Watch out for bald men, okay? And lock your doors."

She laughed. "I watch out for all men, regardless of their hair style. Women have to." She walked away, hips twitching.

Garmo shook his head. Trying to be one of the good guys was a lot harder than he expected.

ANOTHER WEEK PASSED. Another week of shifting pallets and cartons for Parnell. Each day he came home, ate whatever crap food he'd picked up on the way. Then he worked on the letter to his father. When he ran out of things to write he'd crack a beer and watch TV.

The next day he did it all again.

At night he would dream of his old life, planning robberies. Sticking it to rivals. Outsmarting cops and prosecutors.

It all seemed unreal now. Or was this the fantasy life, out where graffiti on a cemetery wall was a major crime wave?

HE FINALLY DECIDED the letter was finished. He had said all he could, if not all he wanted to. He wrote out a clean copy, no scratch-outs or changes. He wasn't sure why he bothered, since the feds would type it up before giving it to the old man. But it seemed important to do the thing right.

The next morning was his day off. He slept late and then called Meisengill.

The deputy sounded strange, like he'd been caught swallowing coffee. "Clancy. I've been meaning to phone you."

"Well, I saved you the trouble. I've got that letter ready for my father. I don't want—"

"Stop." The marshal sighed. "I'm sorry. Your father died yesterday. It'll be in the news this morning."

Garmo said nothing. He could smell the summer flowers out in his yard. Sickly sweet, he decided.

"I want to go to the funeral."

Meisengill was all business again. "Not possible. You know the rules."

"Make it possible, damn it! It's all I can do for him."

"You go anywhere near that graveyard and you'll be their next customer. You know there's a contract out on you and the hit men will be hanging around like hunters in deer season. I'm sorry it happened this way, but—"

Through the window Garmo saw Kathy coming out of her house. She turned to lock the door and—

The bald guy, dressed in black again, burst out of the bushes. He hit her on the head with a blackjack and Kathy collapsed, tumbling backwards into his arms.

Garmo dropped the phone. He ran to his front door, silently cursing his lack of a gun.

Outside, he snatched up one of the long metal garden stakes that was leaning against the wall, still waiting for him to find a place for them.

Then he ran next door.

The bald guy had dragged Kathy into the house and was trying to push the door shut.

Garmo hit the door with his shoulder and thrust it forward, almost into Baldy's face.

The stalker jumped back. He reached into his jacket, obviously going for a holster, and Garmo grabbed the garden stake with both hands and shoved.

Baldy stumbled over Kathy's body and tumbled back onto the carpet.

Garmo followed him down, using his weight to drive the stake deep into the man's chest. He must have hit the heart because blood started to fountain.

Baldy fumbled at the black metal stake and then lay still.

Garmo rolled off and lay gasping. *Meisengill will be pleased. This time when I tried to kill a guy I succeeded.*

Was Kathy dead? If she was, would the cops believe his version of what happened?

He had better call Meisengill, but he had dropped the phone in his kitchen and—

Kathy moaned.

Garmo crawled over to her. "You okay?"

"No. I think my head exploded. What happened?"

"It was the bald guy I told you about. He hit you as you stepped out of the house. I saw it and came over and—well, you don't wanna look."

But she did. "Jesus! You speared him."

"Yeah. He was reaching for a gun, I think."

"Help me up."

Garmo took her arm and led her over to the sofa. She touched the back of her head and winced. "Ouch. I am so lucky."

"I guess that's the best way to look at it. Have you ever seen him before?"

"No. Can you get me my purse?"

Garmo did. "You need aspirin? I'll get you a glass of water."

"That would be nice."

He went into the kitchen and looked for a glass.

"I don't know this guy," Kathy called after him. "But I can guess why he was following me."

"Yeah?" Garmo stopped in the doorway, carrying the water glass.

Kathy was on her feet, a pistol in her hand. "He was trying to eliminate the competition. No one could kill you until your father died, out of respect, so I've been waiting. Him too, I guess."

Garmo heaved the glass, missing her by a yard.

"Thanks for the assist."

The Book of Eve (The First Mystery)

Steve Hockensmith

1.1 ONE DAY IT came to pass that Eve, the mother of all mothers, was going to cook a lamb stew, but her son Abel didn't bring the meat he'd promised. Eve walked around the hill to Abel's hut, but he wasn't there. She climbed the hill and looked out over the fields, yet still she didn't see him. So she returned to the hut that she shared with the father of all fathers.

"Have you seen Abel?" Eve asked Adam.

Adam was experimenting with one of his amusements. He'd dug a hole in the ground the size of his fist, and now he was trying to hit a walnut into it with a stick. He called the game "walnut hole stick hit."

"Of course, I've seen Abel," Adam said, not looking up from his stick.

He hit the walnut. It didn't go into the hole.

"Flutz," Adam said.

He'd also been experimenting with sounds to make when something frustrating happened.

"Well?" Eve said. "When? Where?"

"When where what?"

Adam moved to the walnut and hit it again. It still didn't go into the hole.

"Pronk," Adam said.

"When and where did you see Abel?" Eve asked.

"I've seen Abel a million times all over the place. How could I miss him? He's our son. He lives, like, a hundred cubits away. Flutz, what a dumb question."

Adam lined up to hit the walnut again.

"I meant have you seen Abel lately?" Eve said.

"Oh. Right. Yeah, I've seen him lately."

Adam took a practice swing, passing the tip of the stick over the walnut.

"When?" asked Eve.

"Yesterday afternoon," Adam said. "When he promised to bring you lamb for stew."

Adam hit the walnut. It didn't go into the hole.

Adam cried out unto the heavens.

"Blarm!" he said.

Eve went to see her son Cain.

1.2 CAIN WAS EXPERIMENTING, too. He'd tied a wooden rod to an ass with long vines, and now he was standing a few cubits behind the animal with the rod stuck into the ground.

"I still don't get what we're doing," the ass said.

"I told you. It's gonna help me till the earth," Cain said.

"Yeah, but how?"

Cain wrapped his hands around the rod.

"Just walk," he told the ass. "You'll see."

The ass started walking. As soon as the vines grew taut, the rod popped out of the ground.

"What am I supposed to be seeing?" the ass asked.

Cain tried to push the rod into the earth again. But the soil was hard and rocky, just as the Lord promised when he'd banished Eve and Adam from Eden.

Cain used the word that he preferred for frustrating experiences.

"Excrement!"

The ass stopped and looked back.

"Where? It wasn't me," he said. "Oh, hi, Eve!"

Eve gave the ass a half-hearted wave as she walked up.

"Cain," she said, "when was the last time you saw your brother?"

"I don't know," Cain said. He lifted up the rod and plunged it into the ground. This time it stuck. "Yesterday, I guess."

"Where was he?"

"With his precious flock, of course." Cain grabbed the vines and gave them a snap. "Go!"

"Hey!" said the ass, glaring back at him. "Watch it, man."

"Cain...if you see Abel, tell him I've been looking for him," said Eve.

Cain nodded without looking at her.

"Yeah, yeah," he mumbled.

"You got it, Eve!" the ass said.

Cain snapped the vines again.

"I said, 'Go!'"

The ass stepped forward.

The rod held steady.

The vines broke.

"Fornication!" Cain roared, stomping on big clods of dry dirt. "Fornication excrement!"

"Dude...not in front of your mom," the ass whispered.

But Eve was already heading back to her hut.

1.3 THE NEXT DAY, Eve was even more worried. Abel still hadn't come to see her.

"Relax," Adam said when Eve asked him what they should do. "He's probably just out exploring."

Adam tossed a dried gourd toward a basket he'd perched on some rocks. It was another of his amusements. He called this one "dried gourd basket toss."

The gourd hit the side of the basket and bounced off into the rocks.

"Exploring?" said Eve. "That doesn't sound like Abel."

Adam retrieved his gourd, then turned and trotted about thirty cubits off.

"Yeah, well," he said, taking aim at the basket again. "He's old enough now to realize there's something he ought to be looking for, know what I mean?"

Eve did.

She'd been wondering for a long time if the Lord was ever going to create more women.

Adam tossed his gourd again. This time it went in.

1.4 EVE WENT BACK to Cain's field. Cain was there with a different ass.

"This is gonna help you *what*?" the ass said as Cain wrapped long leather straps around her flanks.

"Till the soil," Cain said.

"I heard that," the ass said. "I just don't have any idea what it...oh, hey, Mrs. A!"

Eve walked out into the field.

"Hello," she said. "Cain—did you ever see Abel?"

Cain gave the leather straps a shake.

"I've been busy, O.K.? You know...trying to grow more food? So we'll have something to eat other than mutton and wild onions?"

"I was just wondering if your brother had returned from wherever he went."

"Well, how should I know? What am I? A shepherd for brothers? A brotherherd? Is that what you want? Me to spend all my time wandering around with a crook looking for Abel instead of growing wheat for bread?"

"I was hoping you'd seen him, that's all."

"Abel's missing?" said the ass. "You should ask the Lord where he is."

"Oh, no no no. Bad idea. Very, *very* bad idea," Cain said. He dropped the straps and turned to his mother. "You know how He is about questions and knowledge and all that. Remember what happened the last time you tried to get some answers? Whammy—out of paradise! With the toil and the hunger and the *death*! Whoo! You want it to get *worse*?"

"No," Eve said.

She was in no hurry to talk to the Lord.

"You can never tell when He's gonna drop by anyway," Cain went on. "He's busy doing whatever it is He does. Who knows when we'll even see Him again?"

Eve turned and began walking away.

"Best just to wait for Abel to come back and not go dragging the Lord into it, don't you think?" Cain said. "Am I right or am I right?"

"You're probably right," Eve said without looking back. "Send Abel to me if you see him."

Cain thumped his chest.

"Not a brotherherd, remember? Not! A! Brotherherd!"

Eve kept walking, headed west.

"I don't think the Lord would be annoyed if your mom asked about Abel," the ass said. "You just have to figure out how to get His attention."

Cain picked up the straps and pulled them tight.

"Oh, shut up," he said.

2.1 EVE WALKED TO the Pishon river and followed it to the garden of Eden. It wasn't that far from her hut, but she hadn't been there in years. It hadn't changed, as far as she could tell.

The cherubim still guarded the east entrance, the four identical, impassive faces each of them wore—man, lion, ox and eagle—gazing unblinkingly at the desolate lands east of Eden. Behind them was the blazing sword that pointed all directions at once.

It always seemed like overkill to Eve. She and Adam weren't going to mess with giant four-faced angel creatures *or* a living sword *or* a living sword that could aim its blade at everything in creation at the same time *or* a living sword that could aim its blade at everything in creation at the same time *and was on fire*.

It wasn't just to keep Eve and Adam and their sons out. It was a message.

Not for you. You blew it. Fornicate off, fornicator.

Yet somewhere beyond the cherubim and the flaming sword, the tree of knowledge still grew. And there was something that Eve really, really wanted to know.

She'd be caught. She'd be punished. Again. But she already knew what was even worse than exile from Eden: *not* knowing where your child is.

Eve stood there a long time, feeling the worry, the pain. Trying to use it to dredge up enough courage to step toward the garden.

"In the mood for fruit?" someone said.

Eve turned toward the voice. It was one she recognized—and never thought she'd hear again.

"It's not that kind of tree of knowledge, you know," the voice went on, though Eve saw nothing but the usual white rocks and yellow soil and tangled coils of black bramble. "It won't tell you where Abel is."

The serpent slithered from the shadows of the thickest, thorniest thicket.

"I could help you, though," he said.

2.2 EVE LOOKED AROUND for a rock the right size—just a little larger than her fist—and upon seeing one she snatched it up.

"Now hold on a second," the serpent said.

Eve lunged at him, raising the rock.

"What have you done to my son, you flutzing excrement?"

The serpent slithered away but didn't dart back into the thorn bushes.

"Me? I haven't done anything!"

Eve chased him in a circle, the rock still over her head.

"You tricked him! Just like you tricked me all those years ago!"

The serpent lifted his head to look back at Eve even as the rest of his body kept writhing away frantically.

"Eve, think about it! The Lord put a curse of enmity on us! Your kids are gonna hate me forever, remember? If I tried to talk to Abel or Cain, either one, they'd do exactly what you're doing now!"

"As they should! Because of you we were thrown out of the garden! Because of you we wear animal skins and have to grow our own food! Because of you the Lord made childbirth *hurt*!"

Eve was suddenly overcome with such rage she screamed and threw the rock at the serpent.

It bounced past him harmlessly.

"Look," the serpent said, stopping and turning toward Eve. "Don't forget that I...oh, come on, woman!"

Eve was picking up another rock.

The serpent fled again.

"I got punished, too!" he said. "I used to have legs! Now I have to slide around in the dirt trying to keep people from pounding me with rocks! All because I was curious!"

Eve hefted the new rock. It was smaller and lighter than the first. Perhaps too small and light to squash a skull.

She tossed it aside and began hunting for something bigger.

"Curious, huh?" she said. "That's why you talked me into eating from the tree of knowledge?"

The serpent paused by the dark thicket he'd emerged from a minute before.

"It didn't take much talking, as I recall," he said. "Neither of us could resist the...the...you know. The *not knowing* of it. The Lord plants something in the garden, right in front of you, and He says, 'This thing is amazing, incredible, mind-blowing. But leave it alone, O.K.? Go eat figs naked all day.' He even calls it 'the tree of knowledge.' And He doesn't think someone's gonna go for it? If He didn't want anyone to touch the thing He should have called it 'the boring tree of nothing special' and planted it a million cubits away. After all these years I still don't get it."

Eve had picked up another rock as the serpent spoke. It was a jagged chunk of soft shale, too brittle to do much damage.

Eve threw it at the serpent anyway.

It sailed over him into the bushes. He didn't even flinch.

"It was a test," Eve said. "And I failed. Thanks to you."

She went back to hunting for the right rock.

"You listened to me because we're the same, Eve," the serpent said. "We're smart. We're curious. We ask questions. We can't help it! You give us a...a *not knowing*, and we want an answer. It's our nature. Is that our fault?"

"Yes!"

Eve scooped up a handful of dusty dirt and slung it at the serpent. It dissipated into a harmless brown cloud before it reached him.

"So you'd rather be stupid?" the serpent said. He shook his head. "No, not you. You had to know, no matter what." He flicked his tongue and dropped his voice. "Admit it, Eve. Leaving Eden sucked, but you're not *really* sorry you ate the fruit."

Eve turned away, shoulders slumping. This was all a stupid distraction.

Where was her son?

"Let me make it up to you," the serpent said softly. "You want to find Abel? I can help."

Eve whirled around. "How do you know Abel's missing?"

The serpent recoiled. But he smiled, too.

"See? An excellent question. Asking comes naturally to you," he said. "An ass talked to some swine who talked to a lizard who talked to a bird who talked to a mouse who talked to me."

"Alright," Eve said, accepting the answer begrudgingly. "But how do I know this isn't another trick?"

"Eve, Eve, Eve...I never tricked you. I never lied. I just made a mistake and now I genuinely, sincerely want to make up for it. Plus, *I'm* curious about Abel, too. Not much interesting happens anymore. I've been bored to tears for years. Haven't you?"

Eve thought it over, frowning, then turned to look at the garden. The faces of the four cherubim—all 16 of them—seemed to be pointed straight at her. The tip of the flaming sword, too.

"Do you know about Adam's sacrifices?" she sighed.

The serpent's smile grew a little wider.

"Is that when he burns twigs and shouts to the Lord?" he said.

"Burns his favorite walnut-hole-stick-hit sticks," Eve corrected. "And asks the Lord to come forgive us." Eve shrugged. "He never does. But the boys have been thinking about giving it a try."

"Yeah?" The serpent slid a little closer. "And?"

"I'm wondering if I should try it."

The serpent didn't hesitate.

"Nah!" he said. "There's no guarantee He'd help. You couldn't even be sure He'd notice. Remember how He figured out you ate from the tree of knowledge all those years ago?"

Eve closed her eyes, returning to that horrible day.

"He came to see us," she said. "And we were hiding in the bushes. Wearing leaves."

Eve opened her eyes again.

The serpent was closer than ever.

"Exactly!" he said. "He didn't just know. He noticed this, noticed that, called out to you, heard your answer, thought about it, put it together. He figured it out from what He *saw* and *heard*. That's what we need to do."

"What do you mean?"

"I'm saying we should do what He did. Look around. Ask questions."

The serpent moved so close he could have licked Eve's toes with a quick flick of his split-ended tongue.

"Investigate," he said.

2.3 ABEL USUALLY SPENT most of his time tending his flock. So Eve went to talk to them.

The serpent went, too, slithering along beside her until they came to the low, rolling hills pocked with grazing sheep.

"Not as many as usual, is it?" the serpent said.

"Not half as many," said Eve.

She looked at the mangy gray animals moving slowly, lazily from one clump of grass to the next. The *big* mangy gray animals.

"The lambs are all gone," Eve said.

"Ooo," said the serpent. "What could it mean?"

It sounded like he was enjoying himself.

Eve scowled down at him.

He zipped ahead.

"Yo! Cotton ball!" he said to the nearest sheep—a ewe with particularly shaggy wool and a missing ear. "Seen Abel lately?"

The ewe looked up from the grass she'd been eating and regarded the serpent incuriously.

"Not for a couple days," she said, still chewing. "It's a bummer, too. We've had lions come by, hyenas, wild dogs. There's an eagle that's gotten, like, six lambs. It's a wonder the jerk can still fly."

The ewe bent her head and tore out another mouthful of grass.

"I can hardly believe *I'm* still alive," she muttered.

"Why didn't you come down out of the hills?" Eve asked her. "Get me and Adam? Or Cain?"

The ewe lifted her head again. But it wasn't to look at Eve and the serpent. It was to glance around at the other sheep languidly grazing nearby.

"What?" she said. "And leave the flock?"

"You could've all come together and...," Eve began.

She cut herself off with a heavy, aggravated sigh.

One problem at a time.

She started over.

"What was Abel doing when you last saw him?"

The ewe nodded at a bluff about two hundred cubits off.

"Taking a couple lambs up to those rocks," she said.

"What for?" the serpent asked.

"How should I know? Maybe he was gonna show 'em the view."

The serpent looked up at Eve. "Shall we go see what *we* see?"

Eve nodded.

"Hey! When you find Abel, tell him to get his butt back here!" the ewe called after them as they left. "We need a shepherd!"

"Yeah! It's not safe around here!" added another sheep.

"Yeah!" said another.

"Yeah!" said another.

"Yeah!" said another.

Then they all lowered their heads and went back to eating.

2.4 EVE COULD HEAR buzzing as she and the serpent neared the top of the bluff. There were insects ahead. Lots.

The serpent picked up his pace, wriggling ahead of Eve.

He came to a sudden stop when he reached the summit.

"Oh," he said. "Ew."

Eve ran the rest of the way up the slope.

"No!" she cried when she saw what was causing the buzzing.

Hunks of black, ragged flesh were strewn atop a large, flat rock. Around it was a swirling cloud—dozens of fat flies that feasted, flew, feasted, flew.

Eve charged toward them waving her arms.

"Get away from him! Get away!"

A black mass of flies rose up from the rock like smoke.

"Hey, back off, lady!" a tinny voice said.

"Yeah, what's the deal?" squeaked another.

Others joined in.

"Don't swat at me, woman!"

"We aren't bothering anybody!"

"Can't a guy eat in peace around here?"

Eve stopped and dropped her arms, and the churning cloud slowly sank back down over the rotting meat.

"Did you see?" the serpent said.

Eve nodded.

Mixed in with the meat under the thick blanket of flies had been leg bones and ribcages and spines. And two skulls small enough for Eve to hold together in one hand.

The flies had been gorging themselves on the bodies of two lambs.

"You thought that was Abel for a second, didn't you?" the serpent asked Eve.

She nodded again.

"What did you think had happened to him?" the serpent said. "I mean, who would...? Ohhhhhhh."

The serpent dropped his voice to a whisper even though whispering or shouting alike made no difference. You could never tell if one or the other would be heard.

"You think He'd do something like that?"

Eve shot the serpent a glare. "You think He wouldn't?"

The serpent just flicked his tongue at that, then looked around the top of the bluff. After a moment he went gliding off toward another flat-topped boulder about thirty cubits away. Something was scattered over it, like the first rock, but the flies were ignoring it.

The serpent lifted his head as high as he could.

"Ash," he said. "And...something."

He sank back down to the ground.

"Legs sure would come in handy right now," he grumbled.

Eve walked over and looked at the top of the rock. The serpent was right: It was covered with powdery gray ash and blackened clumps and long, half-burned stalks.

"Wheat," Eve said. "And I think those are turnips."

"Wheat and turnips? That's Cain's thing, right? Growing plants you guys can eat?" the serpent said. "You think he was here, too?"

Eve stared at the ashes for a long, silent moment before answering.

"He didn't mention it," she said.

"Hm. Interesting," said the serpent. "Hey, flies! You know anything about all this?"

"All this what?" one of the flies replied.

"The lambs, the wheat, the turnips, the fire."

"All we know is the lambs are delicious!"

There were peals of high-pitched laughter.

The serpent sighed and began slithering around the base of the ash-covered boulder.

"So Abel comes up here with a couple lambs, and they end up dead," he said. "And someone brings a pile of wheat and turnips to the same spot and sets it on fire. Weird."

"It was a sacrifice," said Eve.

"A what-a-what?" said the serpent. He stopped and raised his head. "Oh. One of Adam's stick-burning things? You think *he* came up here, too?"

"No. I would've known."

"Hm."

The serpent went back to slithering.

Eve felt something touch the side of her neck, and instinctively, unthinkingly, she slapped a hand over it.

"Frank!" a little voice shrieked.

Eve took her hand from her neck and looked down at it. In the palm was a dot of flattened black at the center of a splotch of red.

"She killed Frank!" a fly screamed.

"Bitch!"

"Should we bite her?"

The black cloud rose up again over what was left of the lambs.

"I think we'd better go," said the serpent. "This way."

He started down the side of the bluff. Eve wiped her hand on her buckskin muumuu and followed.

Behind them, the flies settled back down over the lambs and went back to feasting.

2.5 THE SERPENT ZIGZAGGED down the hill, pausing from time to time to stare at the dry, rocky soil.

"What are you looking at?" Eve asked.

"There's at least one advantage to being low to the ground," the serpent said. "Every footprint's at eye level."

"You see tracks?"

"Oh, yeah. Lots of 'em. They were all over the place up top, too. Crisscrossing, different sizes. A real mess. But these? Headed down into the valley? It's clear as can be."

"*What* is clear as can be?"

"Two people, walking together."

Eve stopped, some part of her suddenly petrified. She looked ahead, at the scrub-pocked meadow stretching out from the base of the hill.

There might be answers there. If she wanted them, she'd have to keep following the serpent.

What if she didn't like the answers, though? What if she were better off not finding them?

Maybe she should turn around. Maybe she should just go home.

Eve started toward the meadow again. She'd stood still barely a second.

The serpent didn't even seem to notice.

"Cain and Abel," he said. "They get along?"

"Of course," Eve said. "I mean...there's a reason they live in separate huts. Abel can be a bit much. Would this please the Lord? Would that please the Lord? Should we thank the Lord before we eat? Should we thank the Lord before we sleep? The Lord, the Lord, the Lord. Sometimes it gets on Cain's nerves."

"Sounds like he's not the only one."

Eve glowered at the serpent. He didn't seem to notice that, either.

"So you say Cain didn't mention anything about a sacrifice?" he said.

"No. Maybe he was embarrassed because the Lord didn't show up again." Eve dropped her voice to a mutter and shot the serpent another glare. "Used to be we didn't even know what embarrassment was."

The serpent finally glanced back at her.

When he turned back to the tracks, he began moving down the hillside a little faster.

3.1 ON THE FAR side of the clearing, under the gnarled branches of an olive tree, was a low mound of earth about two cubits wide and three-and-a-half long.

The serpent circled it, scanning the tracks around it with obvious excitement.

Eve approached slowly, every step a battle again.

"The tracks lead straight to the tree, then get all jumbled up," the serpent said. He stopped and pressed his head in close to the heap of dirt. "Hm. Lotta action in there."

"Action?" said Eve.

The serpent nodded.

"Beetles, worms, maggots, ants," he said. "Hey! Guys! What's down there?"

A hundred soprano voices responded in chorus.

"Food!"

"Well, that's helpful," the serpent sighed. "I'd do some digging to see what's there, but...you know."

He writhed, as if trying to lift up the clawed hands he no longer had.

Eve forced herself to step to the dirt pile, then got down on her knees beside it.

The serpent moved a few cubits off—beyond Eve's reach, but close enough to watch.

This was Eve's last chance to stop. Her last chance to leave it alone.

She started to dig. It didn't take long to unearth what was buried there.

It was the world's first grave, and it wasn't very deep.

Eve collapsed in on herself, curled into a ball, sobbing.

"Oh. Wow. Hoo boy," the serpent said. "Uhh...I'll just be over there for a while."

He slithered off toward the rough bramble that took over at the meadow's edge.

3.2 EVE STAYED DOUBLED-UP for a while, weeping. Then she sat up and wept some more.

When she was finally done crying, she pushed back the dirt she'd dug up, remembering the Lord's judgment from all those years ago.

"You'll have to sweat for your food till you go into the ground yourselves," He'd said. "That's where you came from, you know. You're nothing but dust, and you'll go back to being dust. Ingrates."

Yet Eve had never expected Abel to go into the ground first.

The serpent came sliding from the brush as she smoothed the soil over her youngest son.

"So...Eve. I know you're upset, but...just an FYI," he said. "I found more tracks. One set. They head east."

Not off into the desert. Not back to Eden. Not nowhere, disappearing mid-stride.

Toward the huts.

Eve stood slowly, unsteadily, and dusted off her hands.

"Show me," she said.

3.3 THE SERPENT LED Eve over rolling hills, always eight or nine cubits ahead. Sometimes Eve could see the footprints he was following, sometimes she couldn't. It didn't matter, though. She knew where they led. Where else *could* they lead?

The serpent stopped near a small hut with mud walls and a roof of dried reeds and palm fronds.

Cain's home. He was still in the field nearby, staggering along behind the ass as it dragged his crude plow through the rocky ground.

"It's working!" Cain said.

"Yeah, kinda," grunted the ass. "But I still say we should try it with you pulling and me steering."

"Hands, idiot. You can't steer without hands."

"Watch who you're calling a...hey, look who's back. Yo, Mrs. A! Tell Cain not to be such a jerk!"

Cain stopped and looked back at his mother. She was walking toward him across the field, picking up speed the closer she got.

When Cain saw the fury on her face, he quickly untethered himself from the plow and began backing away.

"What's the matter, Mom?" he asked weakly.

Eve marched up and slapped him.

"What did you do?" She hit him again, then again. "What did you do?"

"Whoa. Eve," said the ass. "All he did was call me an idiot."

Eve kept smacking Cain with a flattened palm, striking the top of his head, his ear, his cheek.

"What did you do? What did you do?"

Cain ducked his head and buried his face in his arms.

"He fell!" he said. "He drowned! He choked on a cherry pit!"

Eve hit Cain again and again.

"What did you do? What did you do?"

"A wolf ate him! A lion mauled him! A snake bit him!"

The serpent had followed Eve across the field, stopping a few cubits behind her.

"Oh, please," he said, rolling his eyes.

The blows kept coming.

"What did you do? What did you do?"

Cain began to cry.

"We tried a sacrifice," he blubbered. "And the Lord came. He noticed and *He actually came*! Only He didn't like my offering. He rejected it. Wheat and turnips I worked so hard to grow. This place is practically a desert, but I get out here and break my back every day and I make food! And when I give Him some, He's just like, 'Big whoop.' And Abel's like, 'Well, how 'bout *this*?' And the Lord's all, 'That's more like it, bro.' Two measly fornicating excrementy lambs! *That* the Lord loved! It was so unfair!"

Eve reached out and placed a hand gently on the back of Cain's head. She mussed his dark hair, tears welling in her own eyes. Then she raised the hand up and brought it down hard.

"What did you do?" she said.

"After the Lord left, I led Abel down to a clearing and I...I... it was so unfair!"

Cain began bawling so hard he couldn't speak.

Eve took a deep breath, then looked over at the ass.

"Don't tell anyone about this," she said. She glared down at the serpent. "*Anyone*."

"Umm...O.K.," said the ass.

"Yeah, sure, whatever you say," said the serpent.

Eve turned and began walking away.

When Cain realized she was leaving, he lifted his head.

"Where are you going?" he whimpered. "What are you gonna do?"

Eve stopped and looked back.

"I'm going to talk to Adam," she said.

Cain wiped his nose on the left shoulder of his dirty sheepskin frock.

"Just Dad, right? You're not gonna try to tell..." He looked around nervously. "You Know Who?"

"No," Eve said. "I'm not going to tell You Know Who."

She started walking away again.

"Mom...I'm scared," said Cain.

"You should be," said Eve, not stopping this time. "I am, too."

3.4 THE SERPENT CAME sliding up beside Eve as she passed Cain's hut.

"You're really not going to tell the Lord?"

"You've seen Him when He's angry," Eve said. "He might kill Cain. He might kill us all."

"So you'll protect Cain even though he's a...a..."

There was no word for what the serpent was trying to say.

"A person who kills other persons?" he said.

"I only have one son left," said Eve. "Yes. I'll protect him."

Tears streamed down her face.

"Why didn't he know right from wrong?" she said. "That's the whole reason we're not in the garden anymore. We're supposed to *know.*"

She wasn't asking the serpent. She was asking herself. She didn't even look down, which is why she didn't notice the serpent coiling and writhing for a moment.

A shoulderless shrug.

"Kids, right?" the serpent said.

3.5 THERE WAS ONE last hill between Eve and the hut she shared with Adam. As she approached it, she saw a thin column of smoke stretching up into the sky like a long, black finger. It pointed at something on the other side of the hill.

"No," Eve said.

She began to run. As she rounded the base of the hill, she could see Adam in the distance, tossing something onto a bonfire.

It was an armful of walnut-hole-stick-hit sticks. He was burning his dried-gourd-basket-toss gourd and his stuffed-hedgehog-kick-into-net hedgehog, too.

When he saw Eve, he smiled and waved.

"Don't worry about Abel, babe—I'll take care of it!" he called out. "I'm gonna ask the Lord where the little pronker went!"

The serpent caught up to Eve.

"Ooo," he said when he saw what Adam was doing. "If that actually works this time...."

He turned and streaked into the nearest bushes.

"Later!" he said.

Eve took a step toward Adam.

"No! Adam! Don't!"

But it was too late.

The Lord was there.

4.1 HE LOOKED THE same, of course. Like Adam, but taller, broader, older, more intense. And dressed in a spotless white robe rather than ragged animal skins.

He only spoke to Adam a moment. Then He turned and started toward Eve, leaving Adam behind Him looking bewildered.

Eve trembled as she watched Him come. She wanted to turn and run. Flee into the bushes like the serpent. But what would be the point?

He can hide from you, but you can't hide from Him. She'd learned that a long time ago.

He said only one thing to her, not even breaking stride to say it. He turned His head and shot it at her as He went stalking past.

"You just *had* to know, didn't you?"

And on He went. After He rounded the hill and disappeared from sight, He spoke again with a voice that seemed to blare at Eve, batter her from every direction at once.

"Cain!" He said. "Where is your brother?"

4.2 EVE COULDN'T HEAR what Cain said, but the Lord's words kept booming through the valleys like thunder.

Abel's blood cried out to Him from the ground, He said.

Cain was cursed, He said.

Cain was marked, He said.

Cain was banished, He said.

Both Eve's sons were now gone to her forever.

She fell to her knees and wept.

4.3 "MY OH MY," the serpent said. "I thought I'd seen Him angry before, but yowza."

He slipped from the brush near Eve. She'd stopped crying, yet she hadn't found the strength or the will or any reason at all to stand.

In the distance, Adam was on his knees, too, sifting forlornly through the ashes of his offering fire.

"I got close enough to hear the whole conversation," the serpent told Eve.

He began circling her, peering at her face, trying to read her expression. Curious, as always.

Eve, hating herself for it, was curious, too.

"Yes?" she said. "And?"

"Cain denied it for, like, two seconds," the serpent said. "But it was obvious the Lord already knew everything. Which confuses me, because last time—when you got thrown out of the garden?—He *didn't* seem to just know everything. Do you think He was toying with us back then? Playing dumb?"

The serpent kept gliding around Eve. Watching her.

She just stared down at the dirt before her.

"Anywho," the serpent said, "the Lord tells Cain he's going to be 'a restless wanderer,' right? And Cain was afraid people would figure out who he was, that he was cursed, and kill him. So the Lord put some kind of mark of protection on him so people would leave him alone. But you know what that makes me wonder? *What people*? Who were Cain and the Lord thinking of? Do they know something we don't?"

The serpent stopped in front of Eve and cocked his head, waiting for an answer.

She didn't give him one.

"Well...apparently, Cain's gonna do his wandering in the land of Nod," the serpent went on. "Ever hear of it? Who named it that? Why? It's like, 'Go forth, exile, to the barren land of Shrug!' Chuh? Who knows, though." He looked around at the sandy soil, the tough, thistly brush, the rocky hills. "Maybe it's better than this place."

Still Eve said nothing.

The serpent sighed.

"Look on the bright side," he said soothingly, slithering a little closer. "It could have turned out worse."

Eve finally raised her head to gape at him.

"*What?*"

"You're here, right?" the serpent said. "The Lord didn't smite you or anything. He didn't even smite Cain."

"One of my sons killed the other, and now my only remaining child is accursed, and I'll never see him again. That's the bright side?"

"Hey, isn't it better to be dirt that's up walking around than dirt that's down in the ground?" the serpent said. "Don't beat yourself up for how things turned out. You and Cain—you were both just being who the Lord made. Now, That Guy..."

The serpent turned his head and stuck his chin toward the east, where the Lord had gone to confront Cain.

"He's the real head scratcher. I've been confused by Him from the get-go. Ya think there's any way to figure Him out? Get inside His head? Cuz I'd sure love to know why He acts surprised when one of you..."

A shadow fell over the serpent.

He looked at Eve again. She was looming up over him with something in her hand.

A rock the size of a pomegranate.

The serpent's round eyes widened.

His curiosity had drawn him too close. The bushes were too far away.

There was no escape.

"No! Eve! Don't!" he cried. "It's not my fault! It's not fair! It's not right!"

Eve lifted the rock.

"I know," she said.

The Woman Who Cried Cat

Kevin Quigley

YOUR CAT HAS been in my garden, the note read. *Get control of your animal or there will be consequences. This is your last warning.* It was signed, *A Concerned Neighbor.* As if Marjorie Field didn't know who the neighbor was. She glanced out the window and caught Kenzie Taylor mincing down Yancy Lane, her bottle-blond hair gleaming in the August sun. That woman was the first woman who had ever lived on Yancy Lane that Marjorie actively disliked. She'd blown in from California three summers ago, newly divorced and absurdly wealthy. Why she'd decided to live here on Yancy Lane was beyond Marjorie; the woman could have lived anywhere. But no. Kenzie had decided that Yancy Lane was where she wanted to put down roots, and Yancy Lane was where she wanted to make the first real trouble the street had seen since those package robberies two Christmases ago.

Marjorie picked up the note again, crumpled from having been angrily stuffed through the mail slot. *Your cat has been in my garden.* There was only one problem with that: Marjorie Field didn't have a cat.

"I got the same note," Kenisha Cerritos said, settling into her chair by the bay window and picking up her coffee cup—bone china that only came out when there was serious discussion afoot. Kenisha did have a cat, a sleek indoor tabby named Harris that had never been within yards of Kenzie Taylor's garden. "I don't care for the tone."

"Nor the implication!" Marjorie agreed. "'This is your last warning.' What does that even mean? She's going to go to the police? They'd laugh themselves silly." Marjorie watched Kenisha; they'd had more than one discussion about what happens when white women cry to the police about Black women's misdeeds. If her friend was ruminating on this, though, Kenisha gave no sign.

"I don't like it, is all. Harris is a good cat."

"At least Harris is a *real* cat." At the sound of his name, Harris suddenly appeared by the side of Marjorie's chair, arching his back toward her palm. She stroked his fur indulgently, and he purred in kind. "I don't even know why I got this note."

Kenisha sipped her tea. "Unless she means Rufus."

"Kenisha, I don't think we're going to get anywhere if we try to apply logic to the stringently illogical."

"You do feed him."

Well, she had a point. Rufus was a neighborhood cat, a grey American shorthair with dark black stripes running across his lean body. For a stray, he didn't seem particularly scuffed or battered, and was positively friendly when he strode boldly up to her covered porch and made his presence known. Marjorie had taken to keeping a bag of Kitty Treats by the side of the door should Rufus decide to stop by. But that had been gradual. For years, the cat had come by the house—had come by every house on Yancy from time to time—seemingly just to check in. A feline neighborhood watch. In all that time, her garden, riot with astors, cornflowers, and bee balms, had gone unmolested. As far as Marjorie knew, the same held true for Kenisha, whose lamb's ears were the envy of the neighborhood.

"You feed him, too," Marjorie reminded her. "I think everyone feeds Rufus."

Kenisha's phone buzzed. It was Kyle O'Brien from three doors down. "I got a note," he told them after Kenisha put him on speaker.

"I think we all did," Marjorie said.

"Should I be worried? Calico's just a little thing. She'd never hurt anyone's garden." Kyle was wonderful—maybe Marjorie's favorite person on Yancy Lane after Kenisha—but the fact that he'd named his Calico cat Calico was alarming ... and she hadn't been a little thing for years. Kyle enjoyed feeding her, letting her have her lethargic run of his place. An absolute unit, was Calico, in no shape to be destroying anyone's garden.

"Well, when it comes to Kenzie Taylor," Kenisha said, "I think a good, healthy worry isn't a bad idea."

"Could I come by? How many other people do you think got the note?"

As it turned out, nearly everyone on Yancy Lane got the note: Tamara Spheeris, who lived next door to Kenzie Taylor but whose cat Tomlinson didn't go anywhere without a leash; Georgie Carmichael, who had a gated yard and whose cat Trinity never went beyond the walls; Ted Nedry, Samira Ahmadi, Wendy Spring. All gathered in Kenisha's dining room with cups of coffee and madeleines Marjorie had brought over. There hadn't been a gathering of Yancy Lane denizens like this in years.

"Maybe we should go to the police," Wendy ventured. "I mean, these notes are threatening."

"They're vague," Samira countered. She'd brought her cat with her, a fluffy ragdoll named Blueberry. Samira rarely went anywhere without Blueberry, who she seemed to think was a purse cat even though she was nearly as big as Calico. "They won't take them seriously."

Georgie spoke up. "But what does she mean, *This is your last warning*? Isn't this our first warning?"

All murmured agreement, and Marjorie held up her hands. "I think we need to address the elephant in the room. *Could any of your cats have been at Kenzie's lawn?*" A mild uproar erupted. "I ask only so we have a good defense. If she starts targeting one of us, I want to know where we stand."

They all discussed this. Ted Nedry, whose cat Monadnock was a hairless sphynx, wrinkly and terrifying, spoke up. "I don't know if I'm being naïve here, but I believe all our cats are well-behaved. I know Mondny wouldn't go after that awful woman's garden ... which, confidentially, is probably better now than before." Nervous titters and murmurs of agreement followed this.

"Now, now, enough of that. If our cats are innocent, we have nothing to worry about. This will pass."

But she was wrong on both counts.

MARJORIE WAS JUST opening the door to offer Rufus a Kitty Treat out of her palm when she saw Kenisha running up the sidewalk. She was in her yoga clothes—sweatpants and T-shirt with the legend #WARRIOR on the front—and that shocked Marjorie almost as much as the expression on her friend's face. When was the last time she'd seen Kenisha look *frantic*? Kenisha mounted the steps and before reaching the porch, she screamed, "That bitch has been at my garden!"

Rufus, unmindful of the sudden shift of mood, purred against Kenisha's leg; distractedly, Kenisha bent and scratched him behind the ears. He purred louder, and some of the frenzy went out of Kenisha's face.

Marjorie said, "Slowly, tell me what happened."

Seemingly calmer now, Kenisha followed Marjorie inside and accepted tea, relaying the story in fits and spurts. She'd been waking up earlier than normal to indulge in her jigsaw puzzle hobby in her basement rec room. "Everyone's asleep and it's me time," she said, her teacup barely shaking now. "An hour of that and then it's upstairs on the Peleton. And you know how I have the bike facing the window so I can look out at my garden. I think I sensed something was wrong immediately, but I was so focused on my workout. Halfway through, I figured it out. My lamb's ears were gone. My *lamb's ears*, Marjorie."

There was never any official competition to decide who had the best garden on Yancy Lane, although Marjorie knew—and experienced—the normal pride and covetousness that comes with a well-thought-out and -maintained garden. To have the knack with zinnias that Tamara Spheeris did, while Kyle openly envied her Hawaiian pink peonies. But no one else on the street had even attempted lamb's ear. Many of the gardens had signs saying, "Enjoy with eyes only, please!" but not Kenisha's. The lamb's ears bordered the whole garden, and they were meant to be appreciated by touch—the silky, indulgently soft feel that offered a whole different dimension to a garden. The beauty of the lamb's ears on the border is that they enticed you to spend longer looking at the rest of the garden, as much a feast for the eyes as the lamb's ears were for the touch. Delicate pastel hues spread across Kenisha's lawn and ended just before the border hedges in front of the house. The sad fact everyone on Yancy Lane knew was that if there *were* a competition, they would all be angling for second place. Kenisha Cerritos would take the gold every time.

Until now.

"What if it *is* a cat?" Marjorie asked. "Like it or not, doesn't this give credence to what Kenzie said?"

In response, Kenisha took Marjorie by the hand and dragged her next door. Immediately, Marjorie saw why her friend had looked so harried, and so sure that a person had done this. Only the lamb's ears, the pride of Kenisha's garden, had been torn up. And not *just* torn up, but *dug* up. That was only the insult; the injury was the clods of sod thrown across the lawn and across the backyard, the lamb's ears still clinging to some of them. One had been hurled at the back of Marjorie's house, leaving an ugly brown stain like a bruise against the pale wood. None of the lamb's ears were salvageable; all had been mashed and crumpled to bits in hands that were not feline.

"She did this," Kenisha said, pacing. "She's gotten it into her skull that Harris tore up her garden."

Marjorie, agape at the blatant destruction, tried to think. "We have to talk to her," she said.

"If by *talk to*, you mean *murder*, then I'm your right-hand woman."

"No one's murdering anyone just yet, Kenisha. Get showered and changed, and then we'll go over there together and talk to her. Not *confront* her. Just talk."

For a moment, Kenisha only watched her. *If this was your garden*, Kenisha might be thinking, *there would be more on the line*. Marjorie didn't think so, but then Marjorie knew she had only a good garden, one that could never compete with that of her best friend. If she had grown something as precious as lamb's ear and it had been so flagrantly destroyed, maybe she would have.

Kenzie Taylor's house was an unforgivable eyesore tucked into the apogee of the Yancy Lane cul-de-sac. The previous tenants, married women named Barb and Erica, had kept nice house and had tended a fair garden, and everyone on Yancy Lane was sorry to see them go. What Kenzie had done with their house was nothing short of criminal. First, she'd had it painted a gaudy, blinding yellow, the color of August blight. Then, unfathomably, she'd installed a *second* bay window, this one looking out not on the street but onto Tamara Spheeris's side yard. The house had gained the countenance of those lizards that look in opposite directions at the same time, their eyes bulging from their faces.

"Sometimes she just sits there," Tamara said during book club one evening. "Staring at my house and my yard. I've had to keep all the window shades closed on that side because you never know if she's watching."

It wasn't the side window she was sitting in now; no, Kenzie Taylor watched them approach perched in the front bay window, coffee cup in hand. The cup said **San Diego** and was hot pink with yellow palm trees all over it. Just beneath the front window, the garden was indeed desecrated: sunflowers were a shambles, baby's breath had gone asthmatic, and the amaranthus—once a lavender octopus crawling from the soil—was so much calamari now. But the garden itself was borderline insane: Kenzie had not only planted a corner of mint—which had already started to infest the rest—but she'd also planted row after row of gardenias. If one gets sick, they all get sick, and then you're left with a gasping garden, invasive cats or no. Besides, the whole thing was just hideous, planted seemingly at random by a person with no concern for science or aesthetics. In Marjorie's opinion, Kenzie would be better off if all the neighborhood cats came and put the garden out of its misery. Or, she thought sneakily, if one of the wild bobcats came out of the woods and laid apocalyptic waste to it.

She stifled a smile and sniffed the air. Some unpleasant odor was coming off the lawn but she couldn't quite detect it. "What's that smell?" she asked Kenisha, who, even in her rage, took a moment to inhale. She wrinkled her nose. "It smells like swamp. Is there a broken sewer line somewhere?"

Holding her breath, Marjorie rang the doorbell. Though they could clearly see Kenzie sitting in her window, the woman didn't get up immediately. "Oh, she's *savoring* this," Kenisha murmured.

When the door finally opened, Kenzie—in a scoop top and skinny jeans—looked surprised to see them; the problem with that was she was about as good an actor as she was a gardener. "What a pleasant surprise. What brings you ladies to the homestead?"

"Cut the shit, Kenzie, I know what you did to my garden," Kenisha said, attempting to storm up the steps past Marjorie. Marjorie held her back. Kenzie's face never changed.

"Why, I'm sure I have no idea what you mean," she said, her tone dripping burnt caramel. "Maybe your cats finally got tired of tearing up my garden and turned on your own."

Marjorie said, "That would only prove they were elevating their taste." For the first time since they'd gotten there, Kenzie's placid expression fell off, twisting momentarily into something hard and brutal, like a sledgehammer coming down on a cat's back.

"My cat never touched your garden, you psycho," Kenisha said, then repeating, "I know what you did."

"The only thing I did was plant a beautiful garden, only to have it destroyed by neighborhood pests." There were so many things wrong with that sentence that Marjorie couldn't respond. "Maybe now you'll think twice before giving your dirty creatures the run of the street."

"We know you did it," Marjorie said, but her voice was shaky. She'd come here stressing calmness and now all she wanted to do was slug this woman in her smug San Diego face.

"Prove it," the woman said, unaware of the irony. That sugar-sweet demeanor dropped entirely. "Because if you can't, I'd suggest you toddle on back home and lick your wounds. And keep your animals off my property." With that, she slammed the door in their faces.

A long silence hung between them. Then Kenisha said, "Can we break in and strangle her?"

"Trust me, I'm considering the same thing." Marjorie, who wasn't thinking exactly the same thing, maneuvered them back out onto the sidewalk. "What's your surveillance system like?"

"Just the porch." After the Christmas robberies, everyone on Yancy Street had had doorbell cameras installed, and still the police had never caught the culprit. "Nothing for the garden. She's right. We can't prove it."

But Marjorie was thinking. "She probably doesn't have one installed, either," she mused. "What if we *could* get proof?"

Kenisha, still likely distracted by the thoughts of her destroyed lamb's ear, didn't follow. Marjorie filled her in, and a slow smile crept across her friend's face. "That might work," she said. It would, and Marjorie was only astounded that Kenzie hadn't considered it herself first. Facts had a way of dissipating even the most lunatic theories. Maybe a dose of reality would even bring Kenzie into the fold a little more. Stranger things had happened.

Marjorie knew one thing: her friends and neighbors on Yancy Lane had always stood with one another. If that meant standing against someone else, well. It wouldn't be the first time.

KENISHA SCRUBBED THE video back again, holding the iPad out of the light so that everyone could see. Kyle threw back his head and laughed theatrically. Marjorie might have shushed him if the entire neighborhood wasn't crowded onto her porch. He held Calico like she was a sleeping baby, her head on his shoulder and his hand supporting her bottom. Marjorie wasn't here to judge. "It's too much!" He'd repeated this several times, but was he wrong?

The answer had been so obvious. The night before, Georgie Carmichael and Samira (who had been reluctantly convinced to leave Blueberry at home) had joined Marjorie and Kenisha in staking out Kenzie's house after dark, all dressed in black and sharing cocoa out of Thermoses. Talk had been at a minimum, even given Samira's continual laments that Blueberry probably felt abandoned, unconvinced that bringing along a cat to a mission that would hopefully exonerate cats was self-defeating. Marjorie only hoped she wasn't wrong about Rufus, who she couldn't picture tearing up any garden. She'd held her tablet in hand, more than halfway convinced that the feral bobcats that lived in the woods had finally gotten tired of suburban development and had decided to start moving into their yards.

The truth was far more mundane. Racoons, of course. They burst out of the woods behind Kenzie's awful yellow house with the bulging lizard-eyes, trundling along in twos and threes. They avoided the mint entirely; racoons didn't like mint. Before making sure her tablet's night mode was on, Marjorie reflected that the most invasive plant in Kenzie's garden was the only one the pests wouldn't touch. The woman couldn't have planted a more nonsensical garden if she'd set out to do it.

Now on the iPad, the racoons swarmed the garden, pulling up flowers by their roots, digging nasty furrows and destroying root systems. The bandits gnawed and yanked, destroying Kenzie's garden with a somehow prim efficiency, their little hands articulate and purposeful. It really did seem as if the garden was being targeted specifically; next door, Tamara's prized roses remained unsullied. Alice Spring's riotous garden to the right, always threatening to overgrow but kept in check by Alice's sure hand, was similarly intact. All you could do was laugh.

"What's so funny?" said a voice. All of them looked around and there stood Kenzie Taylor, her jeans splotched with mud and her shirt smeared with something undefinable. Hectic color was in her cheeks.

"Nothing." Marjorie felt like a girl who'd been caught shoplifting. "Everyone, I invited Kenzie over to show her what happened last night. It's not cats, Kenzie."

She scrubbed to the moment right before the racoons came and handed the iPad over. For a grim few moments, the woman simply watched the screen, her face as tight as a blistered pepper. "You filmed my house?"

"Just to prove it wasn't our cats," Georgie, whose Fluffzilla was safely in her basket swing at home, explained.

Never taking her eyes from the iPad, Kenzie Taylor mused, "These bitches really filmed my house."

Marjorie said, "But see, it's not cats at all. It's the raccoons. They're attracted to your garden. Well, not the mint. You really shouldn't plant mint. It takes over everything. You—"

Kenzie smashed the iPad against one of the porch's columns. The screen shattered into hundreds of shards. Then she hurled the husk of the device down into Marjorie's own pretty garden, crushing a swath of azaleas in the process. "I don't know what kind of CGI bullshit that was, but it's not convincing. You're all covering your asses. And *filming my house*."

"You dug up my garden, you crazy bitch!" Kenisha shouted.

Kyle took up the charge. "And you broke Marjorie's iPad! What's *wrong* with you?"

Marjorie couldn't even process the iPad just yet. "Wait, do you really think we *created* racoons out of thin air to attack your garden?"

"I know what gaslighting is when I see it."

Just then, Rufus, sensing a party he was late for, trotted up the steps toward the porch. Marjorie, still reeling from Kenzie's insane accusation, made to excuse herself to grab her bag of Kitty Treats. Kenzie Taylor hiked back her leg and shot it out, connecting with Rufus' face and sending him flying. The cat arced in the air and hit the sidewalk with a soft thud, bouncing once and landing half in the gutter.

Kenzie said, "Told you there would be consequences. Keep your fucking cats away from me." With that, she left the stunned residents of Yancy Lane on Marjorie's porch and sauntered back down the street. As one, they looked from Kenzie to the cat lying sprawled half-in and half-out of the road. Marjorie and Kenisha were first down the stairs. Already Marjorie was ticking off next steps: racing to the vet, nursing Rufus back to health, finally calling the cops on Kenzie. She didn't know how many years of jail time this got you, but she entertained thoughts of the electric chair.

When she got to Rufus, though, all her plans tattered away. Rufus wasn't maimed. Rufus was dead.

Kenisha looked at her. Everyone looked at her. "What do we do now?"

MARJORIE SAT IN her living room alone. Tea grew cold on the table beside her. A skein of red kept threatening to cover her consciousness, and she fought it back. Anger was no good to you if you gave into it. You had to harness it. Finally she stood, picking up the teacup. The night had come down around Yancy Lane and gloom pervaded her home. As she headed to the kitchen, she couldn't help but notice the bright yellow bag of Kitty Treats by the door. A sharp pang twisted in her gut.

Just then, her phone dinged. The neighborhood group chat had been going since the afternoon, only recently petering out. But this one from Kyle O'Brien sent a fresh chill down Marjorie's spine.

Has anyone seen Calico?

A string of questions clogged her screen, and Marjorie was about to respond herself when a blurry image popped up via Airdrop. Below was a choice: Accept or Decline. With terrible hesitancy, Marjorie touched the ACCEPT button.

A movie began. It was in low light so most of the color had washed out; hints of white cut through the field of brown on brown. Even in the murk, though, it was all too easy to make out what she was seeing.

Calico, Kyle O'Brien's immense cat, sat in the middle of a wasteland of plants and flowers. A few sprigs of amaranth clung to his back, bright and purple in the daylight, bloodred in the gloaming. Marjorie's first thought was, *What, you couldn't force one into his mouth so you settled for this?* Not for a second did the implication of this shot convince. As usual, Calico looked bored, resigned, and unmoving.

Did you break into his house? Marjorie wondered, and then an even more alarming thought occurred: *Did you tear up your own garden just to prove that Calico did it? That's insane. That's...*

The camera steadied itself—as if the person holding the phone put it down somewhere—and someone walked into the scene. They were in overalls and a long-sleeved shirt, a bandana and goggles covering their face. In the half-light, it was impossible to tell who it was. They held something in their hand, and Marjorie realized with dawning horror that it was a garbage bag.

"Oh no," she murmured. "Oh God."

The figure opened the bag and, with some effort, lifted the placid creature and dumped her into the bag like a leftover casserole. For the first time, Calico made a sound: a plaintive, questioning meow that seemed both so distant and so horribly near. Then the person sinched the bag closed, snatched it up, and hurled the heavy end down with tremendous force onto the surface of a nearby paving stone. Marjorie heard the *thump*, followed by a hideous mewling, choking sound, the sound of a creature who knows it is in pain but does not know why.

With barely a pause, the figure grabbed the bag again, hoisting it over their shoulder to achieve faster velocity, and slammed it onto the earth. The only sound now was a wet splat, a water balloon bursting with pudding. Calico, like Rufus, was dead.

Then a gravelly voice muttered, "Consequences." The screen went blank.

And even though she was three houses away, Marjorie could hear the horrible sound of Kyle O'Brien screaming.

THE ONES WHO didn't get the AirDrop watched their neighbors' phones and tablets. None of them dared turn the sound off. They replayed over and over: the choking meow, the deadly splat. Her mind was on overdrive. Never in her life had she felt this angry, or this out of control.

Kenisha said, "Marjorie."

Marjorie wasn't listening. Her mind was on the bag of Kitty Treats.

"Marjorie?"

From behind her: "Should we call the police?"

And: "We need to confront her."

And: "We need to threaten her."

Once upon a time, Marjorie had had her own cat. Friskers was the best indoor cat you could have ever hoped for. When Friskers didn't come for her supper one night, Marjorie had gone out to look for her. What she found was the mangled corpse of her friend tossed unceremoniously into the bushes at the front of the house, the victim of a hit and run. Seeing the blood on her whiskers, the glassy not-there sheen in her eyes, Marjorie had vowed never to own a cat again. It was too much hurt to lose them. Too much pain.

Now that pain welled up in her. She thought she could use it. Neither Rufus nor Calico had been her cat, but that didn't matter. On Yancy Lane, you stood with your neighbors ... and if necessary, you stood for their cats.

"Marjorie," Kenisha repeated a third time, and now she turned.

"She will keep doing this," Marjorie said.

"I know."

"I'm going over there."

"To talk to her?"

"No, Kenisha. Not to talk."

After a very long pause, Kenisha said, "Good."

Kyle O'Brien stood behind Kenisha, nodding. Marjorie took in all their faces, grim but determined. Her mind was on the thief who had stolen all those Christmas presents from their porches that year. After installing those porch cameras, it was easy to figure out who it was. The neighbors of Yancy Lane took care of the problem, because that's what good neighbors did. The police never found him. The police never would.

This was a good place. A safe neighborhood. Marjorie was damned if some lunatic from San Diego was going to destroy her peace of mind.

"Everyone ready?" she asked, and as a one, they were.

KENZIE TAYLOR AWOKE three hours later, her head pounding, her brain frenzied. All of it flooded back to her: that bitch Marjorie Fields showing up at her door, barging in before she could lock it. The Cerritos woman with the hypodermic needle, bearing down on her with staring eyes. The rest of them, all against her since the moment she moved into this awful neighborhood, some of them holding their cats, their fucking *cats*.

Then the darkness had come and tucked her into itself. Her living room drifted away, and now...

She could see the tops of trees. Beyond them, a bruise-purple sky pinpricked with faraway stars. The perspective was off. Was she on the ground? Lying on the ground? Somewhere nearby, there was a noise. Something she recognized but couldn't reconcile with the idea of her suburban home.

It was then she realized she couldn't move.

Just then, a pair of legs tucked into slender jeans came into her point of view. Then Marjorie Fields crouched down, coming into her line of sight. "Kenzie," she said. "I was so hoping it wouldn't come to this."

Kenzie opened her mouth to speak, but her tongue wouldn't work.

"Oh yes," Marjorie said. "You'll find you're quite paralyzed. The effects should wear off in a few hours. By daylight, if not before. But I doubt you'll notice."

That sound again, and closer. A wild sound. Kenzie placed it now, and wanted—tried—to scream. No sound came out.

Marjorie turned toward it and said, "I wonder if you can hear them, too. The bobcats have lived in these woods for centuries, I guess. And then the people came in to destroy their habitat. Poor things. I can empathize. After all, I know what it's like when people destroy your habitat."

Kenzie tried to scream again. A muffled grunt escaped her. That was all.

"Their food sources have become limited—that's the big problem. The other problem is that some of them go rabid out here. Occasionally we have to call animal control, but I don't think we're going to do that tonight. What do you think, Kenzie?"

Another grunt, just as weak at the one before. For the first time, she realized she'd been stripped naked out here, and there was something on her skin. Something sticky, like honey or oil. The smell was coppery, high and sharp. Was it blood? Was it her blood?

"We love our cats on Yancy Lane, Kenzie. We love *all* our cats. Maybe you'll learn to love them, too."

Then Marjorie stood and sauntered off. Some unknown time later, Kenzie heard the soft pad of feet approaching, and cold sweat broke out all over her body. Gooseflesh twisted her skin. It would be Marjorie, come to stop this madness, and if she thought she was going to get away with what she had done to her—

And then the sound: the low, chuckling growl Kenzie had never heard outside nature programs. Not just one but several. And then she saw the eyes: yellowy, floating above the ground like will-o-the-wisps; the shape of a face, feline and horribly large, loomed behind them.

She tried to speak, and when the first claw shot out and sliced her across the face, she tried to scream.

She was still alive when the cats began to eat her.

One Spye After Another

Eve Elliot

NIGEL SPYE COWERED behind his front door, fingers poised on the handle, and risked a glance through the stained glass accent window.

He needed to get out of the house. He didn't often feel the need to leave the twee little Yorkshire cottage he'd inherited from an aunt, but today he was just about chewing the carpet with boredom.

He wasn't asking for much—all he wanted was half an hour to ramble down to the High Street for some fags and a few cans, maybe an extra packet of crisps for the walk home, and to be left alone to enjoy them with his feet up in front of Top Gear. Was that so much to ask?

If only that bloody woman would let him.

Nigel's heart sank as he spotted the blurred shape through the wobbly coloured glass. There she was again, fussing with her gardenias, trimming, watering, cooing at the flowers like they were her pets. Her garden did not need daily tending, it always looked like something out of a magazine—in stark contrast to the overgrown jungle of his that had apparently swallowed a rusted-out Vauxhall Corsa—and yet there she was, every single day, barring his escape.

He blew out a frustrated breath through his nose and stood back from the door, defeated.

Mrs. Enid Spye. Widow of a fourth cousin (in this town everyone was some sort of relation if you went back a few generations, but still, he resented the slender connection). A squat, soft, doughy sort of person, with an enormous bosom that mushroomed out the sides of her white apron. Pink cheeks, wistful blue eyes, a nest of white curls piled up into a top knot, and silver wire glasses with the bottle-bottom lenses—she looked so much like Mrs. Claus that she portrayed that paragon of virtue every year in the town's Santa's Grotto.

She *was* sweet, everyone said so. No children, no relations nearby to help her, just a darling, talkative little old lady who tended her garden and toddled down to the post office once or twice a week with letters to her penpals or her cousin overseas.

Oh yes, she was sweet and lovely and Nigel couldn't bloody stand her.

It was the daily interruptions, the feeble little taps on his door or even his kitchen window, the high, reedy little voice that always began *Oh my dear Mr. Spye, I'm ever so sorry to disturb you, but...* and the endless list of tasks and favours she'd ever so sweetly ask him to do. He'd killed earwigs for her. He'd showed her how to work her remote control at least a hundred times. He'd unscrewed uncooperative preserve jars (and then had to suffer the disgustingly sweet stuff smeared on stale toast as thanks). He'd even smiled with the most sincerity he could bring himself to fake when she'd presented him with a mug that read *World's Best Neighbour* and then served him weak, sugary tea out of it, every single day, as they sat in her spotless kitchen and listened to classical music or *The Archers* on Radio 4.

He couldn't leave the house without cringing at the creak of her front door opening and that fluting little warble *Good morning, Mr. Spye,* like they hadn't seen each other in years. *She must plant herself by the door and wait for me to come out,* he often thought, because he never made it past the half-gate at the end of the garden without being assaulted by that cloying little voice.

He'd only lived here a year, but it had been the worst year of his life, by far.

Nigel kicked aside the pile of leaflets and past-due bills that was growing by the hour, it seemed, and tossed his keys on the hall table. The greasy smell from last night's lasagne still hung in the air, but he was rather getting used to it now, he ate it so often. Two for 99p at Sainsbury's, five minutes in the micro, Robert's your mother's brother.

That was another thing. The microwave bell was too loud. A month ago Mrs. Spye had knocked on his door so timidly, her face full of genteel chagrin, and said, ever so politely, if he would mind awfully not using his microwave after 9 pm, as the bell was so very loud, you see, and it disturbs Harold.

Harold? Who the hell was Harold? Hope had soared in Nigel's heart that perhaps the old biddy had met a widower who could take over the bug-killing and stuck-window-opening for him. But like most aspects of Nigel's life, that faint hope had crashed again like a ten-car pileup on the motorway. Harold was her cockatiel. And in short order, Nigel found out that in terms of auditory disturbances, Harold gave as good as he got.

Now that he thought of it, that bird had been the final straw. He'd been able to live with the daily tea breaks and the six a.m. requests to check the lead on her electric kettle, or fetch a box of her husband's clothes from the cellar so she could put them out for the charity to collect. He could live with the gentle admonitions about the state of his garden, the peeling paint on his front door, or the grimy windows that really ought to be cleaned; he could tolerate the newspaper articles, helpfully clipped out with pinking shears, on losing weight after forty, or the dangers of smoking, or how x units of alcohol a day would rot your oesophagus.

He wasn't a terrible person, of course; he was willing to indulge a lonely old lady, to a degree.

But when that goddamn bird showed up, he'd finally lost it.

The first time the bird had shrieked, Nigel had shot out of bed with alarm, entangling himself in his bedsheets and crashing to the floor in a heap. Heart pounding, elbow throbbing from hitting the side table on the way down, he'd lain on the floor trying to catch his breath and wondering if he'd just dreamed that horrible screeching wail. Then it happened again, and again, and spiralled into a crescendo of ear-splitting rancour that finally ended on one long, petulant scream.

Harold.

She'd decided to get a pet. And instead of adopting some scruffy little terrier or a mangy cat, she'd chosen perhaps the most offensive, irritating, sanity-withering animal on the face of the earth.

Just as he was getting used to the daily serenade of avian outrage, two weeks ago Mrs. Spye had come to his door in tears, blubbering that dear Harold had escaped, and could he please help her find him? *Good job Harold*, was Nigel's first thought, *maybe there is a God*. But he'd agreed to look for the bird, hoping beyond hope that it had met its end with a neighbourhood cat or a kid with a well-aimed rock.

He'd been 'exercising', Mrs. Spye had explained tearfully, blowing her nose into a hankie. Flying around the house on unclipped wings—obviously desperate for a way out, Nigel thought grimly—he'd flown down to the cellar, and discovered the broken window in the corner (another thing Nigel hadn't gotten around to fixing yet). Harold had hopped through the bars and fled, and Nigel had spent hours upon hours roaming the neighbourhood with a pillow case, calling out 'Harold! Here pretty bird!' to the amusement of passersby.

He'd worn his feet to bloody stumps searching for that bird, who, it turned out, had been sitting primly on Mrs. Spye's roof the whole time, staring at him. He'd spent another two hours trying to coax, cajole, threaten and bribe the thing down until Harold had finally grown tired, flown to his shoulder, puffed up his impressive white crown of feathers, and screamed.

What have I done, Lord? Nigel asked this question often, to a deity he didn't believe existed. *What sin have I committed to deserve this neighbour from hell?*

Nigel flopped down onto his sofa, and howled as a lasagne-crusted fork lodged itself in his kidney. He titled his hips up and dug out the offending item, and tossed it onto the floor with the rest of the dirty dishes. He settled back down and closed his eyes, trying to take a deep breath like his therapist had taught him to do. Deep breath in through the mouth, hold it for a few seconds, let it out through the nose. Or maybe it was in through the nose and out through the mouth. He tried it again, both ways. It didn't help.

He felt like he always did—stressed out, miserable, and wishing Aunt Verity had never left him this house.

Well, that wasn't entirely true. He was grateful for the house, considering he'd never managed to keep a job for very long, and didn't really care to anyway. He'd stocked shelves at Boots for a time, but that snooty manageress who wore too much makeup and always looked at him like she'd just smelled something rancid had told him not to bother coming back in. He was off-putting to the customers, she said, in his tatty black t-shirts that didn't quite cover the overhang of his belly and his grungy black trainers with the holes in the toe. What did he care, it was a rubbish job anyway. Verity's house was paid for, and all his, and with his Disability Allowance he didn't have to worry about the stress of earning a living, which his therapist agreed he just couldn't do, not with his level of anxiety.

And it would be nice here, really, even if he couldn't rouse himself to clean the place and didn't really give a toss about the garden. It was comfortable, and warm, and they gave him a discount on the TV license because of his anxiety, and it was only a short walk down to the High Street and the off-track betting and the kebab place. It would be okay to live here, if only he could get rid of the old cow next door.

He'd thought about it often enough. In the bath, whilst her television blared through the wall (*I'm ever so sorry, Mr. Spye, but my hearing is not what it was, and I do enjoy my Coronation Street*), or when trying to take a nap as she banged out *O Promise Me* on her out-of-tune upright, or when that bloody bird started screaming.

How much easier it would be if she would just drop dead. How much quieter, simpler, and easier on his nerves life would be if only she were gone.

They were just fantasies, he told himself, as he envisioned all the ways he could do it and get away with it. He could take the spare key she'd foisted on him (*In case of an emergency, my dear Mr Spye*), sneak into her room one night and smother her with a pillow. It would look like she'd passed away in her sleep, wouldn't it? Hmm...no, she'd probably struggle, and he might not have the nerve to finish her off. Maybe during one of their tea breaks he could surreptitiously put the gas on? No, the rotten egg smell would give it away. A toaster dropped into her bath? Damn, these houses had circuit breakers now, just to prevent that sort of thing.

He closed his eyes and thought up fiendish ways of bumping her off, like in the detective fiction he liked to read. He imagined himself as a cunning assassin, sliding a stiletto between her ribs and guiding her lifeless body to the kitchen lino, or silencing a pistol with a potato and splattering her brains—and potato peels—all over her antiseptic kitchen.

He could never actually *do* any of this, of course, but it made him feel better just thinking about it.

If only she'd suffer a fall, like so many people her age did. There were two flights of stairs in her house, the one with the lurid red carpet leading up to the second floor, and the creaky wooden one leading down to the cellar off the kitchen. Why couldn't she just take a tumble one day?

That's when the idea came to him.

It was simple, and easy to do, and best of all, he wouldn't even need to be there.

If he took a length of fishing line and stretched it across the bottom of the cellar doorway, say three inches off the floor, she'd trip on it the next time she went down to fetch those godawful preserves. He could listen for it, even, imagining the unholy racket her body would make tumbling down to the cement floor. Then he could simply remove the wire, and after a day or two, ring the police for a 'welfare check', concerned as he was for his dear old neighbour.

Nigel sat up slowly. His heart started to pound with the possibilities. A fall like that might not kill her, but that was all right - even if she just broke a hip or something, she'd have to go to hospital for an extended period. She might even need to move to a care home, and sell her house.

She might even need to sell her house!

The next time she went out to mail her letters, he decided, he'd let himself in and arrange it.

Breathless with anticipation, giddy at the thought of freedom from Mrs. Spye forever, he clicked on the television and was finally able to relax.

ENID SPYE CLOSED and latched her front door. She allowed herself a moment, only a moment, to rest her back against it and close her eyes. Deep breath in. Deep breath out.

Nigel Spye had refused to come out. She'd seen his shadow passing behind the decorative stained glass window of his front door, a lurking, cowering shadow (if she wasn't being too fanciful). He was hiding from her, a little old woman out in her garden! She'd fussed with the gardenias and the morning glories as long as she could before finally giving up on him and coming in.

Oh well. Onward and upward.

She pushed off from the door and moved purposefully into the lounge, surveying the room with a practiced eye. Carpet hoovered yesterday (the lines made by the machine still visible); Hummel figurines dusted the day before (their glass cabinet gone over with the spray); throw pillows plumped and artfully arranged (sofa and matching settee hoovered as well, sadly no lines to show it had been done). Lovely. Just as everything ought to be.

In the kitchen she flipped on the electric kettle, and was about to reach for the china cup she preferred when she spotted a blob of something on the base of the kettle. She whipped off a single sheet from the roll of kitchen towel next to the kettle and scrubbed at the blob with vigour until it vanished, leaving the base gleaming and clean. As it should be.

Overall she was pleased. The pale gardenias in the window filled the room with a fresh, delicate scent, and the white cupboard doors gleamed, thanks to last Saturday's day of scrubbing and shining. The floor had been newly waxed, and the window sparkled in the sunshine. Yes, she was pleased. Clean, efficient, with just that slight touch of elegance that revealed her to be a woman of taste and excellent breeding.

She took her tea to the small table near the window and sat, gazing out onto her beloved garden, another source of considerable pride. Surely the Lord wouldn't consider it a sin, she mused, to be proud of one's industry and devotion to order and beauty. Especially when she spent such effort trying to raise the standards of everything around her.

Like that beastly man next door.

Her eyes darted over to his garden, and a shudder went through her at the sight of it. Wild grass and weeds, at least waist-high, a disused fire pit and a mouldering blue bag of lager cans, but worse still, the mortal remains of some kind of economy car.

A car! In the front garden!

It was monstrous that the Council refused to act, despite her many calls and letters. In her day it would have been hauled out of there immediately and the owner presented with a hefty bill and a stern look. These days, the Council were as lazy as her neighbour was.

When Verity Hobbs had owned the place next door (a hard woman in her late fifties, very ropy and lean, who had dressed like a teenager and entertained much younger men), she'd claimed not to know who'd put the vehicle there, that it had been there when she'd inherited the house in the 1997. Gracious, fancy not caring about a thing like that, or doing anything about it for nearly twenty five years. Enid had hoped the new owner, described to her as a bachelor in his forties, would be just the sort of gentleman the neighbourhood needed: someone who would clean up the place and make an attempt to rise to the standard of the other houses on the street.

Oh, how wrong she'd been.

She sipped her tea, and put her cup down delicately, enjoying the genteel sound of a fine china cup settling on a fine china saucer. The more she thought of Mr. Spye, the more precise and elegant her movements became, as if in counterpoint to the utter horror of the man.

She'd watched through the net curtain with great anticipation as the removal company van had pulled up, almost this time last year. Expecting a dapper, neat sort of fellow approaching his middle years, she'd been shocked by what had actually emerged from the passenger side of the van. Huge, stoop-shouldered, carrying at least seven or eight stone more than he should, with shoulder-length stringy black hair that fell across his eyes and had to be flicked away whenever he wanted to look at anything. And the clothes! From that first day onward, she'd only ever seen him in black - not crisp black, however, which could be elegant and hide a host of sins, but the too-many-times-through-the-wash black, all faded and dull.

He didn't work, she'd found out quickly enough. He didn't do much of anything, except play his television too loud and smoke. She'd peek through the curtains and see him trudging up the road with a bag of cans from the off-licence, inhaling package after package of crisps, oblivious to the spectacle of slovenliness he was. She'd ring Louisa, her friend across the street, and gossip about him, and on her way into the post office she'd stop to commiserate with the lovely young mother (married, thank heaven) who'd just moved in at number seventy-seven, but all the furtive complaints in the world wouldn't change the man, and so she'd had to think of something else.

Because he had to go. He simply had to go. He was bringing down the whole neighbourhood, and preventing her beautiful house and garden from shining. Instead of winning the Tidy Streets Competition, or the Garden of the Year Prize, the best she could hope for now was that people didn't actually stop and stare at his place, or point and laugh. So there was really nothing for it, he simply had to go.

She'd read in the Dear Hortense column of *Ladies' Weekly* about a man who was so worn down by his neighbour's constant requests for favours and errands that he'd ended up moving away. This was a splendid idea, she'd thought. She'd simply make such a nuisance of herself that he'd sell the property and take his squalor somewhere else.

At first she'd taken pains to be sweet and doddering, so as to tug on his conscience and make him feel too guilty to say no. That had worked a treat, and soon she was accosting him every day, usually for some minor irritation like a stubborn lid or an earwig that needed to be dispatched. Some days she was the one offering help—in the form of criticism about his weight, his clothes, anything she could think of—most days she made him sit with her and listen to the radio. She'd even bought him a tacky mug emblazoned with the slogan *World's Best Neighbour,* just to lay the guilt on even thicker.

But as the year wore on and he made no signs of moving or—heaven help her—cleaning up, she knew she'd have to up the stakes.

She'd gone to the RSPCA and lied about going deaf, asking if they had any loud birds in need of rescue. Sure enough, Harold was just such a creature, and she'd been delighted the first time he'd let loose one of his unearthly screams. (She hated Harold, there were no two ways about it. Birds were horrendous house pets and entirely too dirty for her spotless house and white furniture, but if he helped get rid of the slug next door, his limited time with her would be well worth it.)

Trouble was, she mused, glancing again at the rusted garden gate next door, even Harold wasn't doing the trick.

She wasn't the sort to let melancholy take hold of her, she was of the generation that didn't put stock in any of that depression rubbish. When she felt her spirits sinking, she rallied and regrouped, which is what she knew she had to do now.

As loathe as she was to take such a drastic step, there really was nothing for it. If he wouldn't move, well, then she'd have to find another way to get him out of there.

She went to the cupboard under the sink and retrieved the insecticide she'd had Nigel use on the earwig. It was amazing they even sold this concoction, she marvelled, looking at the imposing yellow skull and crossbones glaring at her from the front of the box. It contained cyanide, for pity's sake. Cyanide! It was useful, no question, and the strong odour and taste could be easily disguised in sweet tea or preserves, but how irresponsible of the government, to allow just anyone to buy such a thing.

At least *she* had only used it when absolutely necessary, and at that, only twice before—when her husband had grown too feeble to care for himself and had made such a ghastly mess of himself, and then again with that marijuana-smoking tramp Verity Hobbs.

Because really, one simply couldn't be expected to put up with such things.

She picked up the telephone and dialled Nigel's number, while spooning some insecticide into his *World's Best Neighbour* mug.

"Oh good afternoon, Mr. Spye. I am about to walk down to the post office, but I could bring back a *gateau* from the bakery if you'd like to join me for tea when I return?"

AN HOUR LATER, Enid Spye and Nigel Spye sat across from each other at her kitchen table. The sun was glorious, streaming in through her sparkling window and reflecting cheerfully off the cut glass vase of flowers. Classical music tinkled lightly from the radio.

Not long now, thought Enid.

Not long now, thought Nigel.

They smiled at each other as the kettle began to boil.

"What a charming day," Enid sang, rising from the table to make tea. She poured the water into a polished silver tea pot and readied two cups - a delicate white china cup and saucer for her, and the *World's Best Neighbour* mug for him. She fussed with the milk and sugar, careful to add an extra two lumps to the powdery bottom of his mug. "It was such a delightful walk, I do so love this time of year. Such beauty everywhere."

"It's a bit too hot," Nigel replied. "Could do with a bit of rain."

He glanced over at the open door to the cellar. He knew he shouldn't keep looking at it, he didn't want to call attention to it, but the desire to keep confirming that the wire couldn't be seen was almost overpowering. He'd rushed the job, knocking two small nails into the door frame and winding each end of the wire around them until it was stretched taut, watching the clock the whole time.

He needn't have hurried, she'd taken almost an hour to return from shopping. But it was done now, and even in the bright sunlight, he could barely make out a slight glint of light in the doorway—and only because he knew to look for it.

Now he just had to make an excuse and get back home, because it would look very bad for him if he were here when it happened.

"There we are, Mr. Spye," Enid said brightly, placing a tray with two cups and two slabs of chocolate cake on the table between them. She took a seat opposite him and politely offered him his mug before taking her own from the tray.

Don't respond to the comment about the heat, she warned herself. *Don't tell him he wouldn't be so uncomfortable if he didn't insist on wearing head-to-toe black every day.*

Just encourage him to drink his tea...

But he didn't. He just sat there, nibbling on his thumbnail.

"I'm sorry, but I can't stay today, Mrs. Spye," he said at length. "I completely forgot, I have an appointment with my therapist."

"Surely you can spare the time for some of this lovely gateau," Enid said, pushing a plate with the largest wedge of cake towards him. "I bought it especially for you."

He glanced at the cake. "That was very kind of you. Maybe... tomorrow?"

Enid pursed her lips. "Tomorrow I have a meeting of the Tidy Streets Committee." She softened her tone and smiled. "At least finish your tea. Please."

They locked eyes with each other, and inside each of them, a heart began to pound. Like gunfighters facing each other in some dustbowl frontier town, hands twitching above their holsters, eyes keen and wary, the two adversaries waited, barely breathing, for one or the other to make a move.

Nigel decided to move first.

But just as he rose from the table, a flapping, screeching white blur swooped into the kitchen, buzzed the table, and narrowly avoided crashing into him as it angled left and careened off the fridge freezer.

"Harold!" they both cried.

Nigel reached for the bird, almost caught a tail feather, and waved his arms to swat it back into the lounge. Enid rose and tossed him a tea towel, and he flung that at the bird with the same futility. He'd almost herded it back through the kitchen door when it changed direction and, with a steely purpose in its beady eyes, tucked in its wings and, bullet-like, made for the cellar.

Jesus not the cellar! Nigel thought desperately. And without another thought beyond stopping Harold from escaping again, he too went through the cellar door.

The yelp of surprise and alarm as his ankle met with the fishing wire was surpassed in volume only by the tumult of his body crashing down the cellar stairs, his arms and legs bashing against the walls, his head smacking against each wooden step on the way down. When he came to rest, upside down and tangled, on the cement floor at the base of the stairs, his neck was cocked to the side at a wholly unnatural angle. The eyes that stared up at Harold, coolly observing him from his perch on the bannister, were glassy and still.

Enid rushed to the doorway and stared down at the pretzeled pile of man below. Her hand flew to her mouth and she began to pick her way down the steps, not noticing the snapped fishing wire that now lay, invisible and harmless, across the top stair. As she drew closer to the body, she grimaced at the impossible contortion of his neck and how his belly was now completely exposed beneath his torn shirt.

"Mr. Spye," she called, although she suspected he could no longer hear her. Best to make sure though. "Mr. Spye, can you hear me?"

She stepped over him gingerly and bent down to press two fingers to his neck. Satisfied, she stood up and regarded the body.

Perhaps she ought to try to rearrange him a little, for when the police arrived. He did look ever so undignified. She made an effort to tuck his arms in, and tried to shift his bulk so that he wasn't quite so piled up against the wall, but he really was an enormous man, and soon she realized the task was beyond her strength. She resigned herself to leaving him as he was, and made her way upstairs.

She paused to stroke Harold and thank him, resolving to sprinkle the insecticide into his food only after the police had left.

With each step upwards, her jubilation grew. What a marvellous turn of events! She could not have hoped for a happier accident. Clearly, she was entirely blameless for the tragedy, as the police would see, and best of all, she was finally, finally rid of the odious Mr. Spye!

Sweating from her efforts, she plopped down at the table to catch her breath. The day *was* unseasonably warm, and so she absently reached for a cup of tea to quench her parched throat, and took a healthy gulp.

As the sickly sweet liquid passed her throat, she looked down and froze. The *World's Best Neighbour* mug fell from her hands, making an awful mess.

Woops!

Dave Zeltserman

ANOTHER NONDESCRIPT SEDAN pulled up in front of Jack Vance's house. *Probably stolen,* Mitch Erlach thought. He had pushed aside the window blinds so he could use his binoculars to get a good look at the man exiting the car. A hardened criminal, no doubt about it, just like the other two who'd come earlier. Mitch wished he had a camera with a telephoto lens so he could've taken photos of all of Vance's criminal associates visiting him that night. He was sure those photos would be helpful to the police later. If he had that type of camera, he would also have been able to take photos of their cars. Mitch was using the binoculars so he could write down their license plate numbers in the notebook next to him, but it would be better if he could give the police the makes and models. Maybe later if he were gutsy enough he'd sneak outside and take pictures with his cell phone.

Mitch watched the man, who was obviously a criminal scumbag, ring Vance's doorbell. Vance soon came to the door, engulfed his visitor in a bear hug, and brought the man into his home. Mitch knew that they had to be planning a robbery or worse. He wouldn't put anything past his neighbor. Bank robbery, that was a given. He'd heard the rumors, and he'd seen the types who would arrive at all hours at Vance's home. Heck, he wouldn't be surprised to learn that Vance was also involved in drugs, extortion, kidnapping, and even murder. All one had to do was look at the man to know that nothing was beyond him.

Mitch discovered that he'd been grimacing so hard that he had hurt a jaw muscle. He blamed this on Vance also. Wincing, he rubbed his sore jaw as Wendy walked into their daughter Cindy's second-floor bedroom which he was using for his spying. Fortunately their daughter was a freshman in college and had been away at school for most of the time since Vance had moved into the house next door. This had been such a quiet cul-de-sac before Vance's arrival. Just normal people going about their daily, routine lives. Mowing lawns, barbecues, friendly neighborly chats, nothing out of the ordinary, but then Vance and his trashy wife, Lois, had to invade their world. Mitch had no doubt that Lois was an active participant in Vance's bank robberies and crimes. There were rumors that she had made adult films before marrying Vance. Mitch guessed that she was forty now, and with the tight, clingy, and completely family-inappropriate clothes she always wore that left nothing to the imagination, she still had the body to be in those types of movies. This is who had to move into Jim and Ellen Fenston's old house! The worst possible neighbors!

Wendy, her face tense, said, "What do you think they're planning?"

"I don't know, but I'm writing down all their license plates. When the time's right, I'll give it to the police ."

Wendy absently began pulling on her fingers, which was a nervous habit she had. She said, "There have been so many bank robberies in the area since they moved in." Her mouth crumbled as if she were about to break out crying, but showed impressive strength in fighting it back. "I didn't tell you this earlier, but this morning when I went out for the newspaper, the wife was outside doing the same. She actually waved to me! I pretended I didn't see her, but it made my skin crawl. She's as bad as he is, I'm sure of it!"

"So am I. What a pair we had to get stuck with, huh? But honey, this nightmare will be over as soon as I can gather enough evidence of their criminality to bring to the police. Once that happens, they'll be locked away and life will go back to normal here. I promise."

He had pushed aside the blinds covering the window, and car headlights could be seen from outside. "Another of his criminal buddies just arrived," he said to Wendy, nervousness tightening his throat. "This makes four of them." He pushed the blinds further back so Wendy could also see the man exit the car and walk up to Vance's front door. He was obviously a thug, like the others. They watched as Vance opened the door and the two men embraced. Something caught Vance's attention and he looked right up at the bedroom window as if he knew he were being spied on. Mitch let go of the blinds and threw himself away from the window.

"Oh my God," Wendy whispered, her face stark white. "He saw us!"

"He didn't see anything," Mitch lied, because he caught the look on Vance's face, and he knew his neighbor had discovered their spying. Panicked, he wanted to flee the house. Instead, he sat frozen on his daughter's bed, unable move as he held his breath, waiting. He could see Wendy doing the same, her face stricken with fear. A minute passed without anything happening, then another.

"I told you," Mitch said, his voice shaky. "He didn't see us."

The doorbell rang.

Mitch whispered, "He can't possibly know we're home. He'll start thinking he only imagined what he thought he saw, and he'll go away."

The doorbell rang again. Then Vance yelled out from outside their front door, his voice booming as he informed them that he knew they were home.

A muscle had tightened alongside Wendy's mouth causing an involuntary spasm, and it made Mitch even more nervous to see it. Her voice was barely a whisper as she frantically urged him to call the police.

"You better not do something stupid like call the police," Vance yelled. It sounded almost as if he were in the same room with them. "I'll be in your house long before they show up. Now open the damn door before I get mad!"

Mitch and Wendy stared at each other, uncertain what to do next. Mitch felt numb as he got to his feet and led the way down the stairs and to the front door. It was as if he were a condemned man walking to the gallows, but he seemed unable to stop himself. He waited for Wendy to catch up with him before he opened the door. It wasn't just Vance there, but his wife also, both of them grinning widely. His wife was also holding a wine bottle.

"Look at them," Vance said, chuckling. "They look like they'll faint if I say *boo*."

"You're just terrible," Lois Vance said. She slapped her husband's arm, and squeezed past him so she could get into the Erlach home. She took hold of Wendy's arm and led her into the living room. "You and I are going to do what we should've done six months ago," she told Wendy. "You must like Chardonnay, right? Let's get to know each other. I'm sure we'll be fast friends by the end of the night."

Mitch watched all this unfold in stunned amazement. He was even more stunned when Vance, a large bear of a man with a face like a granite block, put a thick heavy arm around his shoulders, the weight heavy on him. Vance, with seemingly little effort, nudged him out of his house.

"Where are we going?" Mitch asked, his voice a squeak.

"Where else? To my basement. That's where I bury the bodies." Vance gave him a sideways glance. "And for Chrissakes, don't piss your pants!"

There was no use fighting it. Vance was too strong and too determined. Mitch was mostly in a daze as he was inexorably drawn into Vance's house, and then down into a finished basement. Sitting around a poker table were the four men that he had earlier seen enter Vance's home. Each of them had a pile of poker chips in front of them and plates of food. Buffalo wings, roast beef sandwiches, crab cakes, stuffed potatoes. There looked to be plenty of alcohol also. Vance introduced Mitch to each of them. The one named Rocco said, "He's the one who was spying on us?"

"Yeah, he's the one," Vance said. He took a seat at the poker table and invited Mitch to take the open seat across from him. "I guess when you got someone a little rough around the edges like me who looks like I do moving into this type of neighborhood, stories are going to fly." He arched an eyebrow at Mitch. "One of the stories I heard is that I'm a bank robber."

Mitch blanched. "I never thought that," he said, his voice cracking.

"Hey, I can't blame you if those are the types of stories going around," Vance said. Somewhat diplomatically, he added, "I'm sure you weren't the one spreading them."

The one named Stick was giving Mitch a hard eye. "So you were thinking we're all a bunch of bank robbers," he said. "I bet when you heard my name's Stick, you thought I got the nickname because I stickup banks?"

"No, I swear I didn't," Mitch lied, because that was exactly what he had thought.

Rocco said, "He got the nickname because as a kid he was as thin as a stick."

The one called Kell—Mitch didn't know whether it was the man's first name, last name, or nickname—said with a straight face, "And the name just *sticked*."

"You ignoramus," the one called Lynch said. "The past tense of *stick* is *stuck*."

"The college professor over there," Kell said.

"High school English teacher," Lynch corrected him.

"You would have been right about Stick, though," Rocco told Mitch with a wicked grin. "The guy's a plumber and he robs his customers blind."

Stick gave Rocco the finger.

"Okay, enough levity," Vance said. "Mitch, this is a low-stakes game. Seeing as I gave you no choice but to join us, I'll pay for your hundred-dollar buy-in. If you end the game with that much or more, you pay me back, otherwise my treat. Help yourself to whatever food you want." He waved a hand toward a table in the back of the room covered with platters of the food he had seen on the men's' plates. "What can I get you to drink?"

"Water will be fine."

"Uh uh," Vance said. "You're not going to be the only one clearheaded and sober among us so you can take us to the cleaners, not with me paying your buy-in. I got top-shelf bourbon and scotch. So what'll it be?"

"I've got to be up early tomorrow for work."

"We all do. Live a little."

"Well, if you're going to twist my arm, scotch."

"Neat, on the rocks, or some water?"

"On the rocks, thanks."

Vance got him his drink, and after he sat back down and Kell handed Mitch his chips, Lynch dealt a hand of five-card draw. When Vance won the pot, beating Rocco's three nines with a flush, Rocco, a hard glint in his eyes, said, "Of course our new buddy here is going to think you're a connected guy, what with your no-show construction job."

Vance threw a chicken bone at Rocco's head, which the other man barely ducked. "Shuddup," he said. "You're going to give Mitch ideas. I bet right now he's probably thinking I spend all day sitting in a chair at the construction site, watching Lois's old movies on my iPad."

Mitch was aghast. He sputtered out, "Your wife made adult films?"

"I didn't say that. I said *movies*. And no, Lois was never in any kind of movie, but I heard the stories going around, and wanted to know if you believed that garbage. Lois was a dental hygienist when we met."

"I'm sorry," Mitch murmured, chastened.

"Forget it. I know how these stories can spread, but maybe you can correct the record next time you hear one of them?"

"I will, I promise."

The deck was passed to Mitch, and the game continued. When Rocco beat Mitch's two aces by drawing an inside straight, he told him he hoped he wouldn't be calling the cops on him for stealing the hand. Other good-natured jibes were thrown his way, but for the most part Mitch was enjoying the company of Vance and his poker buddies. The food was good, the scotch was excellent, and Mitch was holding his own at the table. At nine-thirty Stick's cell phone rang. It was a quick call, and whoever called him did most of the talking. After he got off the phone, he informed the rest of them that his wife had her hands full with their two sons. "I was given an ultimatum," he said. "I either head home now or I get divorce papers in the morning, and I'm not sure she was joking."

Stick left and the game went on. When the game broke up at midnight, Mitch was able to pocket seventy-three dollars after paying Vance back the hundred he was spotted.

"Thanks for inviting me," Mitch said. "I mean it."

Vance ignored Mitch's offered hand to instead bring him in for an embrace. "I'm glad we were able to clear the air," he said. "If my wife's still over at your house gabbing it up, send her home, okay?"

Mitch told him he'd do that. He had lost count of the number of drinks he had had. Seven, eight, maybe more? He felt their effect as he made his way to his home, listing to his right and one time almost losing his balance and having to stutter step to avoid bumping into his recycle bin.

He couldn't help grinning when he found Wendy and Lois both snoring away on the living-room couch, an empty bottle of wine and two empty wine glasses on the coffee table. He admired how sexy Lois looked, even passed out, and then reluctantly woke her to send her on her way. She looked disoriented, as if she were having trouble remembering where she was, and then offered Mitch a weak smile and told him that she and Wendy shouldn't have drunk the whole bottle. "I guess we're a couple of lightweights," she said, as she struggled to her feet. When she got to the door, she waved goodbye, and then she was gone.

Wendy proved harder to wake up, and Mitch wasn't entirely sure she was ever fully awake as he brought her upstairs and to their bed. She continued snoring as he got her out of her clothes and into pajamas. He was nearly out on his feet himself, and was fast asleep once his head hit the pillow.

He woke up gagging, his mouth feeling like he had gargled with sawdust. Too many scotches last night. It was so dark in the room, way too early for him to be waking up. What woke him, a noise? Someone downstairs? The garage door opening? He was too woozy to be entirely sure. Maybe he'd only imagined hearing something. He struggled to look at the clock radio next to the bed. Only ten past three. The thought of getting out of bed and investigating any possible unexplained noises downstairs made him groan. "Did you hear anything?" he croaked out, his voice hoarser than he'd ever heard it. Wendy was too out of it to answer him, and he decided he must've dreamt what he thought he heard. He closed his eyes and it didn't take him long to fall back into a deep sleep.

Later, he dreamt someone was pounding on his front door, and then realized it wasn't a dream. Wendy had woken up also, her face craggy, her skin a sickly white.

"I think I was drugged," she said.

"You're hungover."

"I can't be. I only had one glass of wine."

He was going to argue with her, but he realized that someone really was pounding on the front door. His eyes were functioning just barely enough so he could read the time on the clock radio, and he moaned seeing that it was ten past nine. They had both slept through the alarm.

Wendy asked, "Who's pounding on the front door?"

"I can't imagine," Mitch said, and he really couldn't think of anyone other than his boss. George would've been furious with him for missing the eight-thirty sales meeting, and Mitch wouldn't put it past him to head straight to their house to scold him.

There was more pounding, and then a voice yelled out, "Open up! It's the police!"

That made no sense to Mitch. He nearly crawled out of bed, his head swimming as he shuffled his way to the bathroom to grab a robe. He felt like hell as he plodded down the stairs, and then he remembered all the drinking from last night. He couldn't let himself ever do that again. He peeked out the living room window, and sure enough there was a police car parked in front of the house. Baffled, he opened the door to find two police officers staring at him with ice-cold expressions.

"I'm sorry I didn't get down here sooner," he said. "I must've slept through my alarm, because your knocking woke me up."

"Late night?" the heavier, scruffier police officer said.

This baffled Mitch even more. "I guess so," he said. "What's this about?"

"There was a robbery last night," the other police officer said.

"What?"

"I think you heard my partner," the heavier officer said.

Mitch was now both baffled and annoyed. This made no sense at all. He said, "If there was a robbery you should be talking to Jack Vance. He lives right next door."

"We already talked to him. He's the one who called us about his suspicions. He claimed you got home at three a.m. last night, and that you and your wife were arguing loudly and woke him and his wife up. He also said you drive a white Volvo."

"That didn't happen." Mitch's face scrunched badly to show his confusion. "My wife and I weren't arguing. And we didn't wake anyone up."

Wendy had made her way down from the bedroom and asked him what this was about, which confused him even more. "They say we started arguing at three in the morning and that we woke people up," he said.

"That didn't happen."

"I know."

"Do you have a white Volvo?" the thinner officer said.

Mitch was now more annoyed than anything else. "Yes," he said.

"Can we see it?"

"It's parked in the garage. I'd have to get the keys. They're upstairs."

"It would be better if you told my partner where the keys are. He'll get them."

Mitch couldn't understand why they'd want to see his car, but he told the officer where his keys were, and he stepped aside to let the officer past him. It seemed to take a good deal longer than it should have for the officer to come back downstairs with his keys. Once he did, Mitch and Wendy followed the two officers outside and to the garage. He spotted Vance and his wife in their front yard, staring blankly at him. This made as little sense as everything else that morning. The officer who had his keys handed them to Mitch and told him it would be better if he were to open his garage door. Mitch did as he was asked.

"The license plate matches," the officer told his partner.

"What?" Mitch said.

"Open the trunk," the officer demanded.

Mitch didn't think he should do that. He didn't understand why he should think that, but still, he felt an uneasiness in his chest as he opened the trunk. It barely surprised him when he saw the bags of money and the two handguns. He understood then that the reason he woke up at three a.m. was because he heard someone opening the garage door, and that was so the money and guns could be put in the trunk of his car. The trunk must've been opened earlier in the evening, and left open so this could be done. It also occurred to him that his license plates must've been taken off his car earlier that night and put back on around the same time the money and guns were stashed away. That must've been the real reason that Stick left the poker game at nine-thirty—so he could collect the plates and put them on a different white Volvo that he would use in the robbery. Jack Vance couldn't possibly be mistaken for Mitch—he was way too big, but Stick was about his size. He could see it all then. Wendy must've been drugged like she said, and while she lay unconscious on the couch, Lois set everything up.

Mitch's voice came out funny as he asked the officers how many people were involved in the robbery.

"You already know the answer to that," the officer said, making no attempt to hide his hostility. "A man and a woman. The guard you pistol-whipped is in critical condition, but he'll live. The description he gave us matches you and your wife."

Wendy started running then as if her life depended on it. She was tackled before she made it past the front yard.

JACK AND LOIS Vance waited until the Erlachs were handcuffed and put in the police car before heading back inside. Jack went to the kitchen to make coffee, and once it was done brewing, brought two mugs to the breakfast nook where Lois sat waiting for him.

"What's the matter?" he asked.

"I hate throwing away a job that we spent weeks planning. It's not as if late-night armored car routes grow on trees."

Jack said, "They were awful neighbors. Spying on us and looking down their noses at us. Those schmucks actually thought they were better than us."

"They were the worst," Lois agreed. "But I'd feel better if we had skimmed some of the money."

"The frame wouldn't stick if we had done that. Worse, if money was missing, the cops would keep looking for it, and we might not like where they looked."

"I know, I know." Her eyes dimmed as she took a long sip of her coffee. "I still hate throwing away a hundred and ten grand, even if was for a good cause. And that was a damned uncomfortable job to do. Even with that baggy sweatshirt, I had to wrap myself up tight on top to give myself a snowball's chance of being mistaken for her."

Jack broke out chuckling. "I'd love to see the look on their faces when they're asked about the washed ski masks and blood-stained robbery clothing found in their dryer," he said. "Anyway, Lois, darling, it's not going to be a complete loss. The Erlachs will have to sell their home in a hurry to cover their soon-to-be mounting legal costs, and I don't think there will be too many interested buyers with them being vicious criminals, and me leaning on anyone who might come sniffing around. Stick should be able to buy it for half the price, and we'll have a decent neighbor then."

"That will be nice," she agreed. "Now if the Osgoods would move away, things here would be perfect." She took another sip of her coffee and made a sour face as if it had been spiked with salt. "I don't like the way the husband's been leering at me. I think the creep must've found one of my old films."

"Patience," Jack said. "I'll find a way to get rid of them. Rocco seems to like our little cul-de-sac, and I'm sure if the price were right he'd buy their house. In another six months tops, we'll have good neighbors on both sides of us. Money is money, but good neighbors, that's something else entirely."

Lois closed her eyes, a look of contentment settling over her face, as if she were imagining that future day.

A Little Power

Wendy Harrison

I HEARD A noise downstairs.

Had I forgotten to lock the door? My gated community felt as safe as anywhere else I might have picked to live, but I still kept the doors locked. Religiously.

There it was again. Someone was moving around my living room. I slipped from my office to the bedroom and took the Glock from my nightstand. Making sure there was a bullet in the chamber, I took a peek through the railing overlooking the room below.

"Don't move." My voice was loud and as non-girly as I could make it. Thinning hair barely covered the scalp of the intruder who ignored my command. "I will shoot you," I said and the man looked up.

"Don't be ridiculous, Jeri. You're not going to shoot anyone."

Sam Crawford didn't know anything more about me than the stereotype I had led him to believe. The nice quiet lady, a retired high school math teacher in her 50s who volunteered to drive the school bus. If he moved again, he'd find out how wrong he was.

I held the gun on him and made my way down the stairs as he waited for me. "What are you doing in my house?" He started to step toward me but thought better of it. His first good decision.

"I have a right to be here." His quavering tone suggested he was no longer so sure.

"You do not. You're trespassing. I'm either going to shoot you or have you arrested. Your choice."

"You can't shoot me."

"We're in Florida. Ever hear of Stand Your Ground? I can shoot you for the slightest hint you pose a threat to me." It was an exaggeration of the law, but definitely true when someone shows up in your house uninvited. His face turned as red as the throw pillows on my couch. Cherry tomato red, according to the decorator. "How did you get in anyway? I locked the door."

"I have a key. As the president of the Gulf Coast Pines Homeowners Association, I can go wherever I please, whenever I please." His whiny words were wrong on so many levels, I couldn't decide where to begin. He raised his right hand to show me a master key. "See?"

"Give it to me." When he started to refuse, I aimed the gun at his crotch. "I'm not kidding, Sam. You have no right to go into anyone's home. You're not god. You're the president of the board because no one else wanted it. I know. I was there when you were elected. When you're arrested, you won't be the president of anything."

He changed tactics. "Now, Jeri, I was checking to make sure everything was okay here. It's part of my job as president. I make sure everyone is safe. You weren't even supposed to be home. Why aren't you driving the school bus?"

"No school today. And I know what you were doing. You were snooping to see if I broke any of your stupid, petty rules so you could make my life miserable. It's what you do. You've bullied every woman in the neighborhood, but you picked the wrong one this time. Now give me the damn key, and get your butt out of my house." It didn't take a genius to see his mental gymnastics trying to find a way out of this mess. "Now, Sam."

He let the key drop to the floor and turned to leave. I followed him to the front patio. "This isn't over." His voice shook with rage.

"For your sake, it better be," I told him and was greeted with the sound of applause. My next-door neighbor stood in her driveway, a halo of red hair topping the big smile on her face. I realized the neighbors were able to see me chasing Sam away with a firearm. Not the kind of attention I wanted. I lowered the gun as Sam headed down the street toward his own house.

"Hi, Gloria," I said, my gun hand behind me.

"I've been wanting to do that myself." She walked closer to the property line, still amused.

"Did Sam show up in your living room too?"

She shook her head. "It was a matter of time. He's been hitting on me ever since I joined the board."

"You're way above his pay grade." Gloria was the youngest of the residents, 32, a beautiful woman, and a neurosurgeon to boot. She inherited her house from an aunt. Right after she moved in, we shared an introductory glass of wine. She thought a nice, quiet neighborhood would be the perfect escape from the pressure of her job. I encouraged her to join the board. I guess I didn't do her any favors, by putting her in Sam's sights.

Her smile grew wider. "I can't argue with you, but Sam doesn't take no for an answer, no matter what the question is. What's his deal anyway?"

"The usual. Had his own small business, a housecleaning franchise. He was used to bossing around the poor women who did all the work. When he retired, he discovered he had no one to push around."

She nodded. "Hence the presidency."

"I wasn't kidding when I said no one else wanted the job. You may have noticed we pretty much let him do whatever he wants, as long as it doesn't cost us any money."

"Let's hope you taught him a lesson."

I started to go back in the house, hoping she'd continue to ignore the gun at my side. "Fat chance. Guys like him don't take hints."

She laughed, and I looked back. Her eyes were on my Glock. "Some hint. As a matter of curiosity, would you really have shot him?"

"Little old me? Don't be silly."

She waved and gave me a thumb's up. I hoped I had seen the end of it. Fat chance, indeed.

THE NEXT MORNING, I grabbed a travel mug of coffee and headed to the garage behind my house. I was rich enough to live in quiet luxury even if I set a record for longevity. When I moved into the quiet community a few years ago, I became bored playing with money. It had become more like Monopoly dollars than the real thing.

Then a plea was posted in the community newsletter asking for volunteers to drive the school bus for the handful of resident children. I figured I'd give it a try. For my own convenience, I built a garage to house the bright yellow bus with its automatic STOP signal that flashed when I picked up or dropped off kids. Those kids turned out to be the best reason I had for getting up every weekday morning. They were smart, funny, and happy to keep the old lady behind the wheel up to date on the latest in pop culture. They gave me hope for the future of a disintegrating planet.

I stopped mid-thought and mid-step. The side door to the garage stood ajar. I was sure I'd locked it. Did Sam have a spare master key? I wouldn't put it past him to use it on the garage last night to get back at me. I put my travel cup on the ground to free my hands and weighed my options. I would've preferred to get back to the house for my gun, but it would take too long. Whoever had opened the door might still be inside.

Looking around for anything I could use as a weapon, I saw the machete I used on the wild grasses around my property line. I picked it up and held it over my shoulder like a bat before I looked around through the open door. Cabinets and shelves along the walls held tools and gardening materials. No place for anyone to hide. The bus was still there, so it wasn't out on a joy ride. After I looked in and under the vehicle, I put the machete on the work table and went to check my property.

As I turned the corner of the garage, I saw the body. Sam Crawford, sprawled face down in the lush grass, a knife stuck at an angle high between his shoulders. It must have been a perfect stabbing, past the vertebrae and through the disc, directly into his spinal cord. Either someone knew what they were doing or someone got very lucky. The blood in the grass around him was dark and dry. He must have been killed sometime last night.

I paused when I took a closer look at the knife. It was from a set I had in the garage, so Sam's murder was unlikely to have been premeditated. Someone armed him, or maybe her, self after entering the garage. Worse, it made me a prime suspect. I could kiss my quiet, under-the-radar life goodbye. As tempting as it would be to remove the knife and make it disappear, I could see that scenario ending badly, maybe even worse than all the other ideas I ran through my head.

I pulled my phone from my jeans pocket and took multiple pictures of Sam, with particular attention to the knife. Without disturbing the position of his body, I searched his pockets. His wallet and keys were there, as was the flashy Rolex on his left wrist, so not a robbery.

I had done all I could. Reminding myself the call would be recorded, I dialed 911. "I'd like to report a murder," I said, putting a quaver in my voice. I gave my name and address and agreed to wait for the police. I hung up before the operator had a chance to ask any more questions or tell me to stay on the line. My first priority was to make sure the kids weren't stranded at their stops, waiting for me to pick them up.

I called Art Calloway, vice-president of the board. I could hear the barking and meowing of his patients in the background. I told him Sam was dead in my yard and asked him to have Amy Myers, the board secretary, use the text tree to notify the parents the bus wouldn't run this morning. "Maybe the school can come up with a substitute bus and driver for now."

"I'll take care of it." His voice was calm amidst the furry clamor behind him. "Was it a heart attack? He looked like a good candidate for one. Let me know if you need anything." He hung up, leaving me relieved he didn't ask for more details.

Should I summon up tears as the sirens approached? Would anyone shed genuine tears for the late Sam Crawford? I doubted it, so I put my tear ducts on hold. There were questions I needed answered, preferably at least one step ahead of the cops, who were now running into the backyard from the street. No doubt this was the biggest case they'd had in years. Not much excitement for them in this wealthy town.

I raised my hands slowly and waited for them to come closer. A young one, no doubt new to the job, ran as fast as he could ahead of the others, and pointed his gun at me. "Don't move." I wondered how many times he had practiced that position in the mirror.

"I'm not armed," I said. "I'm the one who called. The body is behind the garage." I tilted my head toward the building.

"I said don't move," he shouted. I was starting to worry he might shoot me from sheer excitement.

A voice from behind him got his attention. "For cryin' out loud, Jackson. Lower your weapon before you shoot somebody." I held my breath, hoping Jackson wouldn't squeeze the trigger from the surprise of what could've passed for the voice of God, or at least James Earl Jones, giving him orders. To my relief, Jackson holstered his weapon. The voice of God added, "Sorry, ma'am. A little too much adrenaline." A tall man in a white shirt and dark pants, a badge on a lanyard around his neck, stood behind Jackson. A detective, no doubt, and an attractive one with short salt and pepper hair, intelligent eyes and, yes, that voice.

"Thanks," I said. "I was wondering if I was going to be the next victim. I'm Jeri Sabo."

"I'm Detective Kensley Lawton. Pleased to meet you."

"I'd say it was nice to meet you too, but..." I waved one raised hand. "This is my home. I drive the school bus, and I found the body when I went out to start my rounds." Slow down, I reminded myself. Let him ask questions. It had been a long time since I was on one side or another in an interrogation. Never volunteer more than you're asked. It was a good rule, whichever side of the table you were on.

"You can put your arms down, ma'am, but for my safety, I'm going have to pat you down for weapons." He walked to me, patted me down thoroughly but with respect, and looked at the gung ho cowboy cop. "Officer Jackson, could you please accompany Ms. Sabo into her house and wait with her? Try not to shoot anyone before I get there." He winked at me, and I led the young officer into the house.

"How about some coffee?" I headed for the kitchen with him close behind. "I never got a chance to drink mine." When he declined, I started a new pot for myself. This was going to be more than a one-cup day. We sat at the counter. He seemed happy enough not to talk, which suited me. I wanted time to think so, as I sipped the hot Guatemalan brew, I came up with a plan. It still needed finishing touches when the detective joined us. He sent Officer Jackson on his way and explained I wasn't under arrest but he was going to read me my rights as a formality. I could've recited them for him but heard him out and then said I'd be happy to help.

After telling me to call him Kensley (I admired his "I'm just a friend having a conversation with another friend" tactic), my buddy Kensley learned I was a retired high school math teacher, 54 years old, single and childless, who knew the decedent from my time on the Homeowners Association board. I admitted to not liking Sam Crawford, but not enough to stab him, and I was happy to share that I wasn't the only one who thought Sam was a pompous bully. When Kensley showed me a photo of the knife last seen in Sam's back, I told him it looked like a set I had in the garage. I wanted to get ahead of the game by explaining why my fingerprints might be on it. I didn't mention the events of the day before. After all, Sam had been stabbed, not shot, so if I had to, I could argue I thought it was irrelevant I had threatened to shoot him.

An hour later, we parted with my promise to come to the station the next day to give a recorded statement. I hoped Kensley assumed I wasn't the murderous type, but if he was as experienced and smart as he appeared, I knew I couldn't count on it.

Checking my texts, I saw Arthur had called an emergency board meeting for 1:00. I wondered if Kensley would show up and hoped he wouldn't hear about it in time. I wanted to have the people with the most reason to loathe Sam all to myself.

ART STOOD IN the doorway of the clubhouse conference room to greet the board members. The meetings were usually boring, painfully, excruciatingly boring, but everyone showed up for this one. I was sure Art had told them the reason for the emergency, and how could they resist? At least we wouldn't have to listen to Sam drone on about what a great job he was doing.

There were five of us at the table plus one visitor. Not, thank heavens, Detective Lawton. The extra chair was taken by Jason, the not quite ex-husband of Amy Myers, the board secretary. I was interested to see she sat next to him. It was no secret Amy had been having an affair with Sam. I wondered if it had been the reason behind the pending divorce.

Art sat across from Amy and Jason. Next to Art was Gloria, my next-door neighbor. At one end of the table, across from me, was our treasurer, Ross Bastian, founder and president of the local bank. He was glaring at Jason. Could he be jealous? Ross, in his 70s, didn't seem a match for Amy, in her 40s, but I'd seen more improbable couples. Could Ross have killed Sam to step into his place as Amy's lover? So many questions, so little time. At the moment, I hoped they all shared Art's guess that Sam had died of natural causes, unless one of them knew better. The one I hoped to flush out.

The room got quiet as Amy set up the recorder she used for the minutes. Art opened the meeting and dove right in. "You all know why we're here. Sam Crawford has died. I'm sure we'll get more details as time goes on, but it's important the board continue to manage the affairs of the Association. I suggest I become the interim president." There was a quick, "So moved," from Ross and a unanimous vote in favor. "Thank you," Art said. "Until we have additional information, it would be wise to have the Association's lawyer monitor the situation. We have no idea what potential liability we might have for whatever happened to Sam." The room got quiet as they realized a position on the board might have opened a Pandora's box of financial disaster. "I'll call Tyler and let him know." Tyler Argent was the real estate lawyer who dealt with routine paperwork for the board. He wasn't an expert in criminal cases, but I kept my opinion to myself. I was the only one who knew Sam had been murdered. Except his killer, who might be sitting here with us.

Ross interrupted and glared at Jason again. "What are you doing here? You don't live here anymore." Hostility turned his voice into a harsh rasp.

Before Jason could answer, Amy jumped in. "Our divorce isn't final yet. Jason is still on the deed and has every right to be here."

"It's okay," Jason said. "He's angry because he's on the hook for the loan I took out to buy Sam's business. He's worried he'll look bad if things go south."

We all knew Sam sold his business to Jason when he retired. He'd bragged about what a great deal he had negotiated. Everyone around the table appeared surprised by the source of the money. Jason had bounced from one losing venture to another, and it was only Amy's income as a nurse that had kept them going. Why would Ross have approved a big loan to someone like Jason?

Amy wouldn't meet Ross's eyes. The age difference between them no longer looked like a barrier to a history of a closer relationship. Did Amy get Ross to give Jason the loan and then take up with Sam? No fool like an old fool, but sometimes an old fool still has plenty of bite. After a quick review of pending

Association business, Art closed the meeting. On my way out, Gloria stopped me. "I'm not going to say anything to the police," she whispered.

"What do you mean?" I knew what she was going to say.

"You know. About you and Sam. The gun? I have to go in to be interviewed later today, but I wanted you to know what I'll be saying. Or not saying." She waited for me to thank her. And maybe to ask me to keep quiet about Sam hitting on her?

Before I could decide the best way to handle it, Amy and Jason walked past. They were holding hands and stopped to talk.

"That was more interesting than most of those meetings." Jason laughed. "Bet Ross is livid. No sense of humor, that guy."

Amy dropped his hand. "There's nothing funny about this."

"You're right, honey. But as many times as Sam stabbed people in the back, he won't be missed."

Amy's face paled. "Let's go." She took his hand again and pulled him away.

I said goodbye to Gloria and walked home. There was a lot to think about. It seemed everyone around the table had a reason to want Sam dead. Jason because Sam slept with his wife. Gloria because Sam had been getting more aggressive in his attentions to her. Ross because the loan to Jason could be costing his bank a lot of money and maybe because he wanted Amy for himself. And Art? Surely he couldn't have wanted to become president badly enough to kill Sam for the job. I've seen stranger things happen, but I'd have to see something stronger before he would go on the list. However, as a veterinarian, he would know the best place to stab someone, even if the victim didn't bark, chirp or meow. Same for Gloria. The means fit her surgical skills. And why would she want a quid pro quo of secrecy from me with the police?

But I had something I needed to follow up with the detective. I called the station and asked for him.

"Detective Lawton will be back in an hour." I asked them to tell him I'd be there when he got in to give my statement. I had one question to ask him. Depending on the answer, I was hoping to be able to steer him toward the killer.

WHEN I GOT to the station, I was escorted into an interrogation room to wait for my new best friend Kensley. There was the usual one-way mirror and cameras up near the ceiling, recording every word and move. The furniture was a step up from the usual battered table and hard wooden chairs. It reflected the affluence of the town. I settled back into the ergonomic leather chair and waited. I was good at being still. Lots of practice. If anyone was watching me, they wouldn't see guilty squirming or sweating. I knew I looked as if I was meditating, which would fit right in with the trendy citizenry.

Fifteen minutes had passed when the door opened. Detective "call me Kensley" Lawton walked over to the table and reached across to shake my hand. "Jeri. Thanks for coming in."

We both pretended I had a choice. After turning down his offer of something to drink (too bad a glass of wine wasn't on the menu; I might've taken him up on it), he asked me about how I came to live in Gulf Coast Pines. I gave him my well-rehearsed story. Grew up in a small town in the Midwest, moved to a bigger city after college, taught high school math until I turned 50 and then headed to Florida, land of sunshine. Never married. No children. If he decided to check me out, my story would hold up to a normal background check. I was going to make sure he didn't see any reason to look deeper.

We went over my discovery of the body from multiple directions, but I had nothing new to add. He asked about Sam's relationship with the other board members and any other neighbors I was aware of. I was happy to give him all the information I had, except for the part where I threatened Sam with a gun. The more he looked at the others, the less time he'd have for me. I couldn't help him with neighbors other than the board members. Sam and I hadn't traveled in the same social circles. I hadn't traveled in any social circles, with or without Sam. I liked my privacy.

I mentioned the emergency board meeting. "It's too bad you didn't hear about it," I said. "You would've had a chance to speak with all of us and maybe saved some time."

"It's all right. I prefer to talk to them separately anyway."

"Am I your first?" The question hung for a minute, but he knew what I meant.

"As a matter of fact, you are. The others are coming in later." Just what I wanted to hear.

"Well, good luck. I hate to think of a killer running around loose." I shuddered, trying not to overdo it. We both stood, shook hands once again, and I left, planning my next step.

I WAITED UNTIL after dinner to make the call. I gave my name and told the person on the other end to meet me in an hour at the garage behind my house. When asked what this was about, I said, "You know. Be there."

This is where in the movies, the audience would be yelling, "Don't go down the basement!" or, in my case, into the garage. I was confident I could handle myself. It wasn't my first rodeo and, knowing my knife from the tool bench was used, I knew Sam's death wasn't a premeditated crime. I wasn't worried about facing down an amateur.

I was at the garage early and waited inside with the side door open. When I heard someone approach, I hit Record on my phone. "I'm in here," I said.

Jason walked in, his hands in his pockets. "Why am I here?" His eyes darted around the garage but he relaxed a little when he didn't see anyone else.

"You know why. You killed Sam. I'm guessing it was self-defense. We all know what a bully he was. How did it happen?"

"I don't know what you're talking about." Jason stopped a few feet away from me.

"You're wasting time. You knew Sam was stabbed in the back. Only the person who killed him could've known how he died." Jason should never play poker. I watched the flash of recognition when he remembered what he had said after the meeting.

"That? It was just a figure of speech." When I shook my head, his shoulders sagged and he clutched at the lifeline I had thrown him.

"You're right. It was self-defense." I watched as he pulled his hands out of his pockets. "I didn't mean to kill him." The words came faster. "He called me to meet him here. Sam didn't like you much. He thought it was funny to use your garage right under your nose. He said he could help me save the business, so I couldn't refuse." His tone was bitter. "He was a bully and a liar. He sold his business to me, but I found out afterwards the numbers were faked. I couldn't prove it, but I'm on the verge of bankruptcy because of him."

"So what happened?"

Jason was moving toward the tool bench, and my hand was moving to my hip. "He told me I was an idiot but he was enjoying my wife. For her sake, he'd get me on track with the business. I lost it. I punched him, but then I thought I heard someone coming. When I looked away, Sam took off through the door. I wasn't thinking. I grabbed a knife and chased him into the yard. I wanted to scare him, show what a coward he really was. I tripped, and the knife landed in his back."

Jason was crying, and I believed him.

"You need to tell the police," I said. "This was an accident." I knew that wasn't completely true, but it was time to wrap this up.

"I can't. I'll lose everything." He whirled around toward the bench. The machete was lying there. I hadn't gotten around to putting it away.

"Jason," I said quietly, "don't."

He paused.

"I'll shoot you if I have to."

When he turned to look at me, he saw the gun in my hand. I was feeling sorry for him, but I wasn't stupid.

As he crumbled to the floor, sobbing, I pulled the phone from my pocket and stopped the recording. I had taken the precaution of putting the detective's cellphone number on speed dial. "Kensley? Jeri. I hope I'm not interrupting anything." Always be polite to the cops. "I think you should come to my house. Right now."

I gave him credit. He didn't ask questions, and it wasn't long before I heard the sirens. With luck, I'd soon be back to my carefully curated uneventful life, driving the yellow school bus every weekday. Drama free, just the way I liked it.

Vengeance Takes a Holiday

Eve Morton

THE FIRST TIME I met Sheila Laherty, she knocked on my door just as I had set the table for Sunday dinner. I was alone, but my mother and sisters always told me to treat each meal as if it was a celebration. My table was clean, with a linen tablecloth, and cutlery placed overtop of napkins on the right side. A spinning daisy in the center held the stew I'd made that morning. I added some wine to the table just before I answered the door.

"Hi," Sheila said. She smiled and revealed slightly crooked teeth. "Mr. Crane?"

"Mr. Cane," I corrected. I'd seen Sheila before in the apartment building. She lived down the hall, one of many neighbors I recognized by sight, but nothing beyond. I wondered how she'd known my name, but figured it was written on our mail slots in the foyer. "What can I do for you...?"

"Shelia. Sheila Laherty," she introduced herself. After shaking my hand in a firm grip, she placed her palm around the swell of her stomach. It was only then that I noticed the bump. It had been fall, then winter, and the expanding clothing she'd adorned herself with I figured was for warmth, if I stopped more than three seconds to consider. "I know this is rather strange, but whatever you're making smells fantastic. What is it?"

"Oh." I sniffed the air, but had been in the kitchen all morning so I'd stopped smelling the spices I was blending for my Sunday meal. "Just a stew."

"What is it, though? Maybe I can find a place that does takeout all the same. I'm not one for the kitchen, but wow." She breathed in deep, her dark eyes popping with delight. "I mean... it just smells so good. I had to come out of my apartment and see what it was. You know, you get a super-nose when you're pregnant. It's sort of neat."

"I didn't know that, actually." The life I'd shared with my mothers and sisters did not include that facet. And my life now mostly revolved around myself and other men. "Would you like some?"

Sheila's dark eyes beamed. I should have seen the devilish way she curled a hand around her ear, tucking away her dark curls slyly, as if the idea had never occurred to her before—when that had probably been the exact reason she'd sought me out. "Are you sure? I don't want to impose..."

"Please. I've made enough for the week. More than enough to share."

I held my door open for her and shut it once she was inside. She took off her shoes next to my own, and revealed remarkably small feet. Everything about Sheila was small; she was barely five feet, her face was round and childish like a pixie, and her hands were no bigger than the feet she bore. She probably wore children's sizes at the stores, until that growing belly of hers came along.

"Were you expecting someone?" she asked when she stepped into the living room. Her gaze flicked from my books to my entertainment center, then to the table that was decked out with a tablecloth and steaming stew and the wine.

"No," I said. "My mother instilled good manners, though."

"I can tell. She did a good job. Are you still in touch with her?"

I shook my head and gestured to the table again. "Please. Sit. I'll grab you a bowl."

She sat in my place setting. I set myself up on the other end of the table. I served us both. Sheila whispered praises about the meal and myself, but once the stew was in front of her, she drew silent and practically inhaled it as if she hadn't eaten in days. Something stirred in my own gut that was not hunger. I should have realized then it was a warning of what was to come.

Instead, I thought it was pity.

"Please stop by any time," I said as she put on her shoes an hour later. "I always have something on the stove."

"If you're sure," she asked, but she was already smiling.

OVER THE NEXT three months, Sheila joined me for Sunday dinner. At first, she only ate what I served, asked questions about the recipes, and probed about my culture and lineage.

Polite topics, especially when sharing a meal. She asked for recipes, which I tried to remember from years of memorization, and she wrote them down happily though she still insisted she was no good in the kitchen.

"I'm not sure how I'm going to feed this one. Maybe I'll get good at warming, as Susan Sontag said she did."

I was delighted at the mention of the cultural critic. We spoke about books and my job at the local college that day, but we always came back around to the food. Even when I was at work, as my business students struggled with passive voice, I'd often browse recipes online. It didn't take long to find some that I believed Sheila would enjoy. I copied them on Sundays, and then she would copy them into a notebook she always had with her. Her writing was neat as she wrote them out, though I know she never made them for herself. I never smelled anything from her apartment, never even saw inside until much later. She always came to me, and eventually, she asked to take some food home.

"Just for tomorrow's lunch. It's hard to balance good meals with working all the time."

"Where do you work?" I asked, realizing I had no idea what she did all day.

"Oh, I work from home. Temp work, mostly."

"What kind?"

"I'm a private investigator, really," she said as if it was nothing. "I find things for people. Mostly missing kids and the like. Cheating husbands are my bread and butter, so to speak."

"Wow. I had no idea."

She gestured to her growing belly. "I don't fit the type, I know. It's a little hard to do the legwork with the baby on the way, so I've taken to mostly doing computer research. I forget to eat, and then that's not good for the baby."

"No, it's not," I had to agree. I gave her leftovers. Then, eventually, I found myself giving her what was in my fridge and pantry. Just small items; oh, I bought some crackers I don't like, would you take them? Some cookies, canned soup, much the same. She took them eagerly and genuinely thanked me.

"You know, you're not like most men I meet in my line of work. Very giving. Thank you."

I didn't say anything to that. I just gave her more and more.

It was not long before she started to make subtle requests. "Have you ever heard of tiramisu? What about jerk chicken or anything with adobe? " She would suggest items outside of both of our cultures and everyday lives, encouraging me to give it a try.

Then she'd take the leftovers without asking. She'd knock on the door at all hours of the day during the weekend requesting more food. She'd leave notes on the door when I was teaching class, notes that started off as kind requests but soon became thinly disguised shopping lists.

"Sheila," I said after we had had one of our Sunday dinners that were growing more and more lengthy. "I can't keep feeding you like this."

"What do you mean?" She tilted her head to the side, her small face and youthful expression making her seem benign. She clasped her hands over her round belly, as if to make me feel guilty. "I thought we were friends."

"We are. Or at least, I'd like to be. But I feel as if I'm being taken advantage of."

"How?"

"The food. You're not even asking me about my job or my life anymore. You're simply making requests and expecting me to meet them."

"How is teaching?" she asked. "You said you were having trouble with a student, right?"

I sighed. "That's not the point."

"I thought you wanted more conversation. I didn't want to ask some things, you know, since I realized your real first name."

"What?" I asked, then swallowed. My real first name, as she referred to it, was a deadname. It was an older version of me, a past I let go of when I moved here and left my family, and my lineage as one of three sisters in my mother's kitchen, behind. The only part of that I'd taken with me were memories, memories I was now transcribing on recipe index cards to a woman who was also a private investigator.

I should have known this would happen.

"You know..." she said, narrowing her dark eyes.

While I focused on what she was about to say, her belly seemed to disappear. I saw what those cheating spouses must have seen when she showed them the telephoto lens, and those black and white images of them caught with their pants down.

"I didn't even need to look you up in a database to find it. I saw the name on one of your letters. The rest was easy to figure out."

"You read my mail?" I asked. I scoffed. "Even you should know that's a—"

"I never opened it. I simply saw the name on the address."

"How do you know it was me, then? There are a lot of people who live in this building—"

"I figured it was your sister. But now you've told me it's you." She rubbed her belly. She smiled in the way I knew the child inside her was moving. "It's not a big deal. I don't care who you were then."

I remained quiet. I could feel the upcoming 'but' under her breath.

"I like your cooking," she said. "Your recipes, both inherited and online experiments. And my baby likes it, too. I can name them after you. I don't know the gender yet, but I suppose it won't really matter. Either one, it'll get a name."

"Sheila," I said. "I think my hospitality has worn out. I'd like you to leave."

"Are you sure about that?"

I examined her. I didn't understand how a small woman, a pregnant woman, could instill so much fear in me. It wasn't just my past, or her nature at digging up dirt on others, either. I was well aware I had rights and could live however I wanted. I was living however I wanted. And there were rules she still had to follow even if she was a PI. But the fear still lingered, enough that I went to offer her the leftovers again, as a small parting gift.

"I didn't like this dish as much," she said. "It smelled good, but the texture was a bit off-putting. You keep it. I'll come again next week."

"Shelia," I said.

"Gregory," she mirrored. When I said nothing, only gestured towards the door, she went on. "You really should consider what you're doing. In all cultures, no matter where you're from, no matter what you serve on the table, you can't deny a pregnant woman food. Or shelter. Or even books she wants to borrow from the shelf."

I wondered what tome in my collection had caught her eye. What piece of furniture she'd asked about next, what part of my past she'd want in exchange for... what? I was getting absolutely nothing in this bargain.

"I thought you were my friend, Sheila," I said. "I don't know about that now."

"Feeling used, Mr. Cane?"

I nodded.

"I get it. I feel like that now. You think I'm a bad neighbor, try having a roommate who's kicking you in the middle of the night and stripping the calcium from your bones. God, I feel my teeth rotting because this beast is taking all of it."

"It's a child, a baby."

"I never asked for it."

"But you have it now," I said, no longer sympathizing with her. "You could have done something, but you didn't."

Sheila gave me a sinister smile. "You're right. I could have, but I didn't. So now I'm merely asking for your hospitality, as you might say. Let me come here for more Sunday dinners. I promise, just Sundays now. And I'll keep your secret."

I sighed. I opened my apartment door. "I have nothing to hide, Sheila. I know who I am."

"And I know who I am. Or at least, who I can become. And Mr. Cane, you haven't seen anything yet."

IT TOOK ABOUT a week for things to go wrong.

I chalked the leaky pipes, a broken hinge on my bedroom door, and the infernal beeping from a malfunctioning fire alarm to the building's general deterioration. Each time I called the super, she came and fixed it all as soon as she could, though she did ask me a few times if I had tried to fix these items myself first. "There are marks on 'em, that's all," she said when I became obstinate that I hadn't touched a thing. "Just looks like you wanted to become a tool guy."

"I'm not."

"Okay, then."

I tried not to let paranoia change my behavior. Even though I dreamed of Sheila slipping in my door, wrench under her arm, I had a hard time imagining her with a large belly getting under the sink and removing pipes. Or climbing a ladder to muck with the fire alarm. It was impossible, downright paranoid. She had better things to do.

But when I was fired at work, my contract terminated early due to a student accusation that I could not track down to prove or disprove, I started to believe something more sinister was occurring.

Finding Sheila's online PI page only confirmed all my doubts. Cheating husbands were not simply her bread and butter, but part of an entire packaged deal she deemed "Revenge Served Cold"; she found cheating spouses and missing children from divorces, and then made the perpetrators pay in ever more creative and ever more elaborate ways. There were dozens of horror stories online about the havoc she had wreaked. *This five foot elf,* a man wrote on a message board. *She ruined my fucking life.*

I exited everything and wiped my computer clean. I knew that she could ruin my life, too. She was already in the process of doing so. The recipe was almost complete.

I paced up and down the apartment hallway, wondering if I should confront her. Would that make it better or worse? I was not a cheating spouse, but she'd still done irreversible damage in my career. What else did I have to lose, other than my apartment itself? My name was changed, my rights in place— for once I was not worried about my gender. But my home. My kitchen. The only family legacy I could keep as my own seemed precarious as the stained recipe cue cards she wrote on, but never used.

I went back to my apartment and tried to sleep. All I heard was the clattering of someone in the apartment above me. Cat screeches from outside. And a slow and unnerving smell that crept up from my toilet.

I called the emergency line for the super, waking her up at one in the morning. "Hello?" her sleep-filled voice answered.

"There's something wrong with the pipes again. I think the sewage is backing up."

"Okay, okay. You're not the first person to mention the smell."

"Am I not? Is it..." I didn't finish. The super was already telling me the pregnant lady down the hall said something, too. "Just after she told me I needed to fix it, or else."

"Yeah," I said. "Sorry about that."

"Eh. She's a persistent one. But I suppose she has a right to be, you know. Baby and all."

I didn't argue. I hung up the phone and barely slept. When the plumber came in the morning, I decided to make a meal in the kitchen. I'd make the first stew that had brought her to my door. I doubled the batch, and added extra spices to entice her. I cooked and cooked, filling the kitchen so much that even the plumber commented as he left. "Good for what ails ya, I suppose," he said. "Good luck feeding the village."

I waited another hour, the table set, until I decided Sheila wasn't coming. I had to go to her this time around. I bundled up a large Tupperware container and headed down to her door. I knocked three times before the neighbor across from her answered.

"She's gone," the woman said. "Having the baby."

"Oh."

"I'm sure she'll appreciate that when she gets back," the woman said, gesturing to the stew. "Sure can smell it from down here."

I was about to offer her some when she made a face. Too much curry, too much spice, I could see in her gaze. I started to feel almost bereft of someone to share it with. Back inside, alone at my table, I even started to long for Sheila. What had she done to me? She was ruining my life and all I wanted from her was another chance to set things in order. Not to serve cold revenge, but warm with stew and kindness.

Did cravings disappear once babies were born? I wondered. I looked it up and found out that yes, they often did. I didn't know if she'd ever want to have dinner with me again.

I realized then she had truly cursed me, made me crazy for something that I had resented, and there was nothing I could do but watch my dinner go cold.

THREE DAYS LATER, when I knew that Sheila had returned
with her baby boy, I knocked on her door. This time I brought
the last of the stew, rather than the first of it. I also had flowers
because, as my mother and sisters told me, when someone
gets out of the hospital, for whatever reason, you bring them
flowers.

"Mr. Cane," she said. She smiled widely. "And some dahlias.
My favorite. Would you like to come in?"

Shelia stepped aside and I entered without another word.
She was back to being her petite self, though she'd just given
birth. It was strange to see her without her large belly—but she
was flat, as if she'd never been pregnant. Even her breasts had
diminished, as if she was binding them like I'd done when I was
in my teen years.

"Where's your son?" I asked. "I heard you had a boy."

"A shame, really."

"A shame?"

"Yeah, all I had picked out were girls' names. Alas." She
shrugged as if this was no big deal. "I guess I'll have to resort to
old case files to find one that fits the circumstance. He's asleep,
by the way. In the bedroom. Come, sit at the table with me."

I followed her through her apartment, a mirror image of
my own. Where I had bookshelves and an entertainment area,
she had nothing. Or next to nothing. There was a long couch,
worn thin on the arms, and some stacks of books that bore
the marker of a local library. A small table was where mine
was, but it was rickety. It leaned to one side as she added the
Tupperware. She went to her kitchen to get something for the
flowers, but all she had was a pitcher one would normally serve
juice in.

"It'll have to do." She added the dahlias to the pitcher with
some water and set it in the middle of the table. She had no
real plates, only paper ones with plastic cutlery, taken from fast
food places where she normally ate her meals.

I felt my stomach surge. Guilt. I'd kicked this woman out of
my life, simply because she'd overstayed her welcome.

"Sheila, I wanted to say I'm sorry. I—"

"No need to apologize," she said with a weary smile. "I was
being, as some of my clients call me, a bitch. I'm going to blame

pregnancy. Certainly made me act differently. I can't wait to get back to normal now. Please."

She gestured to a chair at the table. She sat down after I did, and served us both in paper bowls with plastic spoons. She made all the right noises over the stew, but I could also tell her palate had changed.

"Not the same?" I asked.

"No, not even close." She was about to say something else when I heard a cry. Low and raspy, much different than I thought a baby would be. Her dark eyes seemed tired as she rose from the table. "I'll be right back."

"Let me," I said. I didn't know why I offered. I didn't believe I was good with kids, despite having a teaching degree and many sisters to play dolls with while growing up. Maybe that was why I did offer. I wasn't teaching. I didn't have those sisters anymore. Seeing a young person would have been the next best thing to fulfilling an urge I knew I still had inside of me—not to be a mother, but to be something—no, *someone* kind.

"If you insist," Sheila said. "I bet he'd love to set a familiar face to a familiar voice. You were around him just as much as anyone else."

I had never thought of it that way before. A part inside of me glowed with recognition.

Once again, I should have realized it was another trick, another way of her working her way into my life for the long-term. "It's always the food first," my mother would tell me when I was younger. "That is how you win any man's heart. You feed them, then you love them, and then they never leave." I wondered how my mother would feel about Sheila's bread and butter.

Sheila's son was staying in the room I called my office in my own apartment. It looked to be Sheila's office, too, since a desk was lined against one wall, an outline of a laptop still present in the dust. His crib was along the other side, a bare white cage-like place with no mobile. He was a fussing lump in the center of the big mattress. He wore a blue onesie and had a small hat on. His skin was the same shade as Sheila's, though a little lighter like my own. Once I picked him up, and his dark eyes opened, they were his mother's through and through.

"Ah, a natural," Sheila said. She leaned in the doorframe. I hadn't heard her come in. "I should name him after you."

"Oh?"

"Yes. It means watchful. I looked it up a minute ago. And in general, I think most people should be more watchful."

"That's nice. I didn't know that."

"It's your name, though. I assume you picked it."

"I did. But I just liked the sound."

She nodded. She said nothing else. I waited for her to ask more questions, to pry more into my previous life, but she didn't. Instead, she snapped a photo on her phone of the two of us. "Just for a memory," she said. Then she gasped like she'd forgotten the time. It was an act, and I saw through it, but I also didn't want to see through it. "I have to pick up a prescription from the drugstore," she said. "Do you mind staying with him?"

I told her no, not at all. I did not ask when she'd be back, and she didn't offer a time. She left so easily, with nothing but a purse bulging with her laptop, it didn't seem real.

But by the time three hours had passed, and I'd fed Gregory once from the bottles in the fridge, I knew she'd never return.

PEOPLE IN THE building called her a criminal. People called her other horrible names I'll not repeat here. She was more hated after leaving Gregory than she'd ever been before, despite her business acumen, since only mothers who abandon their children receive worst treatment than people who truly are criminals. Or cheaters.

For once, though, I didn't join in. I didn't know her before she was pregnant, and even while she was, I still had a hard time seeing her as a bad person. Someone stuck in a bad place, a story I didn't know and that she'd probably never tell anyway, but I understood in my own way. She wanted her body back, because it gave her the life she wanted. So she left behind the only part of that she could without guilt. And she only left him behind, because she knew she could count on me, her good neighbor. The only man she ever really liked.

I found out a week later that I'd been listed as the father on the birth certificate. Despite this impossibility, I knew it to be true. I'd fed that baby through her. I'd nurtured him through her. And when he smiled at my voice, Sheila's lies may as well have been the truth.

So he lives with me now. In my apartment, with a better crib than what Sheila had. All the things that Sheila undid with her presence have mostly gone back to normal. A young couple lives in her place. The apartment building is no longer falling apart. And I have a different job at a new school, given to me in part by a stunning recommendation letter that came without asking.

All normal.

Except that I don't have Sunday dinners alone anymore, and when Gregory is older, he'll learn how to cook too, guided by my family memories written in his mother's hand.

Sir Fergus Allison's Bench

Shiny Nyquist

THE DOORBELL CHIMED through the *Ode To Joy* theme before Sharon could reach the hallway to see the shape in the rippled glass of the front door: a shape that shared all the contours and colours of an enormous black bear or some other bulky creature, flapping its arms and swaying from left to right in the cold outside.

For the briefest moment she pictured Ralfy, impatient and keyless after one of his absences. Such thoughts hardly raised a moment's panic these days, and yet she made the effort to calm her nerves by calling to mind the surprisingly grey hollowness of his corpse. That, and the silver-white memorial bench, installed at the height of summer all of three years ago. And of course today, being Wednesday, was her day for writing to Mickey, Ralf's surviving twin, who was still blissfully unaware but safely behind bars in The Scrubs. So no: it could not possibly be Ralfy on the doorstep because Ralf Frost was well and truly dead.

"Coming, coming..." Swathed in her favourite, oversized white dressing-gown—a warm fluffy thing with a big diamond monogram for *big diamond geyser* stitched into the lapel—she shuffled to the front door and cracked it open as far as the chain allowed.

"Mickey!"

Mickey's face was pock-marked and grey, his hair boot-polish black all the way down to the roots, and his eyes dark gleaming buttons that caught the light as he swayed. In a throaty whisper, he said: "You made me wait. What is it with you guys? You and him both."

Feeling she had no choice, Sharon kicked aside the pile of unopened mail and let him in. *Act in the moment as belongs to the moment*, as Ralfy used to say.

A ball of flesh in a dark blue suit, pink shirt, and zebra stripe tie pushed past her.

She didn't actually start to tremble until Mickey was ensconced in the tiny room under the stairs, noisily relieving himself. She thought of wedging the under stairs door shut and barricading him in with the hall table. But he could easily bust through that. And it would only make things worse.

"I—I didn't know..." She said.

"I bought myself a retirement cottage," he said, his words barely audible. "On the dirt track at the end of your rich little cul-de-sac. Close to the woods, like. Away from the main road. Something to put my money into—but not that far from people who is familiar." The loud stream of splashing dribbled to a halt. "I got business here, see."

"Business?"

Back in the hallway, Mickey picked up the framed picture of Ralf from the hall table. "What's this?"

"He's always liked that picture. He's always saying it was a proud moment."

"It's broken." Mickey thrust the picture in her face. "What's this beautiful man doing in some knackered old, botched-up frame? Should be gold for our Ralfy. *Gold!* Nothing less than gold, and don't you forget it. Ralfy was worth that."

"Was?" She leapt at the chance to feign ignorance: "What d'you mean *was*?"

"This is not what I call lying low," Mickey said, jiggling the frame at her. "Not this."

Ralf's face, resurrected in the faded dot-colours of an old newspaper clipping, half-grinned at her from inside the wooden frame. He was holding up an oversized cheque, nestling it under his chin. She cringed at the botched-up superglue job she had done on the frame of this much-stomped-upon reminder of the past.

Mickey returned the picture to the table, repeating the headline: "Heist Twin Breaks Big on Horses. Not what I call lying low. *Mouthy Ralf.* That's what them retards in the press called him. And him getting off like that. And then all that guff about going to Jamaica. No sweetheart, he made his self a marked man for that gee-gee scam, for sure. Besides: there's something not right here. I feel it in my water—like he's a goner: *Mister Ninety Per Cent* went and left the wrong ten percent undone."

"No, no, you're wrong—" Sharon said, "—he can't be dead. He's sure to be back. He always comes back. In the end. You'll see. Any day now. It could be any day now. He could walk through that door, happy as Larry, just like the old days. Even when I saw you—out there in the glass—I thought it might be him, it could be him—*please* let it be him, I thought!"

"Like hell you did." Mickey wrapped his fat fingers around her wrist and tugged her towards the front door.

She grabbed a banister with her free hand.

"Uh-uh." With a quick jerk, he pulled her arm straight and burst her grip. "See, I know who to ask. Ralfy told me who to ask. He said not to trust you. He said to trust next door. To trust that woman with all them artistic tendencies as likes to talk. He said to trust her. She's not streetwise enough to tell porkies, that's what he said. So let's see what she says about your comings and goings, who you been seeing, what you been doing, without neither of us moral guardians around to look after you."

Sharon banged her free elbow on the door frame on the way out, sending shards of pain through her arm. Resentfully, she tried to comfort herself with the thought that next door would be no push-over for Mickey. No, not her next door. Not the neighbourhood Svengali who had lured man after man to his death, and then—*then*—managed to blackmail all the 'grieving' widows for their part in the crime. *No, not her. She'll have you, Mickey Frost, she'll have you for breakfast*. Sharon hoped.

WHEN THE DOORBELL next door went unanswered, Mickey dragged Sharon around the side of the house along the gravel path next to the garage.

She took to whimpering in short indignant breaths and to stomping the heels of her slippers into the loose pebbles, clinging to her act of the falsely accused. Although accused of what she had yet to find out. It might be theft, or murder or, to rub salt into a sore that was already red-raw, blackmail. She felt sick to her soul. All she ever wanted was to escape the gangs and the violence, and yet here she was, putting a brave face on what could turn into a nasty beating—or worse—while forever weighed down by the threat from the photographs glued into that little black book of her scheming neighbour.

Shortly, as she was dragged out from between the house and the garage, and the back garden came into view, Mickey faltered. His grip on Sharon's wrist loosened.

It was not difficult to see why.

As with all these south-facing gardens, a long green lawn dropped away gently down the hillside, giving a clear view of the wooded valley below and of the village beyond, scattered across the opposite slope, with its grey church and its grey slate-roofed buildings.

Sharon never tired of the liberating feeling of walking into this open space nor, even with Mickey within slapping distance, of the frisson of vertigo that the familiar sight stirred within her. But what had stopped him in his tracks—what would stop any first-time visitor—was what was on the lawn.

The lawn was filled with row after row of painted park benches. They stood four benches to a row, no two benches the same colour, and were assembled into ranks that ran from the back of the house down to where the garden dropped away with the hillside. They, in all their fairground glory, stood facing the grey tower of the church on the hillside opposite as if making up one tiny portion of a dazzling amphitheatre, fixed forever in devotion.

Mickey re-tightened his grip. Sharon found herself being dragged towards a large hunched figure in a red and white circus-tent dress who was stooping over a bench (lime green) and was busy scrubbing away lumpy white stains using a pungent disinfectant, probably of her own brewing.

Sharon let out a squeak of faux-friendship: "Violetta!"

Violetta looked up and, after a moment of blank hesitation, her pumpkin face, moist eyes, and wraparound mouth came to life.

"Darlings—oh darling!" She set about crab-walking between benches to meet her visitors. "You *are* Mickey, aren't you? You must be. You are the spitting image! Isn't he the spitting image? My dear, if I didn't know better I'd say long lost Ralfy had been found and returned. Reunited with his loved ones! But your hair looks so nice, and his, well, truth be told: Ralfy was starting to go a teensy-weensy bit grey. But what *am*

I saying? Of course we may find him yet! Oh please Mickey, do say you have word!"

Violetta continued to talk as she prised Sharon free from Mickey's grasp and, soon enough, Sharon was fully tucked up against Violetta's hot armpit, in the bountiful folds of the expansive red and white dress.

"We must celebrate!" Violetta said. "At least one of my wonderful twins deigns to pay call on us! But darling, I forget myself. You must forgive my gardening togs." She made a great show of releasing Sharon and brushing non-existent dirt off the loose-fitting, hide-all-the-lumps dress.

Sharon now worried that these two hardened criminals might get along a little too well, that her reprieve might be only temporary and, shortly, they might even turn on her. So she took a step back, glanced around for an escape route, and noticed that for once the stable-style door at the rear of the garage was open. A route that would, indeed, satisfy all sorts of curiosities, given half the chance.

Mickey was saying, softly, in a voice that made every syllable sound like a threat: "Ralfy said to talk to you. You'd know how to contact him. Where to find him. He trusted you. He always said he'd leave word—with you."

Violetta continued to run her fingers through the swirls of her dress. "How totally sweet of him. So sweet of him. But well, really. He liked to talk. He loved to talk. Though I wasn't quite his *confidante*, you understand. No, no, that was more Sharon's department. There are things only a wife—"

Sharon was suddenly alert and listening, and all innocence, and hoping with all her might that innocence was all that showed on her face.

"If he disappeared legit, like—" Mickey lifted a fold of Violetta's dress and started fat-fingeredly kneading the organic cotton, "—he'd have left a message, a note, a—*indication*—of what he was about. *If* he went off legit. Otherwise..."

"There's always his bench, darling," Violetta said, without flinching. "He did sponsor one of my sun-worshippers' benches."

At the mention of Ralfy's bench, Sharon's stomach became a notch tighter; if they were going to talk benches, the safest place to be really was somewhere, anywhere, other than here.

"What d'ya mean?" Mickey said. "What'd he want with a bench?"

"Each one has its little message," Violetta said.

"He left a message on a bench?"

Violetta pointed distantly, down the lawn. "Yes darling. Now see the row starting turquoise, then pink, then silver-white, then sable? His is one of those. Here now, do let me show you."

She took a step away from him.

Mickey pulled the red and white material of the dress taut, reining her back. "No. You wait here. Don't neither of you twos move." He dropped the fistful of cloth and strode off towards a slither of turquoise half-way down the garden.

As soon as he was out of earshot, Sharon vented her horror in a hissed whisper: "What'd you do that for? When he reads the inscription, he'll know Ralf's dead."

"That's your lookout," Violetta said. "You brought him here. What'd you do that for? He's your problem, darling. Nothing to do with me. Your relation; your problem; you get rid."

"How?" Sharon struggled to steady her voice: "Perhaps you'd, well, like—*tell me how*. You're the expert."

"Yes, darling, but this expert needs paying," Violetta said. "You come up with the dosh, my dear, and maybe, we'll see. You know the rule: no dosh, no doings; you're behind as it is."

"But he could get mad any second," Sharon said. "You can see for yourself... Look—*Please!* I always get up to date in the end, you know that..."

And she could probably do it too: if Mickey disappeared, she might not be left as the owner of the cottage but at least she would be free to search it. There was bound to be something there, if only a left luggage ticket or a locker key.

"You won't be able pay for anything, darling, if he's not alive to tell you where his take of the dosh is."

The sharp crackle of splintering plastic came from down the garden. Mickey had the silver-white bench standing on its end. He was ripping slats from the frame.

"Dear God! That'll cost a fortune to remake," Violetta said. "I'll have to reprocess the whole frightful mess."

"Just look at *him* for one second," Sharon said. "Not your precious bench." She was trying to gauge how much earth

Mickey was disturbing, how deep the bench legs had gone. "What do you think a man like that will do if he actually finds human remains?"

Violetta snorted, unaccountably amused. "That, darling, is never going to happen."

"You seem not to realise," Sharon said, desperate to shake the woman into action: "If anyone has anything to fear from Mickey, it's you. You, who Ralf trusted. You, who would have any note that existed. You, who might benefit from anything it said. It's you Mickey will turn on after he's finished with the bench—not me!"

Violetta's pumpkin face seemed for a moment to lose its shine, and harden.

"I'll help you do it," Sharon said, pressing her advantage. "I promise, I can make it happen. Just tell me what to do."

Mickey finished breaking apart and examining the hollow slats. He started busting up the frame.

Dust lingered in a white haze around him, and, watching him, Violetta launched into her spiel about not milking your own stupidity enough for most men, *darling.*

The spiel where she tells her victim she has Sir Fergus Allison's bench in her collection. Yes, that Fergus, the world famous football manager. Or, if they don't like football, Sir Fergus got it from Mahatma Ali. Or, if they're not into boxing, then try music and the bucket seats came originally from John Lemon's white Rolls Royce. As Sharon waited for the punchline she wondered exactly how Violetta did kill her victims once she had them on the bench—her flypaper, her killing jar, her electric chair... What *was* her weapon of choice? Sharon had long suspected it must be poison, since Violetta had been a globe-trotting biochemist until a mysterious explosion where she worked. But where was the evidence? Whatever the weapon, Sharon had convinced herself it would be found in the forever-locked garage.

Violetta was getting to her climax:

"They just love to put you right, these men, dear heart. It gives them such a warm feeling."

And Sharon nodded and mouthed the words as Violetta spoke them:

"You can't milk your own stupidity enough for most men, darling, you must know that."

"And they want to sit on it?" Sharon said, limply.

"Of course, of course—I can't stop them!"

Thus these men became another entry in Violetta's little black book. And the grieving widow started to pay for services rendered, and that too was entered in the book. The corpse had to be presented once, of course, as evidence, in a little ceremony but always unmarked. And then disposed of, miraculously. No one knew where.

The police might call, but evidence was produced that the middle-aged gentleman in question, after showing a brief interest in the arts, had run off, back to the big city with some floozy, leaving the grieving non-widow to grieve. And any donations to the artist not so accounted for (because a number of names were certainly not locals) "Oh him! Yes, he too, dear officer, sponsored one of my aesthetic installations. There's no crime in that, surely? Come see..."

"This sort of thing happens a lot round here, madam. Strange don't you think?"

"Yes officer, but this is where the installations are, and he was of a certain age, and I do like to think I am convincing when it comes to collecting sponsors. He did talk of an Ashley Martin, or an E-Typical, or a whatchamacallit—Elon's thingummy—a Teaser. So I put it to him straight: you love beautiful things, why not become a sponsor of the arts? Wouldn't that be something to be proud of? But I never really believed any one of them would leave Karen or Rachel or Carletta or Mimsy or, oh dear, oh dear, oh dear..."

Cue impromptu tears.

You can't milk your own stupidity enough for most men.

"Just tell me what to do," Sharon said, convinced that persistence at this moment was her best chance to get in on the secret weapon, "and I'll help you!"

Violetta looked down the garden at Mickey and said, almost scoffing, "Want to help? Okay. I suppose you could make yourself useful. Distract him for a while. Get him back to your place while I ready the bench. Give me fifteen minutes—no, say twenty—then you can suddenly remember all about Fergus Allison, in your own naive way of course, and bring him along to the end of the garden. In return, I suppose I could give you a month's grace to find Mickey's share from the South Ken job. But then I want it all. As a lump sum—no jewellery this time—nor instalments, so be warned."

"I can do more than that," Sharon said. "If you tell me how you do it, then I can make absolutely sure *it* works."

"Really, darling. Allow me to introduce some precision into our relationship: you don't want a close-up look. You might join him."

Sharon couldn't help herself: "But I mean, is there a hidden syringe? Do you have to load it up? Or does the bench leak acid? Or a batteries, does it need charging up? If you tell me I can make absolutely sure he's especially vulnerable to whatever *it* takes..."

Violetta's pumpkin face soured.

"Just get him to the sodding bench, darling," she said. "I'll do the rest."

AFTER MICKEY FINISHED pulverising the silver-white bench, he came back brandishing a strip of polished brass. His swagger reminded Sharon of a child with a toy sword, and oh—*how like Ralfy!*

"These ain't Ralfy's words," Mickey said. "What d'you mean by this?"

"Dear Ralfy chose an apposite phrase," Violetta said, "from a list of pre-prepared phrases on the theme of the big city. I mean, he had already resolved that rural life was not for him. His choice, darling, is the last thought he shared, the last message we received, before he abandoned us."

"*My heart remains; my penance paid,*" Mickey frowned with an intensity that risked forcing his eyeballs into each other. "*Repent—I do my deeds repent; beg mercy and atone.*"

"Darling, it's poetry. It's all mood, emotion and symbolism. It won't mean anything to the uninitiated."

"Ralfy said to trust you," Mickey said, with drops of spittle gathering on his lips. "And you insult him. Behind his back. With this bollocks!"

Act in the moment as belongs to the moment, Sharon thought. The unplanned ten per cent that Ralf always held in reserve.

To keep them people on their toes. She said, "Mickey—oh, Mickey! I just thought of something. It's Ralfy's photo. He could've written on the back of that. I never took it out of the frame. We could look there. That photo might *be* his note..."

"Good," Mickey said. "That's good. Well done Sharon. Well done for thinking. You go fetch the piccy. Me and Violetta's gonna take a look inside her place, aren't we—*darling?*" He raised the hem of Violetta's tent dress with the brass plaque. "Lots of places Ralfy might've found to hide things—*good and close to home.*"

INSTEAD OF A car or van, Sharon discovered that Violetta's garage was home to a mammoth, heavy duty, 3D printing rig. It stood like a huge sewing machine the size of a police Transit and practically filled the available space. Except, instead of being shiny white with blue and yellow squares down the side, the giant sewing machine was gunmetal grey and splattered with globs of paint: pink and yellow and purple and green and loads of in-between colours that she had no hope of naming.

Yet now she'd seen it, the rig didn't feel that important. Okay, so the benches were printed; that made sense, even to someone who had only ever worked as an accountant's clerk.

But, more interesting, this side of the rig and running the full length of the sidewall, was a rusty rack of shelves reaching almost to the ceiling. The rack was loaded to the point of toppling with blue and white polythene sacks, brown stained bottles, and dribble-lidded tins of paint, all piled up, one on top of another, and wedged in at every angle.

It was no doubt the chemicals that caused the sour smell in the air, a bit like the stink of formaldehyde or photographic chemicals from the old days—something like that. She briefly felt the urge to gag and run outside, and yet whatever chemicals were used on Fergus Allison's Bench must be quick acting, and Violetta came in here often enough without protection, and the stable door was still open. Ultimately, though, Sharon might never get a chance like this again, and so far she didn't feel the least bit ill.

Running her eyes along each of the shelves, nothing special stood out. She figured whatever it was would be a one-off: a sack, a tin, a jar, a something that Violetta would not keep in any quantity.

Soon enough though, it was obvious that Sharon would have to squeeze through behind the rig to see the other side. Facing the rear wall, she pulled her stomach in and took care not to catch her dressing gown on the various shoebox-sized display cases mounted on the rear wall which showed off Violetta's collection of miniature sculptures.

Shuffling sideways, she pictured the four black bucket seats near the bottom of the garden that she knew made up the bench. Had she dismissed the idea of an electric chair too easily? Well, no. An electric chair needed electricity, and if there was a power cable, there would be a switch and it didn't take twenty minutes to operate a switch. Yet it took more than twenty minutes, in her experience, to charge a battery—like for instance, a car battery. A battery that would be heavy to carry and difficult to hide...

What about a lethal injection? Violetta would to have to hold the victim down while at the same time stabbing them with a syringe. So no. What if there were hidden syringes in each of the bucket seats? Except, if the victim sat down at the wrong angle, the needles might bend or break. And it would be tricky and dangerous to refill them. Not lethal injection then...

But chemical paint might do it. Poisonous to the touch, like Russian spies used. Especially if it washed off in the rain and was destroyed by sunlight. What was more: painting four bucket seats might just take twenty minutes.

Sharon paused half way across the back of the garage, feeling rather pleased with her TV cop deduction.

She found herself facing the glass-fronted shoebox display of a pink tap, sandwiched between displays of a purple spoon on the left and an orange tube of toothpaste on the right, and she was struck by how deeply absurd both Violetta's lifestyle and indeed Violetta herself were. Biochemist turned artist, murderess and blackmailer. What kind of *screwed up* was that?

Shuffling on, she found the space on the far side of the rig was unused, no shelving and not so much as an oil stain on the concrete floor. She doubled back, focussing on a new problem.

The fact was: there were tins of paint everywhere. How on earth could she work out—and work out safely—which was the one she wanted?

The answer, at least in part, came to her as she resumed her hunt for anything unusual on the racks. All the tins on the top shelf were marked with yellow diamond shaped Hazchem symbols. When the thought arrived it seemed so obvious: poison was hidden in plain sight. Indeed did poison even count as *that kind of poison* if you announced it as poison in the first place. Question was, which tin was the one for the bench? There were a dozen to choose from.

She climbed onto the printing stage of the rig and, leaning precariously, using a rag to protect her hands, she hefted a tin to the ground. As soon she had done it, she knew it was not the one. The lip of the lid was encrusted with yellow paint. The paint for Sir Fergus's bench would have to be black or—better still—transparent.

She climbed up again and, shuffling tiptoe along the edge of the printing stage, inspected the lids of the tins for spills.

She found just one toxic tin of transparent 'paint'. Not only that but a box of heavy duty rubber gloves sat next to it. When she gloved up and lifted it, it neither felt nor sounded like paint.

It slopped about like water.

SHARON FOUND VIOLETTA and Mickey in Violetta's bedroom—or what was left of it; Mickey was giving it the silver-white bench treatment.

"I found something," Sharon said from the open door. She held up the newspaper clipping of Ralf for them both to see.

Mickey snatched it from her, turned it a few times, opened it out, and frowned at her newly-pencilled words. He turned to Violetta: "What's this Fergus Allison bench?"

Behind Mickey's back, Sharon mimed the up, down, and sideways motion of liberally painting one of the bucket seats and gave Violetta a double thumbs up.

"Sir Fergus Allison," Violetta said in a tired voice. Her hair was dishevelled and her dress covered in black smudges. "The football manager, darling. I have a bench he once used. Ralfy

must mean that. You get a wonderful view from it, and oodles
of sun. Why, what does the dear boy say?"

"Says to sit there," Mickey said. "I should sit there and I'll
see something I recognise. And I'll—" he rolled his shoulders
and rocked his head from side to side, appearing to mock his
own brother, "—*get the picture.*"

THE THREE OF them were standing in a hollow at the bottom
of the garden, facing the bucket seats. Sharon couldn't help
shaking, but she couldn't pull her dressing gown any tighter.

"That's the bench, darling," Violetta said. "Fergus Allison,
the football manager's, bench. You can't honesty tell me you
don't know who he is. Besides, Sir Fergus got the bench from
Mahatma Ali, who got all four bucket seats from John Lemon,
from the white Rolls Royce he was so famous for—"

"Save the bollocks for the punters." Mickey slipped the
newspaper clipping into his jacket pocket, peered at the soft
leather and sniffed the air immediately above. "They're wet,"
he said.

Violetta made vulture eyes at Sharon and said, "There was
a frost last night; it's dew."

"Gimmee something to wipe 'em with."

"Use Sharon," Violetta said, and pivoted round to face
Sharon. "Here!"

Sharon felt the needle points of strong fingers dig into her
arms.

Violetta swung her around and planted her in the seat at
the far end, and quickly withdrew.

Something told Sharon she should be screaming but she
was too focused on catching her breath to make a squeak. She
wanted to put her hands out to steady herself, to get up. But she
knew not to do that. She knew to stay perfectly still. To work
out how to get up without touching any part of any seat.

Her two enemies faced each other. Sharon could almost
hear their thoughts:

What's going on? thinks Mickey.

How do I trap him? thinks Violetta.

If ever there was a Ralf moment, now was the Ralf moment,
but Sharon couldn't think of a way to get them both to sit in

a bucket seat. Instead, the harder she tried to come up with a plan, the emptier her mind became.

Eventually, feebly, after what seemed like hours that was probably only seconds, she said, "Mickey, check the bushes. The bushes, Mickey, check the bushes. It's the paint. It's poisonous. She's killed me! She's murdered me!"

Mickey raised a finger for Violetta to stay where she was and, keeping his eye on her, he shifted around the side of the bucket seats, out of Sharon's sight.

"For God's sake darling, don't listen to her," Violetta said. "She spends all her time plotting against people who want to help her. She's delusional. All this time on her own. What else would you expect?"

Behind Sharon, there was the swish of branches being brushed aside. The crunch of twigs and leaves. The metal slithering sound of a paint tin lid being eased off.

The sparkle in Violetta's oversize eyes adjusted to each new sound: now suspicious, now vigilant, now full-on fear...

A great sheet of watery non-paint flew through the air from the far end of the bench-of-four and drenched Violetta, drenched her red and white dress, splattered her pumpkin face and hair, sprayed artificial tears down her cheeks.

Violetta lacked the agility to step aside, or duck. Even after the poison had been thrown, she stood statuesquely still. But her pumpkin face turned first white, then red and she began to wail in a murderous rage and then ran at Mickey and, out of Sharon's line of sight, they must have collided, Violetta embracing Mickey as an act of revenge, and together they must have landed on the ground, producing a hollow thump, whereafter they thrashed about making passionate noises that were anything but.

It only lasted a few seconds.

WITH THE MOST steadfast concentration and delicate care of her life, Sharon moved her hand to the belt of her dressing gown, picked at the cord with her nails, and was gradually able to release the knot, allowing the thick, heavy material to fall away either side, and gingerly, very gingerly, she leaned forward, letting the sleeves slip off her arms and, skimpily clad in her underwear, cold and shaking, she allowed her feet to find ground, until they pressed hard enough on it, through the soles of her slippers, for her to stand up.

With infinite care (and the aid of a twig) she retrieved the newspaper clipping from Mickey's jacket pocket.

She did not linger on the open-mouthed corpses, but she was now bizarrely aware that she had arrived at her goose-bump display of lingerie in full sight of the small grey country church, and in that graceless state, she had picked a dead man's pocket.

THREE WEEKS LATER, two police officers were asking Sharon questions in her living room.

An Icelandic tourist taking photographs from the church tower had reported seeing something out of place at the bottom of the *bench feature* in the garden next door. Subsequently, two bodies had been discovered along with the weathered remains of a dressing gown.

Sharon, in what she thought of as a good show of confused distress, identified the dressing gown from a photo, saying: yes, that was Ralf's monogram; no, she hadn't seen him for years; yes, she thought he'd run off to Jamaica; no, she had no idea he would ever come back, but was it really true that her next door neighbour, that sweet eccentric artist, had actually been murdered?

"We believe they were arguing over the proceeds of a robbery," the police woman said. "Safe deposit boxes in South Kensington. The robbery Michael Frost did time for. It appears your husband killed the other two and made off with the proceeds which were hidden inside one of the benches."

"A lot of deserted women hereabouts," the male officer said. "Many of 'em very generous to your neighbour. Tell me, how much d'you put in?"

"Me? Oh, I—I didn't. No. Not at all. I didn't like to. All seemed rather morbid to me. I mean, why tempt fate, Ralfy not being dead? The bench with his name on was, well—it was all Violetta's doing. For the sake of her art. I wasn't a sponsor. I'm no patroniser of the arts. Of course, now we know why she made it... makes sense."

"You knew about the bench then?" The police woman said. Sharon had to admit that much. But couldn't say when it was installed. Before or after or on the day of Ralfy's departure.

"You see," the male police officer said, "the contributions from deserted women hereabouts don't match the cost of manufacture, or upkeep, so we have to consider the possibility that money was being extorted. Did Violetta van Bruegel ever approach you for money, for any reason?"

"No."

The police officers didn't come back. Sharon concluded they had bigger, or easier, fish to fry. No one seemed to have worked out what she had worked out, but then she had more pieces of the jigsaw than anyone else, including now the 3D printer and those bags of chemicals. They told her where all those grieving widows' husbands had gone. Explained why Violetta had laughed when Sharon had mentioned human remains. And what exactly the benches were made of: Sharon knew.

Anyway, why would the police suspect that the murderer was blackmailing those who commissioned the killings? All would be equally guilty if anyone revealed anything.

Except: when Violetta did away with Ralfy for Sharon, and Sharon had seen the corpse, Violetta had insisted Sharon place an old-fashioned mercury thermometer between Ralfy's blue-grey lips. Violetta had remotely photographed the act, keeping herself out of the frame. Should the photograph ever fall into the hands of the police, well... But what of Violetta if that were to happen? Total denial, of course. An entirely spurious accusation. A fit-up. After all, she could always say: "Where's the corpse?"

The only evidence of her involvement was her little black book.

Thus, the day after Violetta's demise, Sharon had been through that garage with a fine-toothed comb.

She had been on the point of giving up when she had seen what Violetta had hidden in plain sight. One of those arty little shoebox displays contained a book. A black book, a little on the big side, but once extricated from its display case, it turned out to be none other than The Little Black Book.

Worth real money, that was.

King of the Castle

Hilary Davidson

THE SNOW CAME down hard that early December afternoon. At first it looked enchanted, with snowflakes swirling gracefully through the air before landing on the ledge of my home-office window. As they accumulated and covered the trees in my backyard all I could think about was how postcard-perfect my view was. I was busy editing a technical manual for a client who always called me with last-minute jobs. They paid handsomely but inevitably caused headaches. In spite of the looming deadline, every few minutes I lifted my eyes from the laptop and surveyed the glorious scene. It wasn't until my wife, Kait, came home from work that I woke up to reality.

"Fletcher, honey, there's almost a foot of snow out there," she said. "And you haven't started shoveling yet."

It was our first snowfall in our first house. Kait and I had married three years earlier, in a summer ceremony at a manor house up in the Muskoka Lakes. While we'd continued to live in my tiny studio apartment in downtown Toronto, we'd sworn to each other we'd save every penny to buy our dream home. And we had, moving into a semi-detached three-bedroom house on the far eastern edge of Danforth Village, a short walk from restaurants, shops, and the subway. We'd been there for two months, painting and re-grouting and enjoying our new space.

One of our friends had given us a sturdy red snow shovel as a housewarming gift. *Welcome to the wonderful world of homeownership,* he'd told me. *You're your own superintendent now.*

His words were ringing in my ears as I trudged to the garage out back—we didn't own a car, so that was our storage space—and located the shovel. Kait was right; the snow was piled at least a foot deep.

At the front of the house, I took a deep breath and told myself I needed the workout. I'd canceled my gym membership—part of our belt-tightening scheme to afford a house—and had only started setting up a workout space in the basement. At least shoveling snow promised to be a full-body workout. I pumped myself up so much that I cleared not only our side of the house but the next door neighbour's as well. He was an elderly man named Max Bode, and we had yet to meet him, though we'd caught glimpses of his short, bony frame. We considered ourselves lucky because we had yet to detect any noise from him through the wall that our houses shared.

After I finished and returned the shovel to the garage, I noticed the light was on inside Max Bode's kitchen. Like ours, it was at the back of the house. I figured it was as good a time as any to introduce myself, so I headed up his steps. Our neighbour was sitting at a Formica table, his back turned to me as he hunched over a newspaper. Long strips of white hair were carefully combed over an otherwise bald pate.

I tapped on the glass of the storm door.

"Go ahead, Dick, it's open," he said without turning around.

Vaguely I wondered if Dick was one-half of the elderly couple who'd sold their house to Kait and me. It didn't really matter. "Hello, there. It's Fletcher Lemire," I said, pushing the door open. "Your new neighbour. You're Max Bode, right?"

"In the flesh. And I don't care much for neighbours, new or old." He turned in his seat and glared at me with dark, protruding eyes. Up close, he was younger than I'd thought—maybe only sixty or so—but his skin had an unhealthy pallor not unlike the paste we'd used to hang our new wallpaper. "What do you want?"

"You probably noticed it's snowing," I said, fighting the urge to call him *sir*. The neighbourhood had impressed me for its friendliness, and I was caught off guard by his brusqueness. "I was shoveling our steps and the sidewalk and figured I'd do your side, too."

"I don't need your help."

"It's already done," I said. "It's all cleared now."

"Bully for you. If you think I'm giving you one red cent for that, you're out of your mind."

"I'm not looking for you to pay me." I was incredulous. "I'm your neighbour."

"Then what do you want?"

I shrugged. "I guess I figured you should know that you don't have to clear the snow."

His lipless mouth tugged back in a tight little smile. "I don't have to do anything. This is my house. I make the rules. If I don't want to do something, I don't."

"That sounds great, until the city gives you a ticket for not clearing your walk."

He chuckled at that. "No one's giving me a ticket. Bye now, Dick."

"It's Fletcher," I said.

His lips grinned a little more broadly, as if I'd made a joke. "Of course it is. Millennials and their stupid names."

I backed out of his kitchen, quietly closing the storm door with a click and retreating to my side of the porch. He's just a crazy old man, I figured. Lost in his own delusions. Maybe he didn't understand it was even snowing. I patted myself on the back for doing a good deed, but I couldn't keep myself from complaining to Kait.

"Our next-door neighbour is an old coot. He was mad at me for shoveling his walk."

"You think he'd be grateful."

"What were the names of the couple who lived here before?"

"Philip and Ella Marsden. Why?"

"Just curious." Who was Dick, I wondered. Maybe the neighbour who'd lived in the house before the Marsdens? "Did they say anything about the guy next door?"

"Only that he was quiet and never had anyone over."

For all I knew, Max Bode was lost in a foggy mental twilight. I decided to feel sorry for him.

But my sympathy waned the next time it snowed. I trotted out the shovel but decided to ignore Max Bode's side of the house. My back was sore by the end, and when I went inside I thought Kait would be thrilled by the good job I did.

Instead, she said, "You only shoveled our side, Fletcher. Didn't you think of doing the old man's side?" Kait was a guidance counsellor at a downtown high school and sometimes I felt like she looked at me like she did her students.

"Not after he got mad at me last time."

"Hmm." She pursed her lips, gazing out the front window. "He's got to be seventy, at least."

"I've seen him up close. He's younger than that."

"Either way, you should be kinder, Fletcher. I'm going to knock on his door and ask if he needs any help."

There was no dissuading Kait when her mind was made up. She pulled on a navy pea coat and walked across our front porch. I shook my head as she rapped on his front door. Then I retreated to the kitchen, figuring I deserved a cup of cocoa. I was dropping tiny marshmallows into the steaming cup when Kait returned. I heard the front door shut with a slam, which was unlike my wife.

I poked my head into the hallway to make sure it was her. The neighbourhood was incredibly safe and most people seemed to leave their doors unlatched, but you could never be sure. It was indeed Kait, but she was frozen in place. When her eyes met mine, they were shell-shocked.

"He wanted to know where I was from," Kait said slowly.

"You sing the praises of Vancouver?"

"No. He meant... where my family was from. I told him my parents were born in Canada and he wouldn't believe it. He said... they never used to have my kind living around here."

My fists clenched. "Do I need to have a talk with this dinosaur?"

"Don't insult dinosaurs," Kait said. "He's just a creep."

"A racist creep."

She shrugged. "My new plan is to avoid him and hope he moves away. His house is a mess. The eavestrough is falling off. He'll probably be out of there by spring."

I waited until Kait went upstairs before slipping outside and knocking on Max Bode's door myself.

There was hesitation behind the peephole, but he finally opened up. "What do you want?"

"Don't ever talk to my wife that way again," I said. "Because I'm not going to put up with your racist crap."

"Oh, me so solly." He chuckled to himself.

"If you weren't so old and frail, I'd punch you."

"I'm sixty-one and in better shape than you'll ever be." He frowned suddenly as if just noticing that I was almost a foot taller than he was and a hundred pounds heavier. "You're flabby. By the time you're forty, you'll be a real butterball, Dick."

"What is wrong with you? All my wife wanted to do was to be helpful."

"What are you two, the politically correct police? I hate the way things are now, thin-skinned idiots who cry if you look at them sideways." he sighed. "Let me tell you something. There's not a damn thing in this world I have to do. Except pay taxes, because the feds will lock you up if you try to skate on that. Otherwise, I do what I want. No one orders me around, especially on my own property."

I glanced over his shoulder, into his foyer. It was dimly lit, but I could make out a sagging staircase and a crookedly hung painting.

"I'm telling you to be a decent human being," I said.

"And I'm telling you to go to hell." He slammed the door in my face. I stared at it for a moment before shuffling away. I turned when I heard the door open. "Dick!" He shouted at me. Then he slammed the door again.

That was the moment I realized two things: I was living next to a troll, and he wasn't calling me Dick because it was a former neighbour's name.

I didn't bother telling Kait that I'd gone to Max Bode's door. What would be the point? I couldn't talk about how angry he made me, or my one petty attempt at revenge. Out of spite, I reported him to the city the next time snow piled up on his sidewalk. That led to a bureaucrat showing up at his door, and me listening behind the front window for him to get a ticket. That didn't happen.

"I wish I could shovel the walk, but I have a bad heart," Max Bode told her. "I had my first attack after my wife and son died."

There was a gasp. "You poor man," the bureaucrat said. "Please don't worry. I'll put you on the list for the city to remove your snow. It's free of charge."

Behind the door, I wanted to hit my head on the wood. Max Bode would never have to think about shoveling a sidewalk again, thanks to me. Still, it was hard to feel gleeful after finding out both his wife and son had passed away. It sounded like there must've been a terrible accident. That had to be why he was so miserable. It didn't make me like him, but some sympathy welled up. I figured I would simply ignore him.

For weeks at a time, that wasn't hard. Max Bode was as quiet as the proverbial church mouse. He never had visitors and he rarely went out, except for grocery shopping every

Saturday morning at nine o'clock sharp, when he trundled out of his house with a steel cart on wheels.

But that quiet period didn't survive a change in the seasons. Spring showers quickly—and insistently—revealed that our roof had started leaking. When we had a professional inspect it, he found damage on Max Bode's side of the building as well.

"You can't simply repair one side," the roofer told me. "That would be like blowing out tires on either side of your car and only replacing one."

Max Bode wouldn't answer his door when I stood there beside the roofer. Later, when I tried again in the evening, solo, he opened up.

"What now, Dick?" he asked.

"We've got a problem," I told him. "The roof is leaking."

"That's too bad."

"It's your roof, too. Both sides need fixing."

"I'm happy enough with my roof."

"We had water come into our attic. There's damage on the ceiling of the second floor," I said. "You have damage, too. The roofer found holes."

"I don't care what he found. It can stay that way."

"Do you want your house falling down around your ears one day?" I asked him.

"That's fine with me, as long as it's worthless."

"What?" I stared at him, jaw open. "Do you understand how crazy the Toronto real-estate market is? You could sell this house for a small fortune right now, even with everything that's wrong with it! Who wouldn't want that?"

"I don't. If someone gave me a million dollars for this house, I'd burn it." He started to shut the door and paused. "You can pay for the roof if you want, Dick. I don't care."

It was only when I called the roofer that I started to panic. Kait and I could cover the cash we needed for our roof, but there was no way to max out our credit cards beyond that to pay for Max Bode's side of the house.

"You can't just fix one side," the roofer repeated to me. "It's all or nothing."

"Could you patch it?"

"Sure, but that won't hold for long. You need entirely new tiles. A patch job won't last a year."

That evening, when Kait came home, we had a serious talk.

"Our neighbour is a maniac who wants his house to fall down," I said. "He literally told me if someone gave him a million for his house, he'd burn the money."

"Why?"

"Why does a troll do anything? I don't know, but I do know we can't afford the full cost of a new roof."

"We're not going to be able to talk him into it," Kait agreed. "I think we should sue him."

It was a brilliant idea. Talking to Max Bode was a waste of time for us. For a lawyer? It would be a different story.

Or so we thought, until we met with a lawyer who was a friend of a friend. She was sharp, succinct, and to the point. "The city doesn't like for neighbours to sue each other," she told us. "If you need access to his side of the property to get something fixed, we can absolutely do that. But if you want to fix something that he doesn't want to fix, you'll be stuck paying for it."

"But what he's doing is damaging our house!"

"It's damaging our property value," Kait added sagely. "That has to count for something."

"Not much, even if you're actively trying to sell the house. Are you?"

"No."

"The city treats a homeowner like they're king of the castle." The lawyer shook her head. "I've seen people try to fight this in court, but it's a waste of time and money. In the end, you won't get anything. You don't need to sue if you need to make structural repairs. City Hall has an office for that. All you'll pay for is the engineer's time." She wrote down the number for us.

We got referrals to a couple of other lawyers, but their information was the same. The one lawyer willing to take our case wanted a hefty retainer we couldn't afford.

Dejected, I called the roofer and asked him to patch the roof.

I can't say whether or not he did a bad job. All I know is that within a month, we heard scratching above our bedroom ceiling.

"Rats?" I asked Kait.

"More likely a family of raccoons," she answered. "We'll need someone to set a humane trap and take them away."

I didn't even bother to talk to Max Bode about that one. We hired a wildlife-removal expert and got the raccoons out, but while the guy was in our attic he noticed a hole in the wood dividing our attic from Max Bode's. We hired someone else and paid for that repair, too.

"It's insane that he gets out of everything by taking no responsibility," I complained to Kait.

"It doesn't make sense that he wants his house to fall apart," Kait said. "I know we call him a troll, but could he be mentally ill?"

I considered that. None of my encounters with Max Bode suggested he was anything other than a troll. Early on, I'd believed he was calling me the wrong name because he was confused, but even that was a calculated insult. Still, my mind kept tugging at the fact his wife and son were dead. That couldn't be a coincidence. I'd never told Kait about Max Bode's dead family because she had a gentle heart. I knew it would make her want to reach out to him. But it was time to come clean.

"I heard him tell a government worker who came to his door that his wife and son were dead," I said.

"They're both gone?" Kait turned pale. "Did they die at the same time? Was there some awful accident?"

"I don't know." I shrugged. "Maybe he hates the world because of that?"

"Of course he does. Now I feel horrible," Kait said. "I can't believe we were thinking of suing him. Why didn't you tell me this before? It changes a lot."

"No, it doesn't. He's still a rotten person."

"But he's rotten for a reason."

The discovery energized Kait. We'd talked with our neighbours about Max Bode before—generally his name was met with curses and frowns—but suddenly she was determined to get to the bottom of the story. But most of our neighbours had moved into the area in the past five years and had no idea about Max Bode having any family.

Then one evening Kait came home from work, slammed the door, and shouted, "That old bastard!"

I ran from my office to the hallway. "What's wrong?"

"I ran into Leila Grygiel—the widow who lives down the street, near Woodbine."

"The one with the fluffy Samoyed dog?"

"That's her. She's been in this neighbourhood a long time. Max Bode had a kid, all right. A kid who was trans. A decade ago, he threw her out of the house. Told her she should kill herself."

I was speechless. No matter how bad I thought my neighbour was, he would always reveal himself to be worse. "What happened to her?"

"I don't know. Max Bode's wife disappeared after that. One night, she just vanished."

"Vanished... or was killed?"

"What do you want to bet that his wife's body is hidden in his basement?" Kait asked.

I nodded. "Probably a whole bunch of bodies." It wasn't tough to picture.

A week after that, I had another encounter with Max Bode.

It started with me waking up early on a Saturday morning and heading to the basement to work out. That was when I discovered our basement was holding three feet of brown water.

I couldn't understand it. There'd been a pair of storms that hit Toronto that summer, but our basement hadn't flooded either time. I searched for a broken pipe and couldn't find one. I shut off the valve by the water meter, turning off all water to our side of the house. That was when I went out and knocked on our neighbour's front door.

He didn't answer. I tried the bell but it was either disconnected or broken. The newspaper was on his side of the porch, untouched. According to my watch it was six-fifteen. Max Bode would be going out to shop at nine, but who knew when he woke up? And until he did, water would be pouring into my basement.

I couldn't let that continue. I walked around his side of the house. There was a pair of short, rectangular windows that let a little light into our neighbour's basement, just like the pair of matching windows did on our side. It wasn't a surprise to see that his basement was flooded, but I couldn't make out the source.

Instead, I went to Max Bode's kitchen door at the back of the house. The storm door was latched, but all it took was a strong grip to open it. The wooden door inside wasn't locked.

"Max! Your basement's flooded!" I shouted. "Get down here!"

There were footsteps overhead. "What's happened?" he peered at me anxiously from the shadowy landing. "What are you doing in my house?"

"I have to turn off your water valve," I said, heading for the hallway. Max Bode's house was a mirror image of ours; I knew the layout intimately.

"Where do you think you're going?" he demanded, coming down the stairs. His black-and-white-striped pajamas looked like a prison uniform in an old-time movie.

"Your busted pipe is flooding my basement," I said. "I'm shutting it down."

He grabbed my arm but I shook him off. There were dark stains on the walls of the hallway. I looked up and saw the sagging ceiling. There wasn't just water damage in Max Bode's basement. It was through the structure. His house really was falling apart.

I opened his basement door. The water was up to the fifth step of the staircase. I waded through it, and shut down the valve. There had been the sound of rushing water, but suddenly it was silent.

"This is incredible." Max Bode inched down the stairs. "All the times I hoped this house would fall apart. This might actually do it."

"Why do you want to ruin your house?" I gawped at him. "It makes no sense."

"If I sell it, Betsy gets half."

"Betsy?"

"My wife. Estranged wife. We're not officially divorced yet. Oh, she wants me to sell it. Begged me to. She needs the money. Her fault, she left me." He grinned at me. "But I'm going to make sure she gets nothing."

"What about your daughter?"

"I don't have a daughter. I had a son but that freak is dead to me."

There were two small rectangular windows that touched the ceiling and looked out to the backyard. I opened them both, knowing that I'd need equipment to properly drain the space.

"What are you doing?" he demanded.

"We need to dry out the basement. You have a bucket?"

"We aren't doing anything," he said. "They'll need to knock the house down after this."

"You're a psychopath. But this time, you won't get away with it."

"Wrong again. Dick. You can't make me do a damn thing."

I can't explain what happened next. It was a moment of madness, where I stared at this man who'd caused so many problems for Kait and me. I realized he'd never stop so long as he was alive. Without thinking, I punched him in the head and watched him fall backwards into the brackish water. After a moment of splashing and flailing, he resurfaced.

That was when I grabbed him by his scrawny neck and pushed his head underwater.

He slapped and kicked, sending dirty droplets in all directions, but he couldn't free himself. He stopped moving after thirty seconds, except for the occasional jerking of a limb. That stopped after another minute. Still, I waited for a full five. Part of me expected him to reanimate as a zombie.

I guess I'd watched too many movies.

When I finally turned him over, Max Bode's eyes were wide open in existential terror. I left him floating there and I dragged myself out of the water and up the stairs. Soaked, I let myself out the way I came in.

Back at my house, I took a quick shower and dressed in fresh clothes. Kait was just waking up. "There's a broken pipe in Max Bode's basement. Water everywhere," I told her. "I'm going to pick up a sump pump and clear our side. Then I'll have to go over and clear his."

"Unreal," Kait said. "Chalk another one up for the neighbour from hell."

I headed to the 24-hour hardware store feeling oddly light. The guy at the store quickly convinced me that instead of buying a pump I should just call my insurance company and get them to use professional equipment. I phoned on the walk home. They promised to send a couple of guys over, and they made good on that an hour later. They set up a massive machine that somehow hoovered up most the water. Some still seeped through the wall dividing my house from Max Bode's.

"The leak was on our neighbour's side," I said. "I went over and turned it off, but he's so upset about it. Can we clear his side, too?"

"We have to. His leak is damaging your house."

The three of us went out the back door. The lights were off in Max Bode's kitchen.

"Hey, Max?" I called. "It's Fletcher. Can we come in?"

There was no answer. I pushed the door open and led them to the basement door.

"Hey, Max, could you come down?" I called upstairs. Then I opened the basement door.

The overhead light was still on. Two steps down the stairs and you could see Max Bode's body floating face-down in the mucky water.

"Max!" I shouted, as if I cared. I'd been thinking about this moment all the time I'd been out. I couldn't hide that I'd been inside his house. Who knew what I'd touched and where I'd left prints? But I could grab Max Bode, steer his lifeless body to the stairs, and beat on his chest like I was giving him CPR.

No, I did not breathe into his mouth.

First an ambulance came, then the police. They took a statement from me and the insurance guys. They didn't even bother to get one from Kait.

"I can't believe he drowned in his own basement," I said later, after I had cracked open a bottle of whiskey. Someone had given it to us as a housewarming present, and we'd finally found an occasion for it.

"Is it wrong to celebrate?" Kait asked me. "Part of me wants to but another part..."

"No, it's fine. We should be honest about how we feel." More than that, I wanted to spill my guts to her about everything. Kait and I didn't have many secrets between us. I couldn't imagine keeping this from her but I'd have to, at least until the cops stopped sniffing around. Or maybe longer than that, I realized when I noticed tears welling up in her eyes.

"It's still an awful way to go," Kait said. "You can't help but feel a bit sorry for him."

"Not really," I said. "You know that troll didn't have insurance. I wonder what will happen with the house?"

It took a while to figure that out. First the powers that be had to locate Max Bode's relatives—his wife and daughter, both very much alive—and tell them what they'd inherited. Kait and I made nervous jokes about Max Bode: The Sequel. But it turned out that that Betsy and Maxine were lovely, thoughtful people. Without being asked, they paid for the water damage, a new roof, and other repairs to the house. Then they sold it to a guy about my age named Winston Lok, and he brought in his own crew to fix up the interior. When it was done, he let me do a walk-through to see the work. It was beautiful.

"Maybe you and your wife would want to buy it?" he asked. "Own both sides of the house and rent this one."

"I wish we could, but there's no way we could afford it," I said. "We'll enjoy having you as our neighbour."

"You probably won't see me much. I live in a condo downtown," Winston said. "This is an investment for me."

I didn't think about that too much at the time. Then, one Thursday night around ten, heavy bass started pounding through our shared wall. I didn't just hear the music, I could feel it. I think it made my teeth rattle.

"What the heck is that?" Kait asked me.

"Don't worry. I'll get Winston to turn it down."

I went out to the front porch and knocked on my neighbour's door. The guy who answered was maybe twenty-two, with an overgrowth of fluffy pale hair that fell into his eyes. He looked like a puppy, albeit a stoned one. He had a fat joint between his lips.

"You here to party? That'll be a hundred," he told me.

"No, I'm your next-door neighbour," I said. "You need to turn down your music."

"I paid for this space, bro," he answered. "It was advertised as a party palace, and that's what it's going to be."

"You can't play your music that loud. My wife and I..."

"You can't make me do anything," he huffed. "I paid for this space, and I can do whatever I want!"

He slammed the door in my face. Max Bode was dead, but on that dark night, I knew he was laughing at me.

Murder, She Chiselled

Marilyn Todd

IT'S TRUE WHAT they say.

An Englishman's home really is his cavern.

I got up from my bearskin, pulled aside the pelt covering the cave entrance, and sighed. Was I the luckiest girl in the Jurassic, or what! My eyes travelled over the steep sides of the gorge, the river snaking through down below, the sun angling through the trees. Sometimes I almost have to pinch myself. Here's me, a girl from the booncaves, living the high life in Beverly Holes, waking up to the best view in the world, and going to bed with the finest man to ever throw a spear.

I glanced over my shoulder at the rib cage rising and falling under the bear skin. I fell in love with Spruce the moment I saw him. I was gathering berries. He was out on the plains with his best mate, Jagga. The two of them were skinning a mastodon, a mammoth task I can tell you, but despite the blood and stench and sweat, Spruce jumped up, punched the air, and began to sing. I smiled across at the sleeping figure, remembering it as though it was only last year. Well, actually it was only last year. Not the point. It was his voice, carrying clear across the open space, that sent goosepimples down my arms, and I nearly dropped my basket when he looked right into my eyes.

'Tramps like us,' he sang, 'baby, we were born to hunt.'

Tears welled in my eyes then. They still do.

I know it's hereditary, and that all the Stonesteens are terrific singers, but Spruce stood head and shoulders above the rest of his family. Not physically, of course. I mean his voice. His delivery. The way he wove words and chords together. Throughout the months he took me clubbing—and I hate to brag, but I still have some of the bruises—he couldn't stop talking about the plans he and Jagga had for forming their own boulder-and-roll band.

Enough of this strolling down memory lane, though. Spruce was stirring. Time to fire up the George Beforeman grill, and cook my man his breakfast.

'Hello?' a voice called from below. 'Is the Boss in?'

Spruce walked out to the ledge and peered down. 'She sure is. Hold on, I'm sending the elevator down.' He unrolled the rope ladder and let it fall. 'Come on up.'

'Bo!' I squealed. 'Lovely to see you!'

If you want the latest gossip, no one's ear was closer to the ground.

'You, too Dinah.' He heaved off the pack of pelts strapped to his back, and kissed me on both cheeks. 'Marriage suits you, darling. You're positively glowing.'

He wasn't talking to me.

'You can thank your business partner for that,' Spruce gave him an affectionate pat on the shoulder.

Bo and I had worked closely for as long as I can remember. He designed next season's fashions and cut the material to suit, I sewed the pieces together. The famous Bo Nydle and Dinah Sewer, what a team!

'Right, then, that's me off.' Spruce tucked his skinning knife in his belt and picked up his spear. 'What do you fancy for dinner tonight? Bison or antelope?'

'Bison,' I said. I'm not into fast food.

I swear he wasn't half way down the elevator, before Bo started dishing the celebrity dirt. 'You remember Poppy, who modelled stripes for us last summer? Poor darling's distraught. That shaman she moved in with only broke up with her, didn't he? And by cave painting, too, the snivelling coward. Then last night, in the Fight-or-Flight Club, I was just heading for the cave marked Hunters, when guess who I saw coming out of the Gatherers? Merry Berri, no less, talking about Dahlia, the smith's daughter, saying everything she cooks tastes like pterodactyl...'

I drank in all the gossip while sorting through the pelts (he was going for spots this season, then?) thinking it would easy to stitch this lot together, hardly anything there. Gosh, there were going to be some chilly willies this autumn— 'Say that again. The bit about Vlad Pritt.'

'Dead. I know, darling. What a shock.'

'That's the bummer of it, Bo. We eat lean, we eat clean, we keep fit, no processed food, tons of fibre, and dammit we're still dead by the time we hit thirty-five.'

'This wasn't natural causes. Dear old Vlad took the wheel out for a spin, and *pfft*. Never came back.'

'Not another case of woad wage?'

Bo leaned close. 'Don't tell anyone, but the poor bugger fell asleep at the wheel.'

'Holy moon, did it fall on him?'

'Worse.' His mouth turned down at the corners. 'He stopped for a breather and was resting against it, when a sabre tooth tiger pounced. Which reminds me. Have you seen the size of the mastodon Mork Jagga painted outside his entrance? All I can say is, don't believe everything you read.'

'I will not, repeat not, have that name spoken inside my home, and you know it.'

'Sorry, darling, I forgot. Your cave, your rules.'

All those plans Spruce and Jagga made about forming their own band? Dammit, Jagga only went off and started the Rolling Boulders on his own, with himself as lead howler, and not a word about it to Spruce until it was done. I kept telling my husband that it didn't matter. That he'd be great as a solo artist—maybe even better—but it was the sneaking around, the lies, the back-stabbing, that hurt him. Hurt him to the core, and then some.

'If it helps, love, Jagga doesn't have a fraction of the downloads that he had last year. Barely ten chips off the old block, compared to over a hundred for Sprucie—'

'Is that supposed to make me feel better?'

'What I'm saying, darling, is that he's not turning out songs that people will still be humming a thousand years later, and it's not because he's not talented. Just that he's made so many green pebbles, he just wants to spend them, but oh dear, talk about lack of taste. I mean, have you *seen* his art collection? *So* paleolithic, and all those handprints on the walls? I said to him, Mork, you have to stop with the selfies—ooh, is this Sprucie's latest song?'

I looked up from sorting the leopard pelts from the cheetahs to see Bo flicking through my husband's Apple i-boulder.

'Wow, these lyrics are amazing. *You can't stoke a fire, you can't stoke a fire without a spark, this spear's for hire, even if we're just shooting for a lark.*'

That was yet another bone of contention, I told Bo. Spruce's original title was *Jumpin' Black Fish*, but somehow Jagga got wind of it, and next thing you know, he's blasting out his own song under that title.

'Don't let it get to you, sweet. Mork's too busy partying these days to give The Stonesteen any kind of competition. Every night, he's pulling a different girl. Frankly, I'm amazed they have any hair left to pull, and that stuff they smoke? Let's just say they don't call it chickweed for nothing. Honestly, Dinah, if you saw the shenanigans that go on over there—'

'Seriously? I can hardly bloody miss them!'

As if things weren't bad enough, Jagga moved into the cavern right across the gorge from us, after that lovely Glint Westwood moved out.

'Every night there's a dinosorgy, with naked girls prancing about, men glued to their shell phones, that fermented grape juice from Tuskani flowing like water.' I rolled my eyes. 'None of the neighbours can sleep for the music blasting into the wee small hours. Trust me, Bo Nydle. That sacks and drags and boulder-and-roll lifestyle is going to kill Mork Jagga one day.'

A QUARTER MOON later, I was round at Poppy's, consoling her. The poor girl was still distraught over the break-up, and understandably so. The match-making window is short enough as it is, and, thanks to that pig of a shaman, she'd have to wait until the spring gathering of the clans before casting around for a new mate. So I was hoping to cheer her up with a preview of the autumn fashions, and at the same time, since the cut was so...let's say economical...make sure the shaman saw what he was missing. Literally, given the way Bo had cut this season's pelts, but that's not the point. No one took to the catwalk better than Poppy, and it lifted my heart to see the spring in her step as I pinned her into the leopardskin pelt. (Oh, come on. I could hardly bring a cheetah round, could I?) Besides. I wanted to share my good news.

'You remember that patent I put in for?'

'The one where you took some kind of fat and made it lather up, so it cleans all the mud off our bodies?'

'That's it.' Foamosapiens. 'Well, Blakkandecka bought the rights to manufacture and market, and look how much they're prepared to pay.' I chipped open my tablet and showed her the figure. Neither of us had seen so many vertical lines. 'You know what this means, don't you?'

'Oh, hell, yes!' Poppy's eyes twinkled and bulged as she jumped up and down, clapping her hands in excitement. 'Well, actually, no...'

'It means that between Spruce's singing, my sewing and Foamosapiens hitting the market, we'll be able to buy Jagga out.'

No more watching my husband's nose being rubbed in his best friend's betrayal. No more noisy parties. No more chickweed stinking the air. And especially no more having my sister blackmailed into gathering berries for her mother-in-law as well as her own family, or her brother-in-law would show her husband his cave painting of my sister with Jagga.

'Free at last,' I told Poppy.

Which is more than she'd ever be in that leopard skin. I'd sewn it so tight, the poor girl could hardly breathe, but! As I said. Perfect catwalk model.

'Here,' I said, squinting at the hawks, snakes and eyes scored into the wall. 'Are those heiroglyphs?'

'They certainly are.' Poppy twirled and adopted a pose. 'I'm learning a second language for when the clans gather next year, because I want Arno Shortsandkickers to see that I'm not some empty-headed bimbo.'

'Arno Shortsandkickers? For pity's sake, Poppy, he's a lazy good-for-nothing womaniser, who doesn't know his auroch from his elbow.'

'I know. A keeper, right?'

I was *this* close from banging my head against the wall in frustration, when Bo burst in to the cave. 'Have you heard?'

'Heard what?' Poppy and I chorused.

It had to be big for him not to notice the pride of his autumn collection parading round the fire pit.

'Jagga.' He slumped down. 'He's dead.'

'I told you that lifestyle would kill him,' I said smugly, because I might have my faults, but being wrong isn't one of them.

'It wasn't the weed or the booze that did for him, Dinah.' Bo wiped away the tears with the back of his hand. 'Mork was murdered.'

GEESE FLY. TIME flies. Flies fly. None of them, trust me, flew faster than I did that day.

'You were with me.'

Spruce looked up from where he was sharpening his spear. 'I was?'

'You were.'

'And where, exactly, were we..?'

'Here. We were here.' I wasn't breathless from the run. Well, OK, I was. The main reason I couldn't breathe, though, was fear. 'We were home all day, trying to make babies, all right?'

'Someone's been at the goatskin of brandy, I see.'

Usually I love to hear his rich, deep chuckle. Not today. 'This isn't funny.' I scoured the gorge, expecting to hear the clomp of heavy feet. 'When Hemlock Holmes comes asking, you were here. With me.'

'Why on earth would he want to question me?'

'Jagga. He's—'

'I know.'

'I know you know, that's the point.' I drew a deep breath. 'And frankly, I don't blame you. *Jumpin' Black Fish* was the last straw, I understand that. But Holmes won't, and—'

'Wait. You think *I* killed him?' His jaw dropped. 'Babe, Mork was my best friend.'

'Until he wasn't,' I snapped. 'He formed a band behind your back—'

'Only because he thought I was better than playing second fiddle to him. Which, by the way, I can't actually play, but we decided that if he pretended to freeze me out, people would think I had no other choice than to fly solo. And our plan worked. Look at the publicity from that fake feud. Our sales soared.'

'You could at least have told me.'

'Don't be cross, babe. It was such a big deal, and if Bo Nydle found out—'

'How dare you think I'd betray your secret!'

'Not on purpose, but you're so open and honest, Dinah. If you were chatting and accidentally let it slip, there's no way he'd have kept that to himself, no matter how much he crossed his heart and hoped to die.'

True.

'But the song title. *Jumpin' Black Fish?* Jagga stole that from you.'

'That's a load of aurochs. My new song's called *Prancin' in the Park,* fish don't even feature in it.' Spruce spiked his hands through his hair. 'I can't believe you'd think I killed him.'

'You came home covered in blood.'

'Duh. I'm a hunter...'

'But you were back so early! The sun had hardly moved round the sky.'

Spruce pointed to the clearing by the river below. Explained how he was just about to cross, when a stag came down to drink, and hey presto. Venison steaks and venison stew, with a lovely set of antlers for the wall.

'Those?' I was horrified. They were *enormous.* 'You shouldn't have tackled a beast that size on your own. Good grief, those stags can grow up to six feet.'

'Yes, but usually they only grow four.'

'Very funny.'

'I thought so.' He pulled me into his big, strong arms and kissed me and kissed me and kissed me. Before I knew it—well, let's just say, we wouldn't have been lying to Hemlock Holmes about staying at home making babies...

The sun was sinking by the time we wriggled out from under the bearskin.

'Next you'll be telling me that Jagga moving in across the other side of the gorge was all part of the plan.'

Spruce pointed to the fire. 'Everyone's on Smokenger these days, but Mork and I connected through Instasmoke. Much quicker.'

Had I really been too busy stitching pelts to notice what was right under my nose? Sadly, yes.

THE FULL MOON came, and still no news about who might have had it in for Jagga. Rumours abounded. Jealous husbands. Jilted lovers. Drug-crazed fans and stalkers. Angry neighbours driven to their limit was what my little green pebbles were on, only everyone Holmes questioned had an alibi, which of course they would. That's the whole point of clans, safety in numbers. Down in the gorge, the leaves began to turn, there was a chill in the air now, and it wouldn't be long before we'd have to dig out our winter furs. The constellations shifted. Another full moon lit the sky, and as much as everyone pretended life went on as normal, it did not. We were all looking over our shoulder now. Wondering, was it personal? Or was the killing random, are we next? My heart was in my mouth every time Spruce went out to hunt. It didn't stop racing until he returned home safe and sound. In fact, the moon had waned to another nerve-racking quarter before we got to the bottom of the mystery, and naturally, it was Bo who heard it first.

'They got him,' he said triumphantly. 'Turns out it was one of those—what's the term for blokes who don't want to hunt, tan or fish, but go on long, aimless rambles instead?'

'You mean a meanderthal?'

'That's it. Anyway, seems this bloke knew Jagga liked to swagga with a sack of green pebbles on his back, so everyone could see he was rolling in it. And being a lazy sod, our drifter reasoned, why work for it, when you could simply take it?'

Vile senseless crimes committed by vile selfish people? Nothing ever changes, it would seem.

'How did they catch him?'

'He only did it again, didn't he? On the far side of the mountain, except this time there was a witness, who picked him out of the fotofit line-up etched on Holmes' wall.'

'They're just stick figures,' I said.

'And this was a stick-up.'

Which, like Jagga's murder, also went horribly wrong.

I broke the news to Spruce the instant he came home that evening. Especially how Hemlock Holmes was able to tie the drifter to the killing, because he was still wearing Jagga's distinctive sabre tooth amulet round his neck.

'I gave Mork that,' Spruce said. 'The day we made our pact.'

I sniffed. 'I'm so, so sorry I accused you of his murder. I don't know how you managed to forgive me—'

'Easy, babe. You put two and two together, and come up with twenty-two every time, which is why I couldn't tell you about our plan.' He scooped me in his arms. 'You don't have a devious bone in your body, Dinah, but from tragedy comes tribute. Listen to what I've written about Mork—'

He began to sing.

'*Drawing in a dead friend's town, lots of blood when he hit the ground...* I'm calling it "*Drawn to a New Essay*," what do you think?'

I snuggled closer.

'What I think, Spruce Stonesteen, is that now is a very good time to tell you about the baby we're having.'

And cross my fingers that it doesn't look like his father. Mork Jagga's nose was pretty damn distinctive...

One of Us Is Dying

Warren Moore

AT LEAST SHE had the rose bushes in the corner of the picket fence. At least she had her back yard, and at least she had Boots.

Ellen Rivera would tell you her life was good enough for what it was. The MS had taken away her ability to drive, and there wasn't bus service in Ivy Hills. Well, not yet—every year or two, as Ivy Hills gradually became more of a suburb and less of an exurb, there would be talk of extending the regional bus service that way, but it hadn't happened yet. And while Harold would take her to the grocery or WalMart some nights after he got home from work, she could feel his impatience as she slowly made her way down the aisles, using the shopping cart as if it were a walker. So even though it was nice to go out, even to WalMart, she didn't ask Harold to take her all that often, which meant that most of the time—almost all the time—she was home. And home alone at that, except for the company of Boots, the Boston Terrier they had acquired when one of their sons married a woman who was allergic. That was reason enough for the kids not to visit often, Ellen guessed, but had it been the other way around, she might have been willing to sneeze a few times to spend some time with family.

The house was nice enough; it was the first (and she supposed, the only) new home she ever had. They had bought it when Harold got the job in the City, and when they signed the contract, the house was nothing but a vacant lot and a few two-by-fours. She got to choose the countertops, the carpet, the appliances like the ones at the model home. The agent had told them the subdivision "might have sixty homes one day," but the Riveras were the second family on the newly paved street.

That had been thirty years before, and the tract really did fill up fairly quickly, extending from the main road at the Riveras' end to a cul-de-sac a half mile up the hill. There were plenty of neighbors within five years, by the time Ellen was diagnosed with multiple sclerosis. At the time, the average lifespan for someone with MS was supposed to be about twenty years, but Ellen was still here, and still *there*, in the house.

On nice days—in the spring or fall — she could go out back through the kitchen door to the deck Harold had built and sit, or on *really* good days, could work her way down the stairs to the back yard, with her flowers. The perennials, anyway. She couldn't do very much in the way of planting annuals anymore. But she and Boots could go out back and she might pull a few weeds while the dog patrolled the yard or snoozed beside her while she drank the iced tea she had brought. She could even go out in the summer to water the plants, if she went out before it got too hot to stand.

That was the best time to water the plants, anyway. Her father, who had grown the best tomatoes in the old neighborhood, said that you should do your watering early or late in the day, because if you did it in the middle of the day, the sun's heat would burn the plants. She didn't really know how true that was, or if it worked for flowers the same way it seemed to work for her father's tomatoes, but she did it that way anyway, if only because it was easier for her to move around in the cooler times of day.

So she wasn't *quite* a shut-in; she could get outside the house, after all. Still, she thought of herself as being more or less grounded, dependent on Harold to go somewhere, and if he didn't *want* to go somewhere in the evening, she could understand—he worked hard and fought the traffic to and from the City—but it still left her there at the house.

At least the neighbors had been pleasant—after thirty years, Ellen and Harold had become the old-timers in the subdivision, and while there was turnover, most of the neighborhood seemed made up of regular, working folks—the kind of people who might need to borrow a mower from time to time, but who would also be there to help clear your yard if a storm felled your trees. Sure, she'd like to see them more often, but at least they might smile and wave as she and Boots made their way to the mailbox on a sunny day. During the winter, Harold had to bring the mail in—you never knew when there might be ice—or if she just hurt too much, she'd let Harold know when he called from work to check on her, and he'd bring it in when he got home.

But as the years passed, other neighborhoods in Ivy Hills grew. Those neighborhoods were more expensive; the City had grown and more people wanted to live in the suburbs, and some of them wanted to live quite well. Even some of the people moving onto the Riveras' street were buying houses and changing them completely, gutting them or tearing them down, or spiffing them up only to rent or sell them to someone else. It seemed sometimes as though there was as much construction traffic now as there had been when they had moved in.

But it also seemed that while the houses sometimes got nicer, the people in them didn't so much. She'd see them as they pulled their nice cars out of their garages (Ellen and Harold couldn't do that. The garage was full of thirty years of accumulated life, so Harold just parked in the driveway). But she'd see the drivers, men and women, driving without even looking at her—or anyone, really. They all seemed to stare straight ahead, because they were going somewhere, and when they came home, it wasn't to sit in the yard with a glass of tea or mow the grass—they had people to do that. The yards looked nice, Ellen admitted, even if the other lawns she could see from her windows were flowerless expanses of fingerpaint green.

And when the Hersheys moved next door, they had torn down the house that was there, and the new one seemed to be double the size of the old one, squeezing the side yard almost out of existence and reducing the front and back. Ellen didn't like it much, but she wanted to be a good neighbor, so she made some lemon bars while Boots was napping and carefully made her way over, using her cane while holding the Tupperware container in her free hand.

Mrs. Hershey answered the door. Young (well, young to Ellen—early thirties?), fashion model thin, very well dressed, heavily jeweled, carefully manicured. Ellen felt like an unraked lawn. The woman's entire appearance reminded Ellen of the equally well-tended lawns on the street, and perhaps as artfully artificial. "May I help you?" she asked.

"Um, hi," Ellen said. "I'm Ellen Rivera from next door. I just wanted to welcome y'all to the neighborhood." No answer. "I brought you something." She held out the Tupperware container. Mrs. Hershey took it from her, as carefully and reluctantly as if the red plastic were a vial of Ebola virus.

"Well, thank you," Mrs. Hershey said. "I'd love to chat longer, but I have things I need to tend to. I'm sure we'll have another opportunity at some point. Thank you for stopping by." She stepped back and closed the door, and Ellen stood there for a moment before making her way back to her house. As she crossed her driveway, she thought Mrs. Hershey could at least have given her first name. A day later, Harold brought the container in from the mailbox where it had been left. Half a lemon bar remained inside.

A few days after that, Ellen was in the back yard. She had filled the bird feeder and was drinking tea and sitting on a bench that Harold had put in the shade for her. She glanced over the picket fence and saw Mrs. Hershey step out the back door onto her patio. Hershey was talking—loudly—to someone about a Dinner and Event. Ellen heard the capital letters, but stopped paying attention. Boots had spotted a squirrel and was in hot pursuit.

Mrs. Hershey glared their way. Ellen wasn't sure whether she or Boots was the intended target. "Ellen, can you *please* keep your dog quiet?"

"I'm sorry," Ellen said. She wasn't really sorry; Boots was a dog, and dogs chase squirrels, and even if she never caught one, it was good exercise for her, and the dog's waddling run made Ellen smile. But she wanted to be a good neighbor, so she told Boots to hush and come to her. Boots had other ideas, and kept chasing the squirrel, barking all the way.

"Oh, for Christ's sake," Mrs. Hershey said. "Can't I have some peace and quiet without that stupid *thing* yapping?" And then to the dog, "Shut up, damn it!"

That was enough for Ellen. "Mrs. Hershey, we barely know each other. But Boots lives here, and this is her yard just like it's Harold's and mine. She's defending her territory, but she didn't ask you to come out here and have your phone call. I'm sorry it's bothering you, but you know what? Boots is a good dog, and well, we were here first."

The lawyer called them a week or two later. Ellen answered the phone. He explained that his clients were interested in buying the house and would be willing to make a handsome offer that would certainly allow her and Harold to find a nice place in the area.

"I think my husband and I would need to talk about that," she said.

"Talk about what?" Harold asked from the living room.

"Somebody wants to buy the house." Then Ellen realized she was still holding the telephone. "I'm sorry—can you call back another time?"

"Of course," the lawyer said.

"By the way, could you tell me who you're representing?"

"Certainly. I'm calling on behalf of Lynn and Morgan Hershey."

It took Ellen a moment—and she wondered which one was Lynn and which one was Morgan. It seemed as though she had heard both names used by both men and women. "Oh. Well, as I said, we'll need to talk."

"Certainly. What if I were to call you back in a day or two?"

"That seems a bit sudden," Ellen said. "What if we call you after we've decided?"

"Well, the Hersheys would like to arrange the transfer of property in short order, but I can understand wanting to take a little time." After a few politenesses, Ellen hung up the phone.

She told Harold about what the lawyer had said. "The Hersheys want to buy our house."

Harold set the book he was reading to the side. "How much are they offering?"

"I don't know. But I don't like it."

"Why not?"

"Because this is our *home*, Harold. We've lived here nearly half our lives, longer than either of us have lived anywhere else. Think of the Christmases, the Thanksgivings, the boys' graduations. Tommy's rehearsal dinner. It's all been here."

"Well, yes, but if we went somewhere else, there would still be Christmas and Thanksgiving."

"But they'd be different. They'd *be* somewhere else." After a pause, Ellen said, "Have you ever even talked to them?"

"Once," Harold said. "I was down at the supermarket and I saw him. He said he recognized our car, but he was only there to pick up some steaks. We didn't talk long."

"Well, no, I guess you didn't. His wife isn't much of a talker, either."

"I don't know about *that*," Harold said. "You know Jimmy from Growin' Crazy? He told me that they had wanted him to cut their lawn, but when the day came it was rainy—you remember from last week—so he couldn't do it. He said that woman called him at his own home and called him everything but a child of God. He told her he didn't need her business that badly, thank you, and she told him that she'd make sure he didn't find anyone else to do business with, either."

"Yeah," Ellen said. "She's a charmer."

"Something to think about. Maybe we should take the money just to get away from them," he said, and laughed.

"Maybe." But a second later, she said, "But Harold, we've always liked it here, 'til now anyway. Think of all the work you've done here, that *we've* done here. We were here before this was even a 'here.' And just because some people with money want what we have, they think they can just throw some of that money at us and tell us to go away like we're hired help? My daddy didn't raise me to be shoved around like that."

She picked the phone back up. "Who are you calling?" Harold asked.

"I'm calling that lawyer and telling him this house isn't for sale. And neither are we. Then I'm going next door. They can take their money, fold it until it's all sharp corners, and —"

Harold cut her off, "Hold on, old girl. There's no reason to yell at the errand boy. We don't have to take their money, and they can't make us sell if we don't want to, which that look in your eye tells me we don't. And that's fine. But it can wait until tomorrow, can't it?"

Ellen weighed the satisfaction of yelling at the Hersheys against the awkwardness of standing on their front porch while she did it, took a deep breath, and agreed. She could call the lawyer tomorrow, and didn't even have to speak to the Hersheys at all.

And that's what she did. A few days later, she saw Mrs. Hershey out in her own back yard, near the back corner that adjoined the Riveras' yard. Later, after Harold had come home, Ellen went out to water the flowers. When she got to the rosebush in the corner, she saw that where some of the branches had extended into the space between the pickets, the stems had been cut. Likewise, the branches that had grown above the top of the fence and began to droop across the fence's plane had been cut as well.

Ellen didn't like it, but if the Hersheys hadn't wanted the roses even technically in their yard, she supposed they had a right to cut them. The following afternoon, though, when Ellen saw the granules on the Hersheys' side of the fence, it was different. Ellen recognized the herbicide—she had seen it at the plant nursery when Harold would take her to shop. She didn't see any of it on her side, but as the grass around the bush, and then the rosebush itself, browned and died, she knew there had been enough.

The weather cooled as the summer turned to fall, and one evening when Harold came home from work, he mentioned that he had seen the Hersheys on the way home, pulling into the parking lot at Dr. Rabe's office.

Ellen's eyebrows raised. "The obstetrician?"

"He's the only Dr. Rabe I know about, so yeah."

"Are you sure it was their car?" Ellen didn't like to say the name *Hershey* any more—she didn't even like it when Harold brought a candy bar home.

"Yeah," he repeated. "I saw them in the car."

"Both of them?"

"Mm-hmm. And out in the yard a week or two back, I saw her and I thought she was putting on some weight. So I guess it's what you'd think."

"I wouldn't have thought she'd have enough love in her to carry a child."

"Now Ellen, you know you shouldn't say that."

But Harold didn't understand. Ellen had thought being alone all day was bad. But knowing someone as nasty as that woman was next door and wanted her gone? That was worse. Knowing she was spiteful enough to poison Ellen's rosebush? That was worse still.

But it took another week before Ellen broke. It was mid-October, one of those days the television weathermen call "football weather," sunny, crisp, with a sky so clear it seemed like a child's soap bubble. And her legs felt all right for a change, so why not go get the mail? She knew Boots was napping, so she put on her slippers and went from the porch to the driveway, down toward the mailbox.

She could have sworn that she had closed the screen door behind her, but she heard a clatter as Boots shouldered the screen door open and barreled across the yard, toward her. Behind her, she heard a car round the corner and pull onto their street.

Boots reached her, springing up, bouncing up and down at her feet. Ellen reached for her, but lost her balance, and as she fell, Boots leapt backwards as part of the new game. The Hersheys' Grand Cherokee rolled toward them.

It could have been an accident, just bad timing. Certainly that's what Morgan Hershey had said afterwards, but Ellen would believe for the rest of her life that Hershey had swerved. And just like that, it was over. Boots hadn't been a big dog, but she looked even smaller now. Hershey went on, pulled into her drive. The garage door raised. She pulled the Jeep in. The door lowered.

Eventually, one of the older neighbors, someone who had lived in Ivy Hills nearly as long as the Riveras, saw Ellen sitting there on the curb, holding the broken dog in her arms and weeping like a child. And like the dog, Ellen was broken. The neighbor helped Ellen, still carrying Boots, to the house, and even called Harold, who came home from work. He dug the dog's grave near one of the banks of flowers, near where the squirrels liked to run.

After Lynn Hershey got home from work himself, he approached the Riveras' house and rang the bell. Ellen went back to her room, leaving Harold to answer the door.

"Morgan is just so *distraught*," she heard Lynn say. *Not distraught enough to stop.* "She's just *miserable* now, especially with the baby coming. . . she couldn't bear to come over, but we wanted to let you know how sorry we are, and we want to let you know that if you want to get another dog —"

That was when Harold picked up Ellen's cane and told Mr. Hershey that he needed to leave while he was still capable. Ellen knew she would love Harold forever for that. But there were things she needed to do. She took her evening pills, and slept fitfully.

The next day, she went to her medicine cabinet for her morning pills, and then reached under Harold's side of the bed. After she visited her junk drawer, she got dressed, went outside, and crossed the driveway to the Hersheys'. It was slow going, but she had the cane. When she got to the porch, she rang the doorbell, a harmless, broken cripple.

She didn't know if Morgan Hershey would open the door, but she prayed that she would, and whether anyone heard her prayers or not, eventually she heard footsteps, the sound of a turning lock, and saw the door open. Hershey stood there, as perfectly smooth and cold as a porcelain sculpture. Young, healthy, looking even healthier from the glow of the life inside her. "Ellen," Morgan said.

Ellen dropped the cane and pulled Harold's pistol out. "Hello, Morgan. I've come to visit. I don't want to shoot you, but I promise that if you try to close the door I'll pull this trigger as fast as I can. At this range, you'll be hit." Morgan stepped back, pulled the door open. Ellen walked in.

The furniture was nice, of course—Scandinavian, mostly, suited to the spacious, open-concept, neutral-palette layout of this interloping house that was out of scale with all the homes that had once been part of Ivy Hills. But there was a kitchen chair with arms, and Ellen directed Morgan into it, and then told her to use the duct tape from the Riveras' junk drawer, binding first her own legs to the legs of the chair, and then to use her left arm to tape her right arm down. Ellen finished the task, securing Morgan to the chair. And then she sat down across from her.

"You said you weren't going to shoot me," Morgan said.

"No, I said I don't *want* to shoot you. And I don't." Ellen reached into her pocket and pulled out a medicine bottle.

"What is that?"

"It's called Cytotec. They give it to old people like me. As we get old, we have to take things for pain. With MS, I take plenty of them. But they can tear up your stomach.

"So they give you pills that help protect your stomach from the damage the pain pills might do to it. That's how it is—you take pills to balance the pills that you take to deal with the problems you started with." She shook the pills into her hand.

"Matter of fact, I could use a couple myself. Mind if I use your faucet?" She opened cabinets until she found a glass and filled it from the tap. She brought it back, sat down, took a couple of the pills and washed them down. "See? I hurt, so I take some pills, and then I take these to deal with those. And now it's your turn."

"Look," Hershey said. "Lynn *said* we were sorry. I just didn't want to face you. I know we've had problems, but it was an accident, and I panicked, and—"

"You didn't even stop." Ellen shook more of the pills into her hand and put the bottle down. Then, gently but firmly she reached across and pinched Morgan Hershey's nose shut. Slowly—because her hands didn't work as well as they once did, she forced the pills into Hershey's mouth. Sometimes Hershey managed to spit some out, but Ellen picked them up and tried again until she had given Hershey enough. Then she sat back and looked at Hershey.

"When does Lynn come home?"

"About six."

"Well, it's 9:30 right now. In two to four hours, you may start feeling some discomfort. I hear it feels like period cramps. But I get all kinds of cramps, you know. When I was holding Boots after you—after. . . I felt cramps in my back, but I hardly noticed them. When something like that happens, you're supposed to hurt, I think. So it may hurt some, but you'll live, and I'll stay right here with you and keep you company until Lynn gets home. After that, it won't matter much, but from what I've read, the full miscarriage will be done in 24 hours, two to three days tops.

Hershey began to weep then, gasps turning into racking sobs, but not enough to overturn the chair. Ellen had given her more than the 800 milligrams she had read on Google, and sure enough, it took 90 minutes before things started.

Between sobs and screams, Hershey found it within her to stare one more time at Ellen. "You'll go to prison for this. They may put you away for life. The rest of your *life*."

Ellen Rivera smiled. "I've been shut away for years. In a house I couldn't leave, that you thought was only good for tearing down. In a body that fails me a little more every day. All this will be is a change of scenery, a different kind of same.

"But you, Morgan? Maybe you'll have other children; I don't know. But for the rest of life, you'll remember this one, you'll wonder who it might have been. That's where you'll be, that's where you'll spend the rest of *your* life.

"Enjoy your new home."

The author would like to thank Susan Frommeyer, M.D., *for technical assistance with this story.*

Sweet as Satan's Cookies

Kay Hanifen

I JUST WANT to get this off my chest. Liz Coleman's blueberry crumble cookies were not *that* good. Not in the way that everyone went gaga for them. I mean, they were fine, but did they deserve to beat out my award-winning double chocolate chunk cookies at the HOA's Cookiestravaganza? I don't think so. But would I have killed her over it?

Of course not! Like everyone else, I loved Liz. In fact, I was the one who took her under my wing when she first arrived next door. Everyone in the neighborhood watched that moving truck pull up and unload furniture. Once it looked like things had settled down, I knocked on the door bearing a plate of my famous chocolate chunk cookies as a 'welcome to the neighborhood' gift. I must say, I didn't expect what I saw when she opened the door. For a moment, I thought that the Addams family moved in. Despite the summer heat, she was dressed all in black, her dark hair pulled up in a sporty ponytail. She was young, couldn't be more than thirty, and would have been very pretty except, well, the people in this neighborhood have a certain, let's say type, and with her nose piercing and sleeve of tattoos, she would have stood out like a bear among honeybees. Of course, it's not my place to say that, so I just smiled and said, "I'm Tiffany McDonald and I just wanted to say hi and give you a plate of my award-winning double chocolate chunk cookies."

I could feel a touch of judgement as she looked me up and down. Can you imagine? Here I was in my Sunday best, and she had the audacity to look like she'd just stepped in doggy doo.

"Thanks," she finally said, taking the cookies and setting them aside on a pile of boxes. "I'm Liz."

"Is it just you or are there others about? A husband? Kids? I'll have to introduce you to the PTA. They know how to hook your kid up with all the best teachers."

At that, she visibly winced, and I began to feel like I was making a fool of myself. "No kids," she replied, "Just me and my husband."

"In this big house all by your lonesome? What do you do for a living?"

Her eyes were shifty when she said, "I'm a writer, but I'm taking a break for a while. Allan is a neurosurgeon."

"Oh, what do you write? It's such a guilty pleasure, but I love those thrillers you buy in the grocery stores right next to the greeting cards."

"Horror," she replied, and she certainly looked the part if I do say so myself.

"I'm too much of a chicken for that," I replied with a laugh. "You know, the Ladies' Club is having a luncheon tomorrow. Come with me and I can introduce you to the rest of the neighborhood."

Sometimes I regret that offer if only for what came after. When I knocked on the door the next afternoon, she was dressed like some kind of witch, and carried with her a plate of those darn blueberry crumble cookies. "Oh, you're wearing that?" I asked.

She glanced down at her dress and back up at me. "Do you have a problem with my outfit?"

"I just don't want you to make the wrong impression. The people in this neighborhood have certain views about proper attire for our luncheons, and, well..."

"I look like I just walked out of a Spirit Halloween."

"No!" I exclaimed, my face reddening, "It's a very nice outfit. It's just—"

She cut me off, which was a bit rude. "It's fine. I don't mind the funny looks. Morticia is my icon, after all. I own my strangeness."

"Well, then let's go meet the neighbors," I said, leading her to our social club up the street. I must admit, I spent the whole day fretting about what the other housewives would think of the newest member of our neighborhood. She was just so... so...different from what we were used to.

Apparently, all that fretting was for nothing because she immediately hit it off with the ladies. Apparently, she was quite charming when she was talking to other people, and everyone raved about her blueberry crumble cookies. They were a bit too sweet for me, but there's no accounting for taste.

They oohed and awed over her long list of publications and laughed at her every outlandish story. I mean, sure it must have been interesting to spend the night at the Lizzie Borden Ax Murder House with Stephen King, and a part of me almost wanted to channel *that* Lizzie while she showboated about her life. Not that I did, of course. I was just glad she got along with the rest of the housewives with nothing better to do. But I will admit that the story of the séance they held in that house bothered me. I'm sure she thought it was all in good fun, but Pastor Smith warned us about conjuring spirits just about every other Sunday. It opened doors to all kinds of evil, and I would hate for something evil to think it was welcome in our neighborhood, if she went around summoning spirits again. It didn't seem to bother anyone else, though. In fact, it looked like it made her more impressive in the eyes of the ladies at the luncheon. Still, a worry lingered in the back of my mind that she was little more than a novelty to them, someone to be cast aside once she was no longer new and mysterious.

While we walked back, she was the one to break the silence, surprisingly enough. "Thank you for inviting me," she said, staring down at the empty plate in her hands. "I didn't know how much I needed that, Tiffany."

"You're welcome back any time," I said. "The ladies all seemed to love you."

"I just might take you up on that," she replied with a slight smile.

The trouble began a week later. As head of the HOA, I have the unfortunate duty of sending out nastygrams to the people who violate our rules. One such rule was that no one was allowed to leave their trash bins out after eleven in the morning. I had an all-day appointment, and when I left that morning, her trash cans were out. Then, that afternoon, they were still out.

With a smile, I knocked on the door. No response, so I knocked again. There was some rustling on the other side, and Liz opened the door. I could smell the alcohol on her breath, but graciously ignored it. "Hi, Liz, I'm really sorry to come here not as a friend, but as president of the HOA, but there's something we need to discuss."

She squinted at me, and I wasn't sure if she even understood what I said. "What's this about?"

"Well, you're new here, so I understand if you haven't read our bylaws yet, but we have a rule about trash cans being out after eleven. Do you mind putting them back inside?"

"Yeah, sure, I'll do it." We stood in an awkward silence for a moment, neither of us making a move. Finally, she said, "What, right now?"

"Better to do it while it's on your mind," I replied cheerfully. "Lord knows I forget important tasks when I put them off."

"Right," Liz said, pushing past me and putting away the garbage bins. That was the day I discovered that Liz had a vindictive streak. Every trash day, she would leave her bins out until 10: 59 and put them away just as the clock struck eleven. Sure, I understood the little *screw you* for what it was, but she still put her bins away on time, so I was happy.

Then came the matter of Halloween decorations. Given her darker inclinations, I guess I shouldn't have been surprised. We have a rule against blow ups in the front yard. When I reminded her of the fact, she filled the back and side yards with them. She also kept her Halloween out through December, dressing the skeletons with Santa hats when I mentioned that maybe she should have more seasonally appropriate decorations.

The Ladies' Club thought she was a riot. Her little acts of malicious compliance made her a sort of neighborhood folk hero, positioning me as the stick-in-the-mud who wants to murder everyone's fun. Not that I'm a murderer—of fun or anything else. I feel bad crushing flies and I take spiders out in cups. But admittedly, I was tired of the rest of the ladies and their defense of her indefensible spite.

"You're too hard on her, Tiffany."

"Come on, you have to admit it's funny, Tiffany."

"You're just jealous because her cookies beat yours at the Cookiestravaganza, Tiffany."

"She's wily, that one. I can't help but respect her sticking it to The Man."

Dolores, we are The Man! It's our job to keep this neighborhood safe and beautiful. A suburban paradise where we all look after our own, and this outsider was dividing us, turning us against each other one blueberry crumble cookie at a time.

The thing is, though, I knew Liz's secret. She wasn't the loving wife she pretended to be. I began to notice strange people spending the night while Allan was out of town. Men and women, sometimes all at once. They'd sneak in under the cover of darkness and emerge the next morning before the sun was up. I made sure to take pictures as proof. My friend was making a bad decision, and we all needed to come together and help her find her way again.

First, though, I thought I'd confront her with the evidence. One evening when Allan was away, I knocked on the door. Liz looked terrible, almost like she'd been in a fight with a rabid raccoon, and the raccoon won. She wore a torn t-shirt with a bizarre creature on it, a humanoid with angel wings, and a goat's head and hooves. Something about the image was familiar, and it unsettled me in a way I couldn't quite put into words. It just felt evil. "What do you want?" she slurred.

"To talk," I replied, holding up a picture of her with one of her liaisons. "Can we go inside?"

Raising her eyebrows, she blinked and looked at me unimpressed. "Is having friends over against the HOA rules too?" With that, she turned and headed inside without checking if I followed. In the months that I'd known her, I'd never been inside her house. I was struck by the fact that there were no photographs on the walls or tables, and the art on the walls looked like the tarot decks they sell at the mall. No precious memories of her and her husband. The only photo I could find was on the kitchen refrigerator featuring a small family. I recognized Liz and Allan, but the little girl was unfamiliar.

In a corner by the kitchen window, there was a strange little setup of dried flowers and crystals. In the center was a plate with one of those Satanic pentagrams that Pastor Smith warned us about. Did the girl have something to do with this satanic shrine?

I waved my photo again. "Please, her hand is on your heinie. You're doing more than having an innocent girls' night."

With a sigh, she said, "Not that it's any of your business, but Allan and I are in an open relationship. We agreed to experiment with different partners."

"Aren't you worried that he might leave you for someone else?"

Her eyes skirted towards the picture and back. "Not really. If he leaves, he leaves. He deserves that much."

"And you wouldn't mind if I brought this up to your husband?"

Taking a sip from a half-empty wine glass, she shrugged. "Might be a bit embarrassed that you caught me, but that's about it."

"And your drinking?" I blurted out before covering my mouth.

She shot me the kind of glare that made me glad she wasn't actually a real magical witch because it most definitely had a curse in it. "Yeah. We all deal in our own ways. I've cut back a lot, but nights alone are hard."

And then it clicked. "That little girl in the picture. She's your daughter?"

Any defiance still in her face melted away. Deflated, she sat down at the kitchen table. "We lost her last year in an accident. Drowned in the neighborhood pool. We'd only looked away for a second." Her eyes reddened and she sniffled, blowing her nose into a napkin. "I thought moving would give us a fresh start, but I just feel like I've abandoned her."

My heart went out for the poor woman. I can't imagine what it would be like to lose one of my kids. With a sigh, I sat down beside her and took her hand. "Well, if you ever need me, I'm a doorbell away."

"Right. Thanks," she said, wiping her eyes, "You're a good friend, you know that?"

"Oh, you're just saying that," I replied, dismissing the compliment with a handwave.

"It's true. You might have a stick up your ass, but you're not nearly as bad as the Ladies' Club says."

"What do they say about me?" I asked, feeling a sudden and inexplicable spike of anxiety.

She shrugged. "Just that you were uptight. I think Dolores once called you a petty tyrant."

Well, that wasn't nice to hear at all. I thought Dolores was my friend. To hear her call me that hurt beyond words. "I'm sorry she feels that way."

"And since we're all such good friends, don't tell her I said that. I'm such a chatty drunk. Alcohol goes in and the secrets come out." She put her head in her hands and I took advantage of her distraction to snap a few pictures of that satanic shrine. Just looking at it gave me the willies, and a part of me feared that her daughter's death hadn't been an accident after all. Could she actually have been some kind of sacrifice to Satan?

Picking up her head, she wiped her eyes and asked, "Any other questions or is my interrogation over?"

I gave her my warmest smile. "I'll just get out of your hair. If you need anything, you can knock on my door whenever you want."

"Thanks," she said, returning my smile with a lopsided one of her own.

I returned home even more unsettled than before. Of course, what people do in the privacy of their own homes is their own business, but I had the sinking feeling that she wasn't telling me the whole story. Between the witchcraft, the dead little girl, and the comings and goings of her various liaisons, I feared that something much darker was lurking just below the surface, and I was determined to get to the bottom of it.

These late-night visitors seemed to creep around like a secret coven. And the more I thought about it, the less I was able to avoid seeing them for what they obviously were. I took to watching their movements carefully, hitting paydirt two weeks later on a full moon when several people arrived at her house, together as a furtive group wearing hooded robes and singing a song in Latin. I watched them go in and then one by one they reappeared out the back an hour later with a lit candle in each hand. One handed her a shovel and she began to dig a small hole. Another handed her a small parcel and she placed it inside before filling the hole once more. Then, they gathered in a circle and began to chant something I couldn't quite hear. I got it all on video, and once they had gone inside and the lights turned off, I snuck out into the backyard and excavated the hole. The parcel smelled strongly of sage and cinnamon, and inside was a lot of tissue paper, which enshrouded a small, worn teddy bear.

What on earth was this? Could it be evidence left-over from a crime, or—my God—were they planning to kill again? They clearly took this well-loved toy from a child. Was this ritual the precursor to another sacrifice? Whatever it was, it was bad for the neighborhood. Something had to be done about the witch before another child suffered the same fate as her daughter. So, I did what any concerned citizen would do: I wrote a letter to the editor of the local paper about this Satanic threat to our community, making sure to include pictures of what I'd seen.

I guess I shouldn't have been surprised by the knocking on the door so loud it practically shook my house the night after they'd published it. I opened the door to find an irate Liz clutching the paper. "Are you kidding me, Tiffany?" She pushed past me and let herself into my house.

"I was just concerned for the soul of the community," I replied, following her to my living room.

Her breath stank of whiskey. "Bullshit! You've had it out for me ever since that stupid bake sale. You're just so...so...petty and small and you want to make everyone around you small because if they're smaller than you, then you're the big woman in charge."

I'll admit, my temper got the better of me. Here she was throwing baseless accusations, and for what? She owed me for introducing her to all her new friends. "And what are you, exactly? The young, hip girl who thinks she's too cool for this neighborhood but is still lonely enough to attend every Ladies' Club meeting?"

"You're the one who invited me to join the Stepford Wives," she shouted before closing her eyes and taking a deep breath. When she opened them, they were full of tears. "Look, I know I was being obnoxious about the HOA rules, but how could you say those things about me? About my husband? I was just doing a private ritual to say goodbye to my daughter and now people won't make eye contact with me on the street."

"And how could I just sit by and let Satanists worship in our midst? I did it for the safety of the community."

"I'm not a fucking Satanist," she screamed, pushing me.

The next few seconds were a blur. She was going to kill me and turn me into a sacrifice for Satan, so I did the only thing I could do; I defended myself by pushing back. How was I supposed to know that she'd fall and crack her head on the coffee table? I remember standing over her, watching the blood pour out of her head and thinking that it looked like spilled cherry preserves. She was still alive and making the most awful sound, the kind of sound that sets your teeth on edge and I...I needed the sound to stop, so I stuffed a dish towel in her mouth and carried her back to her house, laying her at the bottom of her staircase. She was still breathing when I left. I thought maybe the police would just assume she got drunk and fell down the stairs. She was an alcoholic. Tragedies like that happen. Unfortunate, but not uncommon. And if Sheriff Waites did find something suspicious? Well, let's just say that he wouldn't see a cent from his biggest campaign donor next election.

Finally, I had to clean up the evidence. Do you know how hard it is to get blood out of carpet? Luckily, my husband, Julien, was out of town, so I had the whole night to clean without any interference. I nearly gassed myself to death using ammonia and bleach to get it all up. Then, the police would have had two corpses on their hands, I suppose.

But you have to understand I didn't kill her. Liz killed herself. The alcohol made her wobbly on her feet, and when I protected myself, she fell and died. It was kill or be killed, and I certainly wasn't going to let a Satanist get the better of me and poison this community.

You should thank me. Everyone should thank me! I did what I had to and saved us all from Liz and her coven! If it wasn't for me, every child and neighborhood pet would be sacrificed to Satan by now. So, you're welcome and know that I'd do it again in half a heartbeat if anyone else threatened the safety of this neighborhood.

No Good Key Left Behind

Nick Manzolillo

I FELT IT, that moment I heard the click. My pockets were too light, the check for my rent filled out in that dangerous kind of haste that *always* has consequences. I locked myself out of my apartment like a carefree, country living kinda fool instead of the bunkered-in New Yorker that I should be.

My roommate, Caeser, was off with his girl in Williamsburg. My cousin who I entrusted my spare key to was back home in Rhode Island with *his* girl. I wasn't going to let a locked door get between me and Caeser's junk food so I stuck the envelope with my share of the rent in the mailbox across the street, gathered my courage, and knocked on the door to the apartment next to mine. We share a fire escape.

I'VE NEVER SEEN the people that live next door, though I could hardly be blamed for not waiting by my peephole to find out. I've heard them, late at night (or early in the morning, pending on one's preference for particulars). I'd be doing a last minute English essay in front of the TV and there would be a skittering from beyond the wall. I'd never rule my building out for having rats and other dirty little beasts but it was definitely a person, tap tapping on the walls.

There are at least two people in that other apartment. I've heard someone go clomping into the hallway while an other has stayed behind, scurrying around. Sometimes I've heard garbled singing, like a deaf person humming, but I could feel its intent for rhythm. I've kept waiting to hear somebody getting laid, like they surely listen to Caeser and his girl, same as I do.

The door doesn't open up right away after I knock twice and press the almost imperceptible little buzzer next to their doorknob. My superintendent Hector only speaks Spanish; the weirdos next door are a better option for help, considering how Hector still gives me dirty looks over the time I was a little drunk and mixed up the recycling and the trash bins that he laboriously keeps tidy in the alley out back. If it weren't for Caeser translating my end of the contract, I'm not sure if I'd be able to live here.

I lean close to my neighbor's door. I can hear a distant sort of crackling, like static. The hallway smells heavily of spices from some grandmother cooking up a better meal than any I've eaten since leaving home.

It's the simplest thing in the world to hop across the fire escape from my neighbor's bedroom. My kitchen window's still partially cracked open from when I was cooking bacon and trying to avoid setting off the overly sensitive fire alarm.

There's a heavy click of a lock and the door rolls open and a pale, bald white man is looking at me with pupils dilated big enough for me to toss them onto an olive pizza. Did I mention I'm starving? Perseverance pays off for the promise of junk food: the door is open. I quickly lay down my situation to the Gollum reject standing in front of me. Then I start hoping he can understand English. I held my own enough to pass first year Spanish, but I don't know the words for lock, fire escape, and help. Though I do know 'thank you' so it's not like I'm an asshole or nothing.

The stench from within the apartment is one of sweat: pure, and reeking, fresher than the locker room at the closest gym. The pale man opens the door wide and beckons for me to enter. He's thin, and I wonder if he's sick. That would explain a few things maybe, but as I get a good look at his shirtless body, something about his tattoos doesn't sit right. There are too many skulls etched across his chest. Even my death-metal loving cousin would think there were too many. In the light of his apartment, this guy's front runs the course from pale flesh to pure ink, with a legion of skeletons dancing from hip bone to collar.

"Uh, thanks man." I smile, stepping slowly into the unexplored turf.

The apartment's set up just like mine which somehow makes it seem even more alien. There are stacks of suitcases piled up along the front walkway and acting as coffee tables in a living room filled by a fat, old fashioned TV. There's a drawing on white poster paper taped across the cracked screen and it's drawn nice, at least. It's a portrait of a man with a two long pins, hanging like knitting needles, one piercing each nostril. His eyebrows are lightning bolts and his teeth all seem to be sideways. His curly hair is balding in spots and there are gill-like slits along either side of his cheeks. But it's the big eyes full of dilation that remind me of the pale man that's been so gracious as to let me into his lovely home.

There are too many suitcases, it's almost like a maze once you look toward the bedrooms. I guess my fire escape cuts across the room at the end. This apartment is like the seedy, chaotic underbelly of JFK airport. It's where all the lost luggage goes to die.

"It's one of the bedrooms, I think. The fire escape, you know?" I point toward the bedrooms and the pale man closes the door behind me. He's wearing pink slippers and I want to say, "Hey, I like those," but this isn't a time for ball-busting. Not until I get my keys and thank the ugly man from the safety of my own place.

I try not to touch the suitcases but the stacks on either side of the hallway make it narrower once I reach the bathroom door, and my elbow brushes against them. The suitcases are freezing, almost burning my skin. Past the bathroom, I try and lean away from a suitcase that seems to veer out toward me and in doing so I push against the wrong bedroom door. The one at the end of the hall leads to the window, but this one—I'm looking upon a trash-filled nest and at the center of that nest is a beautiful girl.

Tied up on the floor with a ball gag in her mouth. She might be real pretty if not for the makeup running down her face.

Among the trash on the floor I spy a couple familiar things. Namely the social security card I thought I threw out a month ago, and then there's Caesar's girlfriend's panties, the same panties I took a good look at in his bedroom one day and later, coincidentally (though not to my conscience), I was accused of stealing them, until Caesar tore my room apart and couldn't find them.

"Ah, fuck me," I mutter as the pale man steps up behind me.

Beyond the tied-up girl, who's laying perfectly still on the floor, there are stools that reach up to holes in the blank back wall, close to the ceiling. Little holes big on this side of the wall that surely appear like undetectable pinpricks in my apartment.

They been watching me?

"We just been watching...we just been looking..." I hear a whiney voice from behind me.

The girl on the floor finally notices me, rolls onto her side, and struggles onto her knees. She's wearing sweatpants and a white t-shirt. She grins through the gag.

I turn and cut past the slow, sickly man.

The door at the end of the suitcase-confined hall opens inwards, and out steps the man from the TV screen. The knitting-needle pins aren't in his nose. They're in his hands.

There's a clap on my shoulder from behind. "We go around and around a lot, looking for souvenirs." The voice whines. The grip tightens. "It's not as bad as it looks, citizen." The voice seems to get a little stronger. "Just wanted to see how you livin' is all."

The big man, also shirtless, steps up as close as he can without touching me.

I twist around, forcing the hand from my shoulder.

"We're not from around here." The whiney voice possesses something of a plea. The pale man now rests his hand on one of the suitcases, blocking the way to the front door.

"Can I leave? Can I—can I go—just go, back to my apartment? I'll go out the front, out the front door and—"

"Nonsense," The pale man speaks slowly now, his voice rattling in my ears, "you're locked out."

"You don't touch each other," the big man mutters from the other side of the claustrophobic sandwich, like it's an instruction. Or did he mean me and the girl?

I glance at him and the knitting needles are back through his nose and hopefully that's the only place the needles belong.

I'm so fucked right now.

"We just want to understand you is all," the big man says. "This place is so different from where we come from."

"And um, where is it you come from?" I ask because at this point, at this miserable point, if they're going to kill me, I might as well not have a "Why?" as my dying nugget of satisfaction.

"From the door in our bathroom," the pale man says, pronouncing each word with delicate care. "The door that takes you everywhere. That's what makes here so special. It's the furthest we've gone. We've brought all of our souvenirs with us." He reaches to one of the suitcases along the floor and lifts it up. In a single motion he unzips the bag to reveal some kind of a doll. He hands it to me like it's a gift and it's surprisingly light.

Why the hell am I holding a doll?

From inside the room, I hear the woman call out, slurring through her ball gag, "Let me free. I'm ready. Let me out. Let me up."

"Not finished yet," the pale man raises his voice.

"Uh, could I use the fire escape to get back into my apartment?" I try asking again.

The pale man tips his head, like it's only natural, the polite thing to do, to allow me through.

"We leave soon. We're sorry for watching." The pale man sounds sincere. "But we're glad we got to meet our neighbor."

"That's just fine." I smile, sort of.

The man with the needles through his nose leads me to his bedroom. Of course, it's not a bedroom. There are just three weird, red velvet-looking pod chairs on the floor. The man with the needles takes a seat in one, facing the window, overlooking the street.

I pull the window open, and step onto the balcony, and from there it's a straight shot into my apartment.

I find myself sitting at my kitchen table with nine-one-one on my phone screen, but I don't hit dial. The doll is on the table in front of me. Only it's not a doll. It's a tiny shrunken creature, a bit like a man, in costume, preserved in every detail. I back out of the dial screen.

I grab one of my tapestries, bring it into the living room, and hang it across the wall that my neighbors may or may not have watched me through.

I fold my hands calmly, stare at the tapestry.

Who will replace them when they are gone?

Fifty Something

L. C. Tyler

LIKE MOST FREELANCE copy-editors, I rarely need to resort to murder. I mean in real life. I have, of course, facilitated many fictional stabbings and drive-by shootings through the carefully considered addition of a comma or deletion of an entirely unwarranted exclamation mark.

And why, until now, should I have needed to 'smoke' somebody (as my authors seem to believe young people say)? I ask very little from my fellow men and women. I simply wish to be left alone, preferably in the total silence that I require to do my work. My previous neighbour was, in that respect, exemplary.

I MET HER first, I think, about a year after I moved into my house. I opened the front door, in response to a single commanding ring on the bell, to find on my step a middle-aged lady in a Black Watch tartan skirt and a dark blue cardigan buttoned up to her throat. Her grey-streaked hair was pulled back mercilessly into a bun. She thrust a bulging black plastic sack into my hands.

'You have,' she said, 'permitted your Lonicera periclymenum to grow over into my garden. I have therefore cut it back, as I am permitted to do under English Common Law, to the line of the wall. You are however legally entitled to the return of the cuttings, to compost or dispose of as you choose.'

'Thank you,' I said. 'I shall compost them, I think.'

'That is very wise you,' she said. 'When you have finished with the bag, perhaps you could just pop it over the wall into my garden. Black garden sacks are not cheap.'

'Indeed they are not,' I said.

The second time was about eighteen months or perhaps two years later. Again there was a single, sustained ring on the door bell. This time she was wearing the same Black Watch tartan skirt, but with a green cardigan that seemed to have been buttoned with more haste than accuracy. Her hair was a little greyer than before. She took a deep breath.

'I would ask you,' she said, 'not to allow your dog to bark at night. It kept me awake for some hours.'

'I am sorry for that,' I said, 'but it must have been somebody else's dog.'

'I think not.'

'I do not own a dog,' I said. 'You may search the house if you wish to confirm that there are no canines of any description.'

She considered this for a good ten seconds before replying: 'Thank you, but that will not be necessary. If you give me your word as a gentleman that you do not possess a dog, then I am prepared to overlook the matter *on this occasion*.'

'I am happy to give you an assurance in those terms,' I said.

She nodded, turned on her heel and departed.

The final time I saw her was three weeks ago.

'I thought I should let you know that I am moving,' she said. 'I am going to live with my sister in Cheltenham.'

'You have sold the house?' I said.

'It was only ever rented,' she said. 'I took the lease over from my parents. The cost was not unreasonable then, but rents have risen ridiculously in London. And a house this size ... I simply cannot afford to keep it on and my sister has a spare room. I can't take any of the lovely furniture - my parents' furniture - of course. Fortunately the new tenant wanted furnished accommodation - he has been posted to London for a few years, I understand. A single gentleman like yourself.'

'Thank you for letting me know, Miss ...'

'Merrivale,' she said.

'Thank you, Miss Merrivale,' I said.

'No, thank you, Mr ...'

'Smith,' I said.

'Indeed,' she said. She paused. 'Could I just add, Mr Smith, how much I have enjoyed having you as a neighbour? I shall miss you very much.'

'And I shall miss you,' I said.

'I hope your new neighbour is congenial,' she said.

'Ah,' I said.

A WEEK LATER my worst fears were confirmed. A small van arrived followed shortly after by an SUV. A bald, middle-aged man got out of the SUV, stretched and glanced in my direction. Seeing me standing by the window he gave me a smile and a wave. I drew the curtain immediately.

About an hour later I heard the doorbell ring. Three quick jocular trills. It was the man who had waved to me.

'Hi!' he said. 'I thought I'd better introduce myself, since we're to be neighbours. Also to apologise for the fact that all of my boxes are currently blocking the sidewalk.'

It was the last word that struck fear in my heart. 'You're an American?' I said.

'Certainly am! Joe Zakrewski. Delighted to meet you.'

He held out his hand. I shook it cautiously.

'Born in Chicago but raised in New York,' he continued. 'I've travelled round the world a lot since then, of course. Singapore. Shanghai. Montevideo. Now I'm in your lovely city of London. How about yourself?'

'I've always lived here,' I said.

'Lucky you! Wonderful place! Shanghai was the pits. Don't even think of going there.'

'Do you intend to stay long?' I asked.

'Open-ended assignment. Could be a couple of years. Might decide to stay for ever. Is it always as sunny as this?'

'No,' I said. 'You certainly should not count on good weather when making your decision.'

'And what do I call you?' he asked.

'I'm Mr Smith,' I said.

'Hell, I can't call you that! I mean your first name.'

'Peregrine,' I said.

'I bet your friends call you Perry or something?'

'You are utterly mistaken,' I said. 'They do not.'

IT WAS EARLY in the afternoon when my concentration was again disturbed. I was trying to see how a very long sentence could either be broken down into several shorter ones or made more comprehensible through a few well-selected punctuation marks. I had just seen a very exciting way forward when the bell rang.

'H!' said Joe. 'Look, I'm not going to be able to cook tonight, not until I get all of my stuff unpacked, so I thought I'd order in a pizza or two - I wondered of you'd like to join me? You and your wife.'

'I'm not currently married,' I said.

'Divorced too, eh? I just parted company with my third wife, the scheming bitch, hence having to live in a rented place with somebody's grandparents' furniture - God, you should see some of that stuff your former neighbour sold us. Total junk. Well, if it's just us boys, I guess we could risk a beer or two as well, eh? Maybe three? What do you say, Perry?'

'I fear that I shall have to work all evening,' I said. 'I'm a freelance copy editor. I have to take what I can get and the deadlines are fairly tight.'

'That's too bad. You sure?'

'Absolutely. I probably won't get time to eat at all.'

'Those publishers sure are slave-drivers. Well, if you change your mind, just drop round. It would be great to get to know you better.'

I did in fact have some work that needed attention, but I'd finished by seven o'clock and started guiltily when the bell rang again. It was not in fact my neighbour. It was a pizza delivery man.

'You've come to the wrong house,' I said.

'No, it's the right one,' he said. 'Your neighbour ordered a couple of pizzas and told me to bring this one to you. He said you had to work all evening and he was worried you wouldn't have time to order anything for yourself. He sent this round, with his compliments. No charge.'

'I'm a vegan,' I said, eyeing the box suspiciously.

'It's a vegan pizza,' said the delivery man. 'He said he thought that's what you'd probably like.'

'Thank you,' I said.

'You're lucky you have such a thoughtful neighbour.'

'Ah,' I said.

THE FOLLOWING DAY it was a parcel. I'd just got back from shopping at the local Waitrose.

'The Amazon delivery guy was about to go off with it when he found you were out,' said Joe. 'So I dashed over, grabbed him and signed for it. He was a bit surprised. He said the soured-face old dame who lived here before never took in a parcel for anyone.'

'Miss Merrivale was a very good friend of mine,' I said.

'Was she? Sorry, no disrespect intended. She doesn't seem to have been very popular in the street though.'

'You've spoken to many people in the street?'

'Hell, yes. I've been here three days now. I know most of them.'

'Thank you for the parcel,' I said.

'Any time, Perry,' he replied. 'I'm sure you'd do the same for me.'

IT MUST HAVE been less than twenty four hours after that when I caught a glimpse of him over the garden wall. He waved.

'That's *Lonicera periclymenum* isn't it?' he said.

'I apologise unreservedly,' I said. 'It does tend to grow quite quickly. I shall cut it back so that it doesn't disturb you.'

'Disturb me? Not a bit. It's lovely the way it tumbles over that old red brick. Let it grow just as much as it likes. I might plant a clematis on my side and let it fall over onto your side. That would be swell, eh?'

'Clematis takes a while to grow,' I said.

'Oh, I don't think so. Anyway, I reckon I'll stick around long enough to see it develop,' he said. 'I'm not planning to go anywhere. I like it here.'

'What sort of clematis?' I asked. 'One of the small flowered ones?'

'No, I'd like giant purple flowers everywhere,' he said. 'Masses of them. I thought, maybe, *General Sikorski*? Hey, what if one day a year we all opened our gardens to each other, and wandered up and down the street, just taking in the flowers and maybe enjoying a martini. We'd get to know each other so much better.'

'Our own *private gardens*?' I said. "Open to anyone who just fancied wandering in?'

'That's the idea. Cool, eh?'

It was at that point that I knew he would have to die.

I SPENT THE evening Googling 'how to hire a hitman'. The results were not encouraging. They began by saying that, if you seriously planned to kill somebody, the very worst thing you could do was to Google 'how to hire a hitman'. Nothing you Googled ever left the Internet. If you found yourself a suspect, the first thing the police would do was check your search history. It got worse. I would need in any case to interrogate the dark web and would have to download something called Tor. That too might, in itself, arouse suspicion. Finally, most of the websites on the dark web offering assassination services were scams, designed to take the money of the unsuspecting client and deliver nothing in return. The remaining sites had all been set up by the CIA to catch aspiring criminals. I'd either end up with my bank account cleaned out by the Russian mafia or in jail somewhere in the American Mid-West. Neither prospect was inviting.

I wondered if I could perhaps just frighten him off. I tried drafting a letter, all in block capitals, saying that he was being randomly targeted by a gang from eastern Europe. His movements were being watched. Unless he contacted a certain number at once and agreed to make a payment in Bitcoin, he would be kidnapped and murdered. He'd be booking a ticket back to nice, safe Shanghai before the week was out. But, rereading the death-threat with a copy-editor's eye, it didn't seem that convincing. It was clear in its meaning, but perhaps just a bit too literate for a hardened killer. And what would I do if my neighbour cheerfully paid up? I decided it wasn't worth putting into an envelope for delivery.

I also considered whether I could do the killing myself. Having already Googled how to hire a contact killer, I reckoned I had nothing further to lose in Googling how to kill somebody you knew well, but the results were similarly bleak. We spread our DNA like confetti at a summer wedding. I would leave his house covered in his DNA while he would be generously endowed with my own. Actual cases of murder in the news were mainly family members killing each other and getting caught. Only total strangers - primarily people who had just happened to be in the wrong place at the wrong time - were really safe to kill. I had of course read dozens of crime novels, which should have acted as a practical manual for safe homicide. But I suspected that people rarely died as neatly and cleanly as suggested; and many of the plots, especially the short stories, seemed to rely on some improbable coincidence for them to work.

I closed the computer down, left the draft death-threat lying in my pending tray and went to bed.

RETURNING HOME THE following morning—I had been out shopping again—I noticed the door leading from the side passage into my kitchen was slightly open. I was horrified. Not only was Joe interrupting me at every opportunity, but he was now actually entering my house in my absence - doubtless to drop off a plateful of 'cookies' that he had just baked to his grandmother's recipe.

It was something of a relief to discover a youth in a hoodie ransacking the kitchen.

'I'd be grateful,' I said, 'if you didn't disturb the contents of that drawer. It is carefully arranged and there is nothing in it of value.'

He looked up at me. 'You're not kidding, are you, mate? I mean, there's nothing worth nicking here at all. How old is that TV of yours?'

'I can't remember,' I said. 'I could check my receipts file if you're genuinely interested to know. Otherwise, I would suggest that you leave at once, now, before I call the police. I'd merely like you to empty your pockets first. On the work surface there, if you don't mind.'

He scowled at me. 'You can't just order me around like that.'

'I think you'll find I can.'

He pulled a neat little gun out of the front pocket of his hoodie and pointed it at me. 'This says you can't. OK?'

'On the contrary,' I said. 'If you fire that, my neighbour will hear and be over immediately. I wish that wasn't true, but it is. Moreover, just before I came in, I took a photo of you through the kitchen window. It has already been uploaded to the Cloud. There's nothing you can do about it. Shoot me and the police will have a picture of my attacker. I assume you are already known to the police?'

'Maybe,' he said.

'You'd better empty your pockets and trot along then,' I said.

'Don't think this is the end of it,' he said. 'I'll get you. I don't just turn over houses like this one. I'm a contract killer, I am'

I laughed. Then I said: 'Really?'

'Really,' he said.

'And have you done many jobs?'

'Loads.'

'You look very young.'

'Nineteen. That's old for this game. I'm already thinking about retiring and going straight.'

'How could I confirm the quality of your work? Do you supply references?'

'I'm not on bleeding Checkatrade,' he said.

'But you have been largely successful?'

'Every time I've done it. God's truth.'

'And what do you charge?'

'Who do you want killed?'

'I'd like to know your rates first, then I'll tell you if I'm interested in having him smoked.'

'Smoked?'

'I'm told it's the correct street word for "killed".'

'Not round here.'

'Just give me a quote,' I said.

'OK, what sort of a job is it? London?'

'Yes.'

'House or flat?'

'House.'

'Does the geezer live on his own?'

'Yes.'

'Famous?'

'No.'

'Bodyguard?'

'No.'

'Dog?'

'No.'

'Burglar alarm?'

'I very much doubt it.'

'It wouldn't be a problem anyway. OK, I'll go away and price the job up for you.'

'Can't you tell me now?'

'I need to look at the figures and factor in the overheads and stuff.'

'You've never actually killed anyone before, have you?' I said.

'Course I have. Let me have your mobile number. I'll give you a call tomorrow.'

I gave it to him.

'I look forward to hearing from you,' I said. 'And now, if you'd just like to empty your pockets before you go?'

He placed six silver teaspoons on the work surface.

'Early Victorian,' he said. 'Hardly worth the effort of fencing them.'

THE FOLLOWING DAY I was moderately surprised to receive a call.

'I've got you a contract killer,' he said.

'I thought you were one?'

'Didn't fancy the job,' he said evasively. 'But I know this bloke who'll do it.'

'I'll speak to him,' I said.

'You can't. He's in Bulgaria.'

'That could be tricky. The job's in London.'

'He comes over every now and then, does a few, then goes back. If the police aren't after him over here, he flies back a few months later. Kills a few more.'

'Is he any good?'

'The best. Straight up. A real pro. He'd strangle his own grandmother if the price was right.'

'What happens now?'

'He'll phone you. He thinks I'm called Danny, by the way.'

'And are you?'

'As if. Don't tell him any more than you have to. No unnecessary detail, especially about yourself. Just keep it all really simple and you won't go wrong.'

I GOT THE call an hour afterwards.

'Danny says you got job for me.'

'How much?' I asked.

'For me, ten thousand. Pounds, not Dollars. And a thousand to Danny for setting up.'

It wasn't cheap, but I might have paid that much to fix dry rot or rising damp or anything else that would have made the house uninhabitable.

'OK,' I said. 'Do you require payment up front?'

'After. When is dead.'

'That is very trusting of you,' I said.

'You not pay me, world not big enough for you to run, eh?' He laughed at this *bon mot*. 'I get you, cut your guts out, then maybe kill you too. When is dead, give money to Danny. He come your house. Cash. Pounds or Euros. No Bitcoin. He give to me. All done. I don't grass you to police. You never hear from me again. Everyone happy except dead friend.'

'And you trust Danny?'

'Danny know me too well to cheat me. I know where he live. I know his name not Danny. He cheat me, I take his sister and sell her in Baku.'

'And what's your name?'

'Boris.'

'That's the truth?'

'Sometimes is truth. Other times is not. What you care?'

He said something I didn't quite catch.

'The line's not good,' I said. 'But Danny says you're in Bulgaria.'

'Bulgaria? That's what I tell him.' He laughed and said something else that was lost in a crackling noise. 'So, where do I find the friend you want to kill?' he added.

'52 Lauderdale Avenue,' I said. I added the postcode for good measure.

'Sorry - bad line. I not hear. He live at 50?'

'No, 52. I live at 50. Next door.'

'Still not hear. He live next door to 52?'

'He lives at 52,' I said. 'I live next door at number 50.'

'OK, got that,' he said above the static. 'I go there tomorrow night. Kill him. All very quiet. You not even notice. Relax. All over now except pay me or have guts taken out. You choose, eh?'

'Just repeat back the address you have,' I said. 'For God's sake, just repeat back the address.'

But the line had gone dead. I tried calling him back, but the phone didn't even ring, wherever he actually was. Had he got the right address or the wrong one? I cursed myself for not listening to Danny's advice to tell Boris nothing that he did not need to know, especially about me.

My fault of course. My fault entirely. How could I - for whom the nuanced semi-colon was a way of life - have hired a contract killer with the communication skills of a slab of reinforced concrete? It was, I told myself, a joke. A complete joke.

Then suddenly all became clear. Boris did not exist any more than the kidnappers in my threatening letter to Joe existed. This was all part of some elaborate hoax on Danny's part - revenge for my humiliating him and making him empty his pockets. Why hadn't I suspected that from the very beginning? Fine. Let him think he had given me a scare. At least I hadn't parted with any money. In fact, when I thought about it, no harm had been done at all.

YES, IT WAS as much a surprise to me as anyone when my neighbour was murdered. Contract killing the police reckoned. A single shot to the head while he was asleep in bed. I told them: I'd only just moved in next door to him. I can't say I knew him well - not yet. But Perry seemed the very last person who'd get mixed up in organised crime - unless being a copy editor was just a very clever front. Back home in the States, all sort of people seem to get caught up in mafia stuff. You'd scarcely believe it. The police checked his computer of course. He'd apparently been googling all sorts of stuff about hitmen, suggesting he was worried somebody was after him. Then the police found a letter - in his pending tray oddly enough—all in block capitals saying that he was being randomly targeted by a gang from Eastern Europe and that he'd be killed if he didn't pay up. It had no finger prints on it other than his own—a professional job. The police couldn't find the envelope the letter must have come in, which strangely proved quite an important clue in its way, because the police checked his recycling and, when they couldn't find it there either, they deduced that the letter must have arrived more than a week before and the envelope had gone out with the refuse in the previous week's collection. Clever reasoning, eh? I mean, real Agatha Christie stuff. Which in turn meant Perry had probably missed the deadline for payment. So, they concluded, that was almost certainly why he was shot - 'smoked' as they say round my way. He'd just been really unlucky. In the wrong place at the wrong time. Hell, they could have just as easily chosen me.

Poor Perry. He seemed such a nice guy. I admired the way he stood up for that chiselling, sanctimonious former neighbour of his, who ripped me off over a sun-bleached table and a few moth-eaten chairs, and who must have been a real pain in the arse for him. But was he a good neighbour? A bad neighbour? Too soon to say, I suppose. All I can really tell you is that he never did me any harm.

I Found Me a Bigger Flea

F. D. Trenton

WHEN I HOPPED off my pushbike outside Zsa Zsa Juice Bar in Bayswater Road, the vehicle that was following me came to a halt. Behind me, its engine continued to tick over quietly. One of its windows purred open. Still I did not turn around. I steadied myself for the usual tirade of *bloody cyclists, why don't you...!* Although I couldn't think of anything I'd done—cut him up, missed a hand signal, nothing like that. However, this time it was not abuse; this time someone called my name:

"Alan!"

A thin olive-skinned man with a beard, wearing a brilliant white keffiyeh and a tailored silver-grey suit opened the back door and slid out of the people-carrier, which was bulky, black, and had gold diplomatic plates. He smiled broadly. "Alan!"

"I'm terribly sorry," I said, "but I don't quite..."

"Alan! You've stopped for a juice! I'll join you—no, no, you'll have one on me. How simply marvellous to see you!"

He was getting close now, his hand out. I recoiled. We were only just at the end of the first Covid lockdown. "I'm afraid my mind's a blank, you're going to have to..."

When I didn't offer my hand, he draped his arm across my shoulder. As if I wasn't uncomfortable enough, he wore a strong sickly-sweet perfume that made me want to sneeze. I didn't even have a mask on.

"Come now. We lived together five years. Shared the biggest part of our lives. What have you been drinking that has turned all those neurons of yours to slush?"

As if mechanically, my brain ticked back the years, until:

"Ahh! Karim! Of course!" I said. Only the most brutal fast-bowler in our year, that's who. Mister sportsman. Only the boy who shagged the housemaster's daughter, and was dishonourable enough to let everyone know. "Karim! How the hell are you? What are you doing in London?"

"Posted here. By my uncle."

"What the K-I-N-G?" It was all coming back, now. Ten years of history melting away. Karim and his exotic extended family.

"Yes my friend, the K-I-N-G." He smiled again, and now I recognised that broad, big-toothed smile with its sardonic little twist in the corner of the mouth.

We had reached the outside serving hatch, which was as much of the juice bar that was open. He ordered us both something I'd never heard of. No money changed hands.

"You were always a bit of a nerd," he said, playing with the paper straw that poked out of his deep paper cup. "You still nerding it around, or have you, well, what are you up to these days?"

I explained that I was writing apps, developing a must-have app of my own.

He said that he'd just landed the job of managing the Royal Estate in the UK. "Poacher turned gamekeeper, you might say," and he laughed.

I don't recall what incident he had in mind. Perhaps something no-one ever discovered. He soon established (it was not difficult to get out of me) that my work had all but ground to a halt. That I was pretty much prevented from focused thought by noisy neighbours, by lack of sleep at night, then unable to escape for more than forty-five minutes exercise during the day, what with lockdown restrictions...

"I have the perfect solution for you," he said. "A most beautiful place to live. And your government continues to allow you to move home, so... But you must do this yourself, no mention of me. All above board, this time. I promise."

Again, I didn't know what he meant. In fact I wondered whether he was confusing me with someone else. But he went on:

"The Royal Estate includes a great land-holding just outside Exeter. It was the special retreat of the late Princess Malika, *may Allah shower blessings upon her grave...*" He paused, briefly grim-faced, then continued as if reciting a brochure: "There are numerous detached properties on the Estate, many for rental. You should check out the agents, Ratsloe & Poltimore, search their website for Todmorton Hoe. She was a great woman, The Princess. A believer in people. She would have approved your enterprising spirit."

I wondered briefly what relation she was to him. But I don't understand all these family ties, and before I could find a way to ask without causing offence, he announced that he was being paged, handed me his juice, and dashed back to his diplomatic people-carrier.

"YES, VALE COTTAGE at Todmorton Hoe," I said.

There was the clatter of a keyboard at the other end of the phone. It was 8:31 a.m. the next day. I wanted to make sure I was the first person the rental manager spoke to that morning.

"Uh, yuh, there we go. Got it," he said.

"It's beautiful," I said. "It's exactly what I want. I'd buy it if it was for sale."

This was true. The two bedroom thatched cottage stood in a small oval of land on a hillside, surrounded on three sides by a field. It was neat, clean and light inside, and nicely done out—although I would be renting unfurnished. And outside, it was a quarter of a mile from the nearest house, which was the estate farmhouse. A mile from the nearby village and its shop, and the right side of the hillside to get a 4G mobile signal. I'd grown up in a cottage like that. It wasn't cheap, but it was exactly what I wanted—and needed, after yet another noisy night of broken sleep.

"Still available?" I said.

"That'd be true," the rental manager said. He had reluctantly identified himself as Dennis.

"And not wanted by anyone local? I mean if I trek all the way down to see it, you're not going to greet me with 'Oh sorry it's gone to the kid on the corner'?"

"We had some local interest," Dennis said. "Signed up he did. But then he dropped out. Must be all of three weeks ago. Got a job in Bristol, he did, moving out of the area. Should go pretty quick though. You seen the pictures. Where you living now?"

"London."

"How'd you propose to see it? I mean, seeing as you're so keen."

"I'll come down today."

The truth was, I'd spent the whole of the previous evening researching the place. *Nerd-that-I-am* I had located it on Google satellite view (all of two miles from where the estate agents marked it on their website map), and I had worked out how to cycle to the cottage from the local market town of Bekworth. I'd even travelled the journey by Google street view and memorised the landmarks and the road junctions, some of which possessed sign posts, others not.

"I'll pay the deposit, today, as well. If I like it."

Understand, in lockdown, many people wanted to escape London for whatever Covid-related reason. Me, I needed to escape the neighbours so I could do some work, get on with my life. Immediate action and a quick decision were called for.

"How'd you say you'd be travelling? All the way from London, you say?"

"Train and bike," I said. "I can be there, meet you at the cottage—I've found it on the map—for say, 2 p.m.?"

"You'm won't be able to cycle there," Dennis said authoritatively. "That'd be your non-starter for one."

He went on to explain that it was too far from the station, and too hilly, and that I would have to get a taxi. He was a cyclist of long-standing *his-self* and he wouldn't do it. It looked like a couple of miles on the map, but it would take him an hour, easy. And he was ten furlong's fitter than any townie he'd ever met.

"There's a cab rank at the station," he said. "There's always someone there. Use them. I can do you for one o'clock. Nothing doing for two."

Since my earliest train got me to Bekworth at 12.30, I had to agree and gave up on the idea of taking my bike on the train. The bike would get me as far as Paddington, at least.

"See you at the cottage at 1pm," I said, now in a hurry to book and catch my train.

"Make it the main farm building," he said. "Todmorton House. In the yard."

WHEN I GOT off the train at Bekworth, I was greeted by bright sunlight.

After dull, laborious lockdown-London, I was suddenly aware of the wide open space, the low horizon, and the big sky. Not only that, but the warm air of the late English summer gave me a feeling of buoyancy. It was as if I had been suppressing something. As if for months, if not years, I had abandoned any hope of anything new, of any kind of renewal. The truth was, I realise now: I was as thrilled as a schoolkid at the prospect of adventure.

On this, the penultimate stage of my journey I had been one of three passengers in a single carriage train out of Exeter. One of the other two got off with me, an elderly lady dressed in lavender blue, including beret with a black feather jauntily fastened to it.

I was wearing my hi viz cycle jacket and carrying my cycle panier. Although scuffed and grimy, it contained my cycle helmet and a puncture repair kit. I had to bring them with me since there was nowhere safe to leave them in Paddington, although carrying them made me feel a bit lopsided.

We had emerged on the far side platform from the ticket office and faced a fenced-off car park. I approached the elderly lady with some trepidation, feeling not a little out-dressed. "I wonder if you could tell me," I said, "where I might wait for a taxi?"

"There ain't no call for them things round these parts," she said. "Them's all long gone. Need to go to town you do, if it's a taxi you want, and then maybe you lucky, but most probably not." And she walked off, shaking her head, making the black feather in her beret bounce.

I crossed the footbridge and found the ticket office closed.

A cafe next to it appeared to be open, albeit with a placard outside saying, "Railway Tea Room. No entry. Ring for service." There were three people inside, unmasked and chatting.

I rapped on the glass of the part-open door to make my presence known (I only noticed the miniature hand bell resting on top of the placard *after* I had made my noise). A woman of about thirty in a Charlie Brown pinafore, with billowing brown hair and a soft wide face came to the door, putting her face mask on as she approached.

I explained the purpose of my visit, my need to get to the estate by one o'clock, and did she by any chance have the number for a taxi?

"Used to live on the estate myself, I did," she said. "Beautiful place. Go back like a shot I would, given half the chance." She extracted a mobile from the pocket of her pinafore. "Don't you worry now, I'll get you your taxi. Such a shame about the Princess." She thumbed in a number. "Real woman she was. Showed us all what can be done. Built that herd—you know about the herd? Thoroughbreds they were—built them up from nothing. Won shows, she did—Oh hello, AB Cab Co? Can you do me a cab from Railway Tea Room to The Princess's Estate?" She listened, frowning. "Yes, Todmorton, that's the one." And then, "What d'you mean, *closed for lunch*, never heard such."

She held the phone at arm's length and shook her head at it.

"Well now, there's their competitor in Kikford," she said. "I'll try them but if they're coming from Kikford you can't help but be late." She thumbed in another number and made a similar request.

Eventually she finished and announced: "You got the luck of the devil, I must say. Their only cab is dropping off hereabouts, can be here in ten minutes. Reckon you destined to get that cottage, and that's saying something."

Given that I was used to the London mindset of *me-first-and-me-only*, I was surprised and touched, not to say a little embarrassed, by this woman's kindness. I established that her name was Charlotte, and I promised to visit her tea rooms on my way back, to stock up with cake and whatever I might need for my return journey.

I am sorry to this day that I was unable to keep that promise.

"YOU AIN'T HALF lucky I come along when I did." The cab driver's voice was muffled by his mask and almost lost beneath the chug of the engine and the rattle of the windows, but it was definitely a London voice.

The framed registration in the back of his old-style black cab named him Ken McCreedy. The photo rendered him square-jawed, clean-shaven, about fifty, with a military haircut. All I could see were the tattoos on his left arm and the side of his head. He continued, "Your working cabbie is hardly likely to hang around a two-bit station like this. One train an hour ain't worth the candle. Tell you that for nothing. Round here you either walk or get a motor. Ain't that the truth. Even if I am talking myself out of a job."

I said I'd been assured there'd be a cab.

"That's the other thing," he said. "People in this neck of the woods ain't no more nor no less reliable than cityfolk. They present it different, is all. That AB Cab Co. *Cab Co*—there's a name for something that's not—they got a reputation for picking and choosing. Pick and choose! What honest cab firm does that? If you're a cabbie, you're a cabbie, you take all-comers. That's what life's about, that is. I hope you know where you're going, by the way. I can get you to Congleton Junction but after that, well, you'd better know where you're going is all I can say. Mostly I do conferences and hotels round here. And there's only one place does that in Bekworth."

I assured him that I could give him metre by metre instructions if needed.

About a mile out of Bekworth he decided to phone in his fare to his office and failed to get a signal.

"Too late," he said. "I knew hereabouts I'd lose it. Hope you don't need no signal where you're headed. Don't need signal do you? Probably get something on higher ground. Leastways, if you choose your spot. You can always choose your spot. Know what I'm saying?"

Congleton Junction turned out to be a blind left turn off the main road and a signpost obscured by bushes. We were now about two miles out of Bekworth and three miles of country lanes lay between us and Todmorton House.

The main road had been busy, with traffic moving so fast I doubted many drivers would even notice the turning. On the single track lane, however, we encountered nothing at all. Thankfully I remembered the way and we arrived at the farm only five minutes late.

I asked Mr. McCreedy for his business card and he wrote his competitor's number on the back. He took his mask off and said, conspiratorially, "Don't tell 'em I give it you. But next job's the last job of the day for me, so I can't help you. Not unless you stay overnight. You don't want to get stuck out here, so here you go."

As THE JOLT and clatter of the taxi faded into the distance, I was swamped by silence. Not a tree stirred in the warm air. Not an insect buzzed. Not a bird cried out. Under the bright sun, the green and gold of the countryside became numbing and oppressive. I could have been the only creature left alive on the planet.

To my left, a low fence which had been patchily whitewashed stood between the yard and the farmhouse, while to my right a high breeze block wall served as one side of a large barn. A yellow tractor, with a large spiked bucket (and not a little rusty) was parked straight ahead on a track that led off along the side of the barn towards some woods. However, squarely in front of me a metal-framed shed more or less blocked the way. The word "office" was painted above the door and a large sign hung in the window demanding: "All visitors must dip their boots before entry."

I was in trainers.

Besides which, there were no buckets, nor troughs, for dipping anything. Mainly though, I was worried that the estate agent had been here already, and left.

I explored a little, not sure if I was being terribly irresponsible, but remembering my route in case someone needed to disinfect the ground after me. Although, as best as I could recall, hadn't the last foot-and-mouth outbreak been when I was still at school?

In any case, the farmhouse was deserted. Everywhere, grass and weeds were growing through cracks in the concrete. The cowsheds were deserted. The stables were deserted. It couldn't have been clearer had the place been stamped all over with the words "abandoned" and "disuse."

I decided to wait. I told myself I should allow at least half an hour. The estate agent might be running late from a previous appointment and I figured they probably booked viewings in half-hour slots.

After twenty minutes of intense listening for any sound from any vehicle travelling any part of the road, I caught a rumble, and shortly a man appeared in a dusky green Range Rover and wound down the window.

He was bald with a puffed up red face, bulging blue eyes, and a goatee.

"Dennis?" I ventured.

He looked me up and down. "So you'm be from London then. Am I right? Come to see Dandelion Lodge?"

"No, Vale Cottage."

"You're not Alan Gregson then?"

"I am Alan Gregson and I've come to view Vale Cottage."

"They give me the wrong details then. Sure you don't want to see Dandelion Lodge?"

I assured him I knew what I wanted. That we had spoken earlier.

He asked if I minded being driven. I said I didn't, even though I knew from Google maps it was only a hundred and fifty metres and seemed hardly worth getting into a car for.

He drove us along a rough track to the cottage. The location was everything the photographs had promised.

However, when Dennis got out of the Range Rover he was not quite the athlete I'd expected; he had bandy legs and a darts-player's stomach—with full trouser overhang—and he was a good six inches shorter than me.

We clambered down a steep flight of steps to the front of my prospective new home.

What struck me first about the cottage was the thatch—and I'm no expert on thatch (the family home having been covered by a slate roof). The thatch was grey, had moss growing on it, and wisps of grass growing out of it. Surely it should have been treated or even replaced some time ago?

Then the front door and the window frames all needed a coat of paint to cover the naked grey of the timber, and the front door wouldn't open so we had to go in at the side.

Inside was grubby. Every horizontal surface carried a layer of dust. It could not have been cleaned since it had been vacated, and my guess was that it must have been vacated some years ago. Certainly the photos I had seen were ten, even twenty, years out of date.

I looked around, upstairs and down. It was, in terms of location and space exactly what I was after. But it was difficult to see myself living here, even if I spent a week cleaning it up, not least because none of the windows would shut (they all seemed to be jammed half an inch open). They would all have to be eased—or whatver it was carpenters did.

And then there were the flies.

The cottage was built on a slope, going down the hill lengthways, with three separate areas at three different levels and two or three steps between each level. In the lower reception room, the windows on both sides of the cottage, and at the end, were covered in flies. Living, buzzing flies. And when I say covered, I don't mean dozens or hundreds, I mean carpeted: thousands.

I sniffed the air and, confident I did not have Covid, nor any other excuse to suppose any loss of any sense, I caught not the least whiff of damp or decay. There was no explanation as to why there should be so many flies. Except: four empty Kilner jars stood on the mantelpiece above the fireplace, and I was struck by the bizarre thought that the flies had been imported and released especially for my edification.

However, I was not put off so much as curious. After all, everything I had seen could be remedied, even the windows, by anyone who had a mind to.

Dennis made a great show of trying to open one of the windows to let some of the flies out, but couldn't dislodge the window from its frame.

"We'll have someone look at that," he said.

Eventually we found ourselves standing once more outside, facing, I must confess, a deeply disappointing prospect.

He said, "So what you reckon?"

"No other enquiries?"

"Only been on the market a few days. Estate's only just signed over the papers. If you're wanting it, you'm best snap it quick."

I didn't mention the alternative history he'd fed me earlier.

"I like it," I said. I decided to make up my mind in my own time. There was sufficient doubt that if in the meantime it went to someone else, so be it. Most importantly, how was it I didn't feel the same way now about a cottage that an hour earlier I would have raced across the hills of England for? Was I some kind of mollycoddled, city-living weakling, defeated by the reality of country living? I had been so convinced; so what had changed?

"I can't deny," I said, not very convincingly, "it's everything I'm after. Although being here and facing the prospect feels strange. I will say a provisional yes, but see how it sits with me when I mull it over on the train going back." I didn't want to commit either way until I'd had the chance to think properly about my own reaction.

"Your call. Like I say. I'll get the carpenter in. It'll need an electrician too. Probably could have it habitable for you, say, in three, maybe four, weeks."

"The website said available immediately."

He ignored that. He said, "I got another appointment, another rental. I can drop you off at Congleton Junction. You can walk back easy from there. Along the main road, like. Nice walk it is too. Nice views. Touristy. You'll like that."

"I noticed a footpath," I said pointing along a rough track, aware I had two hours to kill before my train. "I thought I might walk back to the station through the fields."

"Not signposted, that path," he said. "Some round here take against city folk. We're not an amusement park. Valuable land this. Best use the road. Can't get lost on the road."

He dropped me off at Congleton Junction.

"Just turn right," he said. "Follow the main road."

"Thanks but I'm going to walk back towards the cottage. See how difficult it would be to cycle."

I'm a great believer in gears. I'd seen nothing here that would defeat my pedal-power. And I doubted Dennis had warmed the seat of a pushbike since he'd attended junior school, if then. Another driver who had a problem with cyclists, obviously.

He gave me a dirty look and drove off.

I DECIDED TO walk back in the direction of Todmorton Hoe for half an hour and see how far I might get. I owed it to myself to enjoy some of my day far away from London, enjoy the peace, as well of course, as getting a feel for the place.

I was coming to the end of my self-imposed half hour, and had only been disturbed by two cars on the road, when a third car came from behind me and pulled up in front of me. It was a small yellow runabout. I don't know the make, I'm not an expert on cars, but it was the sort of small car you'd expect from a middle class family with two cars and a drive to match.

The window on the passenger side slid open. A young woman in the passenger seat with straight brown hair, a pink face and freckles said, "We're trying to find—mum, what's it called?"

The mother, in the driving seat, leaned over across her daughter. Her brushed back blonde hair flopped a little but her piercing blue eyes sparkled as she said, very precisely, "Todmorton Hall."

"I'm terribly sorry," I said. "I'm a stranger here myself." I made a sweeping gesture. "This is all the Todmorton Estate, so you're broadly in the right place. I've heard of the House, but the Hall—I don't know."

"Where the Princess lived," the young woman said helpfully.

"I've just visited a cottage on the estate. That was Vale Cottage. I don't know what else there is." It occurred to me briefly that we might be competing for the same rental, and they were being sly and reticent. I felt a frisson of the competitive spirit, but it turned just as quickly into a subliminal shrug.

"Not to worry," the mother said. "We've allowed plenty of time."

Half an hour later I was back at Congleton Junction and resigned to the twenty minutes or so I estimated it should take to get back to Bekworth Station.

It was then that I discovered the main road had no footpath.

To my right, there was a low embankment, strewn with branches and leaves, but nothing more. I set about tramping toward Bekworth, facing the oncoming traffic, through the detritus on the embankment, a few feet off the ground.

After a hundred and fifty metres the embankment ran out. I could just make out another embankment on the far side of the road, a hundred metres further on but I would have to walk in the road that distance before crossing. I was not best pleased. The road was busy, with a single carriageway each way. And yet if I walked all the way back to Vale Cottage and tried the footpath which was supposedly grown over, I was definitely going to miss my train.

There was nothing for it and I was wearing my yellow hi viz jacket, so I started to walk against the oncoming traffic keeping hard against the now tall, unclimbable embankment.

I'm not sure how far I walked before I decided this was close to lunacy. I still clung to the belief that one could walk to Bekworth along this road as the estate agent had claimed. I rationalised the belief by imagining a path would magically appear any moment.

I think the event which defined my deluded lunacy was an oncoming tractor and trailer. When I say tractor I'm talking something with wheels taller than I am and a trailer the size of a shipping container, probably larger.

Any cyclist will tell you the danger is not from the person coming straight at you so much as from the driver behind them who has no idea you exist until they are upon you. Even as it approached apace, a queue of cars was quite apparent, following the trailer.

I leaned into the embankment, at least choosing a spot where I was not hidden by bramble.

Without the hi viz jacket I have no doubt I would have been killed.

The tractor was rolling along at the best part of forty miles an hour but could not move over into the middle of the road because at the last minute a truck came charging along in the opposite direction on the other carriageway. The tractor wheels passed six inches from my face.

A loose flap of clothing and, well...

I held onto the embankment and tried not to think about wing mirrors.

At the next gap in the traffic I ran across the road and along the opposite carriageway to the opposite embankment.

Now I could see how bad the road was up ahead, around the next bend.

There was no footpath and no raised bank on either side. The bend ahead was blind, and to judge from the pattern of the road, and the valley rising steeply on both sides, the next bend was followed by others equally as tight and narrow.

There was no mobile signal. Not here nor at Congleton Junction which had only just disappeared from sight, but clearly getting back there was the only option and my first priority. Once safely off the main road, I could worry about how to get to the station to catch my train.

WHAT HAPPENED ON my return to the junction has all the hallmarks of the most remarkable coincidence. Looking back however, a cool, rational analysis renders it inevitable given my fondness for time-management by the half-hour.

The putative coincidence was this: just as I returned to the junction, as I stepped off that last stretch of raised embankment (and not without some struggle to arrive there safely) the mother and daughter in the yellow car pulled up by the signpost.

The car was indicating left, away from Bekworth.

I waved, ran across to them, and the mother wound down the window.

"Any chance of a lift to Bekworth?" I said. "Only I was told I could walk there but plainly the road won't let me." I added, "I have a train to catch, and I would be so, so grateful."

The woman consulted her daughter and between them they took pity on this strange man in a cycle-soiled hi viz jacket. They masked up and let me in the back of the car.

I don't remember exactly what niceties we talked about. I know I gushed gratitude, especially now I was taking notice of how impossible the road would have been for any pedestrian.

I do remember several foil trays of Cesar dog food in the floor well by the daughter's feet and BBC Radio 4 FM sputtering on the verge of stereo reception. The mother's name was Liz and the daughter Gillian. And yes they had viewed The Hall where the Princess had lived, but had been disappointed. For one thing the kitchen was not in the main building since the Princess disliked the smell of cooking in her living quarters. For another the place had the feeling of neglect and not being ready for habitation.

They had travelled that day from Bristol. Liz was looking for a place to rent, close to her son in boarding school. Gillian was at college, but on holiday.

They told me about the Princess. How she had bred cattle. Was world renowned for it. She had provided work for many locals, had built up the business on a good reputation, sound finance and good business sense. How she loved this country and this corner of this country, and how terrible it was that she died so young. She was not yet fifty.

I started to feel the loss, and the tragedy, of the neglect of her estate since her passing. The indifference to her works, the casual decay that had been allowed to take over. She had left an enormous gap that no one had been big enough to fill. In every way, the estate had died with her, her life's work wasted. A long shadow cast where she had shed only light.

However, in that moment, I owed Liz and Gillian an enormous debt of gratitude for going out of their way to help. Unless they read this account of events they will never know the extent of it.

They returned me to the station where I found the tea rooms closed.

I had a half-hour wait for my train and towards the end of that time the elderly lady in the lavender blue beret joined me on the platform. As she passed my bench, heading for the only other bench a few metres beyond, she paused and spoke to me. "I had a friend," she said. "But she died. I keep forgetting."

Soon the single carriage train came and I went home.

THE NEXT DAY I was back in my lockdown routine, queuing for a healthy juice outside Zsa Zsa'a, having emailed Ratsloe & Poltimore saying I would not want the cottage. It was too badly neglected.

For now, I would be struggling with my app in the continued stress of sleep deprivation and noise. In fact, I was close to giving up, and had an idea for something simpler, less ambitious. A piece of programming I might turn out in my sleep.

"Alan!"

Ahh! How was I going to tell my old school friend that his property wasn't the salubrious mansion he supposed?

He clasped my shoulder (jumping the queue and flooding me with what I realised now was rose-scented perfume). "How was your day trip to the English countryside?"

After my experiences, I felt a certain directness was in order. "To be honest, the agents cannot seriously be trying to rent the property. They tried to stop me leaving London. The location was wrongly indicated on the map, by two miles. They didn't want me cycling because I might get there. They said there was a local taxi service and there wasn't. And once I got there and expressed my interest, they made it punishingly hard, not to say dangerous, to get back to town—I damn well nearly got killed. What their game is, I can only guess. Maybe they want to collect deposits, property unseen, confident that if anyone ever finds the place, they will find it uninhabitable and write off the cost to experience. Who knows? But I'm not the only one. A woman I met—by pure chance—was similarly put off when she visited a property that she'd seen advertised on the same estate..."

"Wo, wo, wo!" Karim tightened his grip on my shoulder. "Slow down mate. I get the picture. I had no idea. No idea at all that the rumours might be true."

"Rumours? *What* rumours?"

"It's all right," he said, "You're alive mate. But in the last six months there have been four mystery deaths on that stretch of road."

"*What!*"

"The local paper's branded it the Bekworth Stretch—sort of local version of the Bermuda Triangle. Complete strangers have materialised out of nowhere, dead in the road. The authorities claim it is a statistical blip and cite long Covid *confusion*."

I couldn't believe what I was hearing. He had sent me there knowing this? I pulled away from him.

"A Liverpool man, a widower with a life assurance windfall," he said, "goes to bed as usual one night, next day he's found dead, mysteriously transported to the Bekworth Road—no rhyme or reason why or how he got there. A single woman, a furloughed supply teacher, from Ipswich. A student from Portsmouth about to start a sabbatical. A pension adviser from Northampton..."

"And you didn't think to tell me something strange was going on? Did you suspect it was part of a scam against your uncle—aunt—or..." At that point I made a very sudden and bad connection. The Todmorton Hoe estate, run so remarkably well by the Princess, sister of the K-I-N-G, or married to, or well—was She his mother?

He straightened his keffiyeh.

"I needed an unbiased view," he said. "An honest view. No private investigator. Someone with some good sense and who would act in earnest..."

"Act in earnest! You nearly got me killed!"

I walked away, wheeling my bike to the kerb.

He shouted after me: "The deposit scam wasn't the half of it. There was so much more at stake..."

I lost the rest of what he said in traffic.

I TRIED TO forget my encounter with Karim. I was going to put it down to one more misery imposed on us by lockdown. But I was still angry about being used so, instead, I sent him a test version of my new app. It was a simple point-and-click shooter. My working name for it was *Click2Kill*.

Click2Kill turned the whole sorry saga of the cottage on its head.

The truth was, *Click2Kill* was spyware. Childish payback by me, I know. Once Karim had installed it on his mobile—which he did a couple of minutes after he opened my email—I could see everything he saw on his screen, hear everything he was saying any time the phone was turned on, and I could download any files from his phone to the *Click2Kill* server on my own PC.

Karim drank, womanised and gambled, none of which surprised me, and he did so in the company of a clique of high-end estate agents. They swapped stories about how they had ripped off everyone from the naive retired postman to the super-rich oligarch, and they ranked each other not on the basis of money earned *per se* but the rate at which they could suck up cash: one hour to pull in a commission of fifty thousand pounds trumped four hours pulling in a commission of one hundred and fifty *thou*.

Karim, in one of their conference calls, had started talking about the Princess's estate and how they should go down and "*Have a butcher's*, what d'you think lads?" and "*Grab some of the action*," the coming weekend.

The following Monday he shared a video with them that makes me sick, even today, merely thinking about it.

The clip started with a good deal of fumbling and heavy breathing and the words to someone out of sight, "Sure, wish I'd thought, could've got the whole thing." The mobile was walked across what was obviously the farm yard at Todmorton Hoe, settling eventually on a dark green Range Rover and the rusty yellow tractor with the bucket, in front of the breeze block wall.

The armature at the front of the tractor was fully extended and the bucket was embedded, spikes down, into the bonnet of the Range Rover. The windscreen of the Range Rover was smashed and, impaled on the bonnet, was what looked like a large sheep, broken into two pieces (it would be too nice and wholly inaccurate to say 'cut'. Bludgeoned maybe). There was blood everywhere. Bits of pink flesh and red and white bone were sticking out, catching the sunlight. But it was not a sheep, though it was a terrible jumbled mess. What it was—what it had been—was a man in a white shirt and light trousers. He had been severed, almost, in two. His head, with a white blood-splattered goatee, rested near the front of the bonnet staring up. His feet lay dangling through the broken glass of the windscreen...

I didn't watch any more.

The police at the local station took my details and listened to my hypothetical question about this guy who'd played a prank on a mate using spyware and seen footage of a grisly crime. "I mean," I said. "What should the otherwise law-abiding citizen do to serve Justice but not himself end up behind bars?"

"Tell your friend," the police officer said, "that the name and address of this theoretical victim and the theoretical perpetrator would be the right place to start." He added, "Not forgetting date, time and place."

Four days later two plain-clothed police officers turned up at my flat.

"We need the mobile," the officer who did all the talking said. "And we need it unlocked, seeing as we can't use what you've given us. How do you feel about engaging this Karim Karbala in conversation in a public place? Try and get him to use the phone. We'll have officers standing by for when he unlocks it."

I thought about the massive forty-mile-an-hour tractor thundering along Bekworth Road and about the sheep-shaped carcass on the bonnet of the Range Rover.

"When and where?" I said.

THERE WOULD BE no rehearsal, I was told some days later. Just be natural.

I no longer frequented Zsa Zsa's. I'd substituted a new habit, a new cycle route. So this meeting had all the appearance of chance.

I went up to my old school acquaintance in the queue.

"Karim?"

He turned on the toothy smile. "Alan! I thought maybe you had moved out of the area, succeeded in your great escape. How the devil are you? I'm so glad you're still around I've been wanting to catch up."

He pulled out his mobile phone.

"I know you have every right to feel bitter. But you need to see this. It's not something you'll find in the papers, or online, even from the most ardent conspiracy theorist."

He flicked through a series of photos, found the one he was after, and showed me.

It was a still from the video clip.

I'd already started having flashbacks of the scene and, in the way that sometimes the mind latches on to some specific detail and won't let go, I had been fixating on the arrangement of the head, body and legs.

He was waiting for my reaction.

I had concluded it must have taken a team of five to mete out this punishment. The estate agent was face up, so he had not crashed through the windscreen into this position. I believe he had been held down. That would have required one man each side for each arm. And I can't believe that any less than two men would have been required inside the Range Rover to stop him kicking and wriggling. And then one more to operate the tractor.

They would want him to see it coming, of course. And they wanted whoever received this photo, or the video clip, to know that he had seen it coming. *Pour encourager les autres.* Whether the bucket came down quickly or slowly, I couldn't say. I guess a forensic scientist would be needed to judge that. But what need was there for an investigation when those who needed to know would be told directly, and the remains disposed of on a private estate without any prospect of discovery?

As was fast becoming habit, I focused on calming the quiver in my stomach.

Clearly getting impatient, Karim said: "The estate agent, you know, had been paid by a would-be purchaser to devalue the estate to get a cheap sale. The quarter of a million he made from his rental deposit scam has nothing on the sums involved in the bigger picture."

"Oh," I said.

"Is that all you have to say? The man who tried to kill you is dead. You might be happy."

"He wasn't the only one, though, was he?" I said, knotting my stomach muscles to keep it still. "Who tried to kill me, I mean. You know what sticks in my craw—what *really* sticks in my craw—is the casual indifference with which these people use others. The indifference to the suffering they cause for the sake of lining their own pockets. You with me? Know who I mean?"

He smiled nervously.

"Like my app did you?" I said.

"Your *app*?"

"*Click2Kill*, like it, did you?"

"Sure."

"You play it enough. Average sixty-one minutes a day, according to the statistics I collect."

The nervous smile morphed into a frown. "You spy on your users?"

"Just you. You have a special version," I said. "It has features."

I could tell from the uneasy shifting of his eyes that he was thinking like crazy. Worried, I should say.

"Yes features," I said. "Collects certain data, you see. So much for *Nerdy-boy Gaga Gregson*. Just another disposable asset. *Gaga*. Yeah. You bet."

"What've you done? You got to tell me what you done!"

Two bulky men arrived out of nowhere, each grabbing one of his arms. One of them lifted the phone out of Karim's hand.

"The local police are not impressed by your personal style of Justice. And your embassy is not impressed by the embarrassment caused by one of its citizens—kind of stretches the diplomatic immunity thing a bit far."

I tipped my head in the direction of his people-carrier.

He glanced at it.

Two uniformed police officers were standing next to it, accompanied by a heavy looking Arab gentleman.

"You were quite happy to sacrifice me. Have me believe the Princess was your mother. That some great universal Justice was being served. But it seems you've been muscling in on the dead estate agent's action. A real shit, aren't you? Always have been. The real school shit. Just covered it up better than the other candidates for that role."

He mangled his face into a twisted snarl.

"You always were a loser," he said, showing a nervous tic. "Always will be. Always have to go begging, cap in hand, to someone bigger than you to get you out of trouble. I pity you. Yes, man, I pity you."

I shrugged. It seemed like the best response.

I guess after that he got shipped home. I've heard nothing more about him since, and the truth is: I'm no longer interested enough to make enquiries. Forgetting him strikes me as poetic justice.

If only it was as easy to be rid of the flashbacks.

And as for me and my neighbours: I've given up on apps. I've taken up breeding flies.

TINNITUS (novel excerpt)

Jack Calverley

Chapter One

SANDY AMADEUS arrived at a quarter to nine even though the woman had said, "About nine," and not to worry. "It's difficult to find."

In the narrow entrance hall he now risked straining his voice to make himself heard above the ghetto-blaster on the floor which was playing house music and above the relentless banging of a hammer on the far side of a nearby wall:

"Vic Victor!" He felt like his throat would scratch itself dry. "I'm looking for Vic Victor!"

The guy behind reception had scarlet headphones clamped to his ears and continued to stand, motionless, staring at the screen of a desktop computer that was perched on the counter. He wore his hair straggly and black (showing at the roots) and was definitely on the anorexic side of wiry but trying to appear bigger than he was under a loose, age-creased black leather jacket.

Sandy couldn't have been more obviously in front of the guy and had to wonder whether being ignored was the penalty for getting close enough to be noticed.

A scatter of freebie magazines littered the counter, a little further along, mostly with Princess Diana on the cover, although one had an ad for *Phantom* on the back. However Sandy wasn't looking to kill time in the hope that eventually someone would come for him.

The counter itself hugged one side of a flaking white-painted corridor that was badly lit and led off into the building. He felt tempted: but you couldn't just walk in, could you?

Behind him, every so often, a body would jostle past, hefting a tea chest out of the building, whereupon a different body, wiping hands on jeans and squeezing through sideways, would pass in the opposite direction, to collect another chest.

Sandy decided he couldn't stay here.

Minutes ago, from the outside, the glass fronted building, no wider than a sandwich shop, had mirrored the trees of Hoxton Square, with their black and grey trunks and greenery that, presumably for the whole summer, would conceal the broken-windowed warehouse opposite. In the bright sunlight of that Monday morning, the outside displayed all the promise of something ultra-modern and elegantly cool.

Inside however, the building ran only to gloom, the mousy scent of tea chest wood and an unending, nail-screeching din.

Sandy stopped the next person coming into the building as she tried to squeeze past him, a floppy-haired young woman with a pink face, watery blue eyes and a *Cats* t-shirt. She was hardly older than he was.

Leaning into her ear, he said, "Vic Victor?"

Against the din, in a Liverpool accent, she said, "Next door kiddo!" But she jabbed her finger the way she was headed, deeper into the building. "Make yourself useful!"

Sandy had spent over an hour that morning finding a look to suit the occasion. He had ironed his mustard yellow shirt, untangled his bootlace tie—even polished its silver guitar clasp—and had carefully brushed dog hairs and fragments of rosin from his grey paisley waistcoat. He wanted to capture something of the authentic Western *bolo and vest*, yet add his own touch of jazz. The showman, the performer, that was the first impression he needed to make. Finally he had tied his ponytail with a dark brown bungee that exactly matched the colour of his hair, but decided that any kind of a hat would undermine the casualness of his urban cool.

In his head, and in the mirror, he had rehearsed and revised the posture and the voice of the creature he wanted to be: the professional musician who took life in his stride while always on the lookout for an exciting—no, an ambitious—no, no, sir, mister Victor, sir, that is to say sir, an *unmissable*—new musical.

Never mind that Sandy had to scrape pennies together to help his mother meet her rent—and pay his own—while struggling to stay in the industry, to keep that foot-in-the-door. Any work, any time, any place: he would do it. *Just set me down close to the stage, close enough to smell the sweat. I will do the rest.*

But now, with this young woman's request to be useful he saw only dust, dirt, breathless dishevelment, and fits of coughing. The failure of his audition loomed large. The failure of this chance of a lifetime. The only First Impression he would ever make on the indomitable Vic Victor and the one time he needed *not* to get his hands dirty—and he had to show willing!

With mixed feelings, he accepted her invitation.

At the back of the building, beyond a concealed stairwell, he came to a single large room that was flooded by morning sunlight from a wall-size metal-framed window.

A woman in a blue boiler suit, with a wide, dimpled face and her hair up, was lifting box files in threes and fours from the lowest shelf of a metal rack and dropping them into the last of a row of tea chests.

The tea chest closest the door was overflowing with loose papers. Sandy contrived to lift it while minimising any contact with his clothes and just hoped he didn't have to carry it far.

'Next door' turned out to be three doors along, up one flight of steps outside, and up three flights of stairs inside. In the brief pauses for door-openings and door-kickings-shut he established that the woman in the *Cats* t-shirt called herself Pauline.

When eventually he reached it, he found the whole of the top floor was given over to a single gable-ceilinged room that spanned this and the adjacent building. On the side of the room where he stood, an open French window let air in at the front while, across the whole of the double wall at the back, a single long set of metal-framed windows let the sun in, full on, forcing him to squint. Thankfully, he had left all the noise of the street at street level. The hammering was barely audible. The ghetto-blaster not at all. You could hardly hear any traffic, either from the Square or from the streets nearby. The only real sound came from two people sharing a desk under the window at the back who were quietly talking on their phones.

The air was filled with the smell of roasted coffee beans, but for now that was a luxury he must resist. He added his tea chest to an orderly pile and started picking detritus off his waistcoat.

Pauline, close behind him, called out: "Vic! Someone for you!"

While the whole top floor was obviously a single room, as much as a third of the floor space was taken up by a stage, with a green velvet curtain around it, front and sides.

From behind the curtain came a polished but distinctly London-bred voice, a man's: "Linda! Where's Linda?"

"Not back yet."

"If it's the Mozart fellah, then okay."

"That's the one."

The flat of a hand pressed into the small of Sandy's back just as he himself started to move, ready to rise to the challenge of anyone who would risk repeating the tired old school-yard gag in his hearing.

When he got to the overlap at the centre of the facing curtains, he pulled the heavy drape to one side and stepped up, onto the podium, letting the material fall back behind him. There he paused, precarious on the inside edge of the enclosed stage, needing to hang onto something.

The stage—he couldn't think of it any other way—was bathed in a dim orange light and dominated by an enormous bed in front of him, while to his left a grand piano stood with its lid open, and to his right there was an upright, and a sink, mounted on the back wall.

A man with a square face, pointed chin, not much hair and half-moon reading glasses sat on top of the bed in a red silk dressing gown, propped up by pillows. With a flurry of the stapled sheets of paper he had been reading, he ushered Sandy to the piano. "Let's hear you play."

Three single-sheet pieces were set out neatly on the music rack. Sight-reading, Sandy faced a single melody three times over: once treated simply, once as a jazz piece, and once as a sour, moody violation of standard music progressions.

Was it too much of a risk to play each piece in his own voice—to do what in any other circumstance would count as *showing off*? Yet if he was aiming high, if he believed one day he might reach the top, he had to have his own voice. He had to rise above the prosaic.

To be *anything* you had to *be* something. So he set to it.

The melody, he played with humour. The jazz, he mangled into blues. For his sour, moody offering he remembered a stand-in organist at a rehearsal for a piece composed by the head of his music school. The stand-in had played the music exactly as set down in the score, and had got the music wrong. You had to hear the music in real life to know how to play it. Sandy examined the piece before him. What was the composer trying to do? The real music lay hidden in plain sight—as if defying the muscular precision with which the notes were set down.

He could only guess. He would have to guess. So long as the piece felt like a unified whole, was consistent, and advanced with emotional force, yet with subtlety...

He played.

Before the last note died, Vic Victor said, "Which do you like best?"

That was not difficult. "The last."

"Why?"

"It holds my interest."

"It says here you act."

Sandy rested his hands on his knees to stop them shaking. "Sure."

Vic Victor turned his head to address the curtain. "Linda? You here?"

The curtains at the end of the bed parted at the overlap and the woman in the blue boiler suit stepped up onto the stage carrying a pile of newspapers and the mail.

"A newsreader," Vic Victor said, "reads out a newsflash of a plane crash and realises that his wife is on board. Okay?"

Sandy put his hands to his face, filled his lungs and stiffened his back—as much to buy time as to prepare his body for a role.

He imagined he was on-stage in the West End in an experimental performance that mixed fact with fiction. He imagined he had volunteered for the factual role. His job in the production was to read real, live newsfeeds from autocue in front of a camera. His factual piece and the on-stage fiction would be broadcast live, simultaneously, side by side, in split-screen. His imaginary director said, "Be yourself. Speak clearly." Sandy didn't even have to act.

He relaxed before the camera, which he imagined next to Vic's face but by a trick of the low orange lighting, not visible.

Sandy put his finger to his ear, and listened. "We are just receiving reports," he said, "of a plane in difficulty over the

Atlantic—," there are planes in difficulty all the time, are there not? Bird strikes, lightning strikes, an engine on fire. Plenty of things go wrong, most of them routinely dealt with by professional crews. The words he was speaking were literally true, somewhere. No need even to act, "—being diverted to Shannon airport."

Sandy sort-of remembered the format of flight numbers, but the question was, how to authentically conjure up a non-existent wife who was on board? Well, there had been that American girlfriend Curtis, the other music scholar at Pemberwell college. They'd been pretty close. But they'd split up when she was forced to go home. It was not beyond the possible that she had taken it into her head to come back. Just for him. With one intention only...

And they fly everywhere in The States, don't they? It was not beyond possible that she was in the air at this very moment.

Listening intently to his earpiece, Sandy carefully repeated the flight number that was on the ticket on her lap as she sat on the plane.

Then he spoke the phone number that the public should call for more information, desperately tying to memorise each digit as it passed his lips, so he could dial the number himself, as soon as he was off-air.

"You sing?" Vic Victor said.

Remaining in character, staring at Vic Victor and the imaginary camera, Sandy nodded.

"Anything you like," Vic Victor said, but added, "unaccompanied."

This was the one thing Sandy had prepared for. His party piece. The one he used to shock old school friends when they visited him from up north, doubting that he would amount to anything, and anxious to see him fall flat on his face.

Except, after the newsreader, he was all out of wind, and emotion, and energy.

"Glass of water?" Linda said.

"Thanks," he said, with hardly any voice.

She filled a tumbler of water at the sink on the far side of the bed.

"In your own time," Vic Victor said.

Sandy stood. His throat was still dusty, he'd had no time to warm up, and he'd just bruised every emotional muscle he possessed. How well could he do this? He called to mind the limp oval face of Gary Palini, the mouthy school bully who had come up to London with the others to see the graduation show that Sandy had penned, expecting, Sandy had no doubt, to see some amateur production and to find ample opportunity to mock. *Mock* they did not.

Sandy held Vic Victor's eye and tapped into some of that *I'll show you, you bastard* spirit.

He started to breathe for his song like he was being counted in and, with the invisible tuning fork of the mind, he summoned the key, the timbre and the first note he would deliver to this hostile audience. He willed surprise on the face that challenged him:

"Che bella cosa 'na jurnata 'e sole...

He held eye contact, and he knew, he just knew, when he started the chorus of *'O sole mio* that he had hit the spot. He had done the best he possibly could, and if they really honestly didn't like that, The Musical Theatre Company was not for him.

Shakily, he finished the glass of water and sat down.

Beyond the curtain someone wolf-whistled and there was applause.

Vic Victor said, "You do realise, in this company, everyone turns their hand to everything. No one is special."

"I read that," Sandy said.

"Know what we're working on?"

"Only rumours."

"That's because we're at the starting line. What I want, what I need, one month from now, is for you, or Linda, or Pauline or whoever, to be sitting where you are now, with a true story in your hands, explaining to me how it captures the essence of a tragic life. Of love won and lost, of death, perhaps murder, of betrayal, injustice, tragedy and redemption. We will make the audience laugh; we will make the audience cry; we will relieve them of the burden of the daily grind. Take them to a place they have never been before—well at least not since *Gaius*. How are you with that?"

"A researcher?" *Know the role, be the part, make it true* had been the mantra of his tutor at Pemberwell, and if Sandy was in on the story—a true story at that—from the start...

"Researcher this month," Vic Victor said, "next month, who knows?"

"Absolutely," Sandy said, a little more enthusiastically than he intended. He couldn't help himself. To join the company any way, any how. "Please! I'd love to." He was shaking his head in appreciative agreement. "In from the start. Absolutely."

"Linda?" Vic Victor glanced towards the curtain. "Envelope."

Linda took an envelope from the top of the pile of newspapers on the bed and handed it to Sandy.

"There are some newspaper cuttings," she said, "of a story a superfan sent us as a suggestion. Most likely it will come to nothing, but it will get you off the ground. You never know..."

"Back here nine a.m. tomorrow," Vic Victor said, "and you'll be introduced to the rest of the team. You started working for The Musical Theatre Company forty-five minutes ago. Pay is weekly in arrears for the first two months. Then when we know we're all madly in love with each other, you move onto the permanent payroll. There's some sheet music I've ordered from Chappell. Bring it with you tomorrow. Just say my name. They'll know."

Sandy gripped the envelope, his hand trembling.

He parted the curtain and stepped off the stage.

"WHAT DID I tell you?" Linda Turnbull said, after a suitable pause. She was nicely satisfied that Ruby Rattler had yet again come up with the goods, this time in the form of Sandy Amadeus.

"Sure. I'm feeling T-O-L-D," Vic Victor said. "But I may just have engaged another Barry."

"Without Barry there would have been no *Gaius*." Linda was reluctant to stand up for Barry. But he had made all the difference. Once you'd seen the man, or heard the voice, you couldn't look away, couldn't listen to anyone less, that's what they needed. Barry's downfall was, well, just bad luck, even if, kind of, foretold.

"Any post?" Vic said.

Linda passed him the accountant's quarterly income report, which was what he was really after.

"Down again." He placed his hands behind his head, leant back and closed his eyes. "I need the next show, like yesterday. Until then, *someone* must know: what can we use eight hundred seats and a stage for?—and don't you dare say the B word."

Linda believed in The Musical Theatre Company. She believed in Vic Victor junior. She believed in the stage musical as the most magical, most moving expression of the human condition; she was hardly likely to say bingo. Nor was she about to repeat any of the dead-end suggestions she'd heard over recent weeks and months, none of which could busk a dime in the face of MTC's looming crisis.

"Everyone we negotiate with," she said, "arrives at the negotiation either believing we're desperate or believing we're loaded with royalties from *Gaius*. To a man they believe they can write their own terms."

"Find the zeitgeist," Vic said. "We live in a time of change. We need to tap into the change. You're the one with contacts. All those ears to the ground. Find the tomorrow thing. What about this internet people are raving about? Is that set to be the next big one? Maybe we can do something with that?"

He opened his eyes and levelled his head. "Even if Sandy Amadeus is the talent we need, it's going to take time. Even if we hit on the right story, like tomorrow, it's all going to take time. Is it too soon to tap Sponsor Numero Uno for more cash? That'd be useful. Really useful. *Heh!* Perhaps your Ruby Rattler can lend us a few bob. What d'you think?"

Linda switched on her most patronising smile.

For sure, for sure: Ruby Rattler had been a great source of industry news to MTC. She had pointed Linda to Sandy Amadeus and his self-penned graduation show. She had offered priceless insider info in Linda's campaign to keep MTC afloat, to help Linda pay her debt of gratitude to Vic Victor senior. But no-one, least of all Linda, had the faintest idea who Ruby Rattler was.

Tinnitus is available from the usual stores or visit:

www.jackcalverley.com

TINNITUS, a novel

by Jack Calverley

WHEN SANDY AMADEUS searches for real-life stories for the musical theatre he finds a clutch of real-death stories instead, and becomes a player on a larger stage.

Sound is the weapon. Noise is the crime.

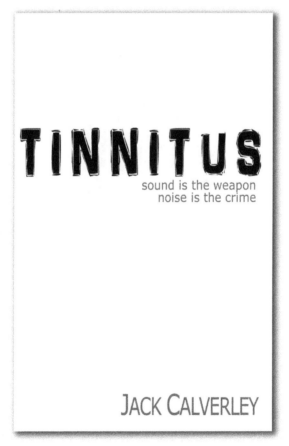

Available from the usual stores or go to **jackcalverley.com** for links.

Also published by The Logic of Dreams:

CB's Top 100 Writing Tips, Tricks, Techniques and Tools from the Advice Toolbox: Break the Rules, Not the Writing

by Carter Blakelaw

Available from the usual stores or go to **carterblakelaw.com** for links.

Gift Ideas

Riffing on Death of a Bad Neighbour

The **six original** cockerel-themed ads that appeared in **Private Eye** (issues 1570-1575) are available on lap trays, place mats, and other bitingly wicked domestic items (**in full colour**) to torture your friends and loved ones (...even your neighbours) with.

Cockerel memorabilia © 2021 Jack Calverley

These and other cockerel-themed *objets d'art* are available from the online store at **doabn.com**.

The Heavy-Footed House asks:

Are you a patron or sponsor of the arts?

The Logic of Dreams is looking for a retreat where a writer can spend a sabbatical, where interruptions are few and far between.

If you own an isolated house in Scotland that remains unused most of the year round, or a boat on the English canal system that needs to be kept ticking over, or some other, similarly remote dwelling place, would you consider adopting a writer as a house-sitter?

If you think you have the right place and are willing to accommodate the writer, please email:

sponsor-a-writer@logicofdreams.com

April 2022

The Heavy-Footed House logo © 2022 Jack Calverley

Lightning Source UK Ltd.
Milton Keynes UK
UKHW012250220422
401922UK00002B/412

9 781739 688707